Stage Fright

Stage
Fright

Christine Poulson

Thomas Dunne Books
St. Martin's Minotaur ⚭ New York

THOMAS DUNNE BOOKS.
An imprint of St. Martin's Press.

www.minotaurbooks.com

ISBN 0-312-34074-5
EAN 978-0312-34074-2

First published in Great Britain by Robert Hale Limited

First U.S. Edition: May 2005

10 9 8 7 6 5 4 3 2 1

'He who fights with monsters might take care lest he thereby become a monster. And if you gaze for long into the abyss, the abyss gazes also into you.'

Beyond Good and Evil, Friedrich Nietzsche

'Dead! and . . . never called me mother.'

(*East Lynne*, by Mrs Henry Wood, dramatized by T. A. Palmer)

Acknowledgements

THE Everyman Theatre is a product of my imagination. Readers who know Cambridge will realize that I have placed it on the site of the old Festival Theatre on Newmarket Road. (Thanks to Carola Hicks for that idea). Sadly since I began writing this novel, the shop, the Racquet Kings, has closed down.

Earlier ideas and drafts were much improved by the comments of Peter Blundell Jones, Sara Dunant, Sue Hepworth, Amanda Rainger, Gillian Slovo and Jonathan Waller. My thanks to them all.

I learnt a lot about the practicalities of rehearsal from Alan Ayckbourn, Heather Stoney, and the cast and crew of *This is Where We Came In*, who very kindly allowed me to sit in on their rehearsals. It was a fascinating experience. I need hardly add that none of them bear the remotest resemblance to any of the characters in this novel.

I greatly appreciate Jude Liebert's generosity in allowing me to draw on her many years of experience in the theatre. Paula Shirley kindly shared with me her knowledge of documentary film-making and much else. Last but not least, I am grateful to Roger Forsdyke and Sandra Perry for advising on aspects of police procedure.

Chapter One

I can pinpoint exactly the moment that everything started to go wrong. It was when I saw Stephen's car parked outside the house.

Up until then it had been a perfect day. The rehearsal had gone like a dream and as I drove home across the fens, a warm breeze flowed in through the open windows of the car. It was one of those rare August days that has a Mediterranean quality. The vast fenland fields stretched out on either side of me, golden in the haze of mid-afternoon, and far off in the distance a tiny tractor moved in a cloud of wheat dust.

The motion of the car had worked its usual magic on Grace and she was fast asleep. She wasn't an easy baby to settle, but one thing you could say about her: when she did at last drop off, not much short of an earthquake would wake her. I slipped a tape into the cassette-player. A bass voice and a soprano swooped and soared, mingled briefly and parted, as they sang of the love of a woman for a man, of a parent for a child, of passion and pain and renunciation. It was the scene in *La Traviata* where Alfredo's father pleads with the courtesan Violetta to renounce his son.

The Old Granary, where I live, is a few miles south-east of Ely. And it was as I bumped down the long rutted track to the house that I spotted Stephen's Audi. I hardly had time to wonder what he was doing home so early, because the next instant a dark shape shot out of the bushes by the gate. I'd swerved before I knew what I was doing. The gatepost loomed up in front of me. I was about to stamp on the brake, when I thought, Grace! She was buckled into her car seat, but . . . I hauled the wheel round, missing the post by a hair's breadth. The car lurched and shuddered over the ruts of the track. It was heading for the water channel that runs through the garden and under the house. Now I did slam the brakes on and the car juddered to a standstill.

I turned to look at Grace. She was still safely strapped in. Her eyes and mouth were round with astonishment, but she didn't make a sound. The breath had been jolted out of her. The cassette player was still belting out *La Traviata*. Violetta on her deathbed was pouring out her love for Alfredo. I reached over with trembling fingers and switched off the music. I got out of the car. I was breathing hard, and my legs were so wobbly that I had to lean against the bonnet. A few more inches and we would have plunged down through the reeds and chickweed into two feet of water.

I looked back. A black-and-white collie dog was loping away, its tail between its legs. It disappeared round a bend in the track. Silence settled over the garden and the surrounding fields. I could smell the fragrance of grass crushed under the car wheels. The dustbin by the gate had been knocked over and across the lawn there was a trail of chicken hones, tin cans, and shreds of kitchen roll.

The door of the house opened and Stephen appeared on the doorstep. Grace got her breath back and began to wail.

'Cass, what's happened?' He came running towards me.

'A dog. Ran straight out in front of me.'

He put his arm round me and I leaned against him.

'Are you all right? And Grace. . . ?'

'She's just shocked, I think.'

By now she was yelling her head off. Stephen opened the back door of the car and reached in to unbuckle her.

10

'Come on, little one,' he crooned. He lifted her out and hoisted her on to his shoulder.

'I've already chased that bloody dog away once this afternoon,' he told me. 'Found it rummaging in the bin when I got home.'

'A stray?'

'Looks too well fed for that. Must be from one of the farms.'

'What are you doing here anyway?' I asked. 'You're not ill, are you?'

'No, I'm fine. But I got an urgent call this afternoon. I've got to go away for a few days.'

These business trips had been happening increasingly often of late. Stephen is a partner in a small firm of solicitors that specializes in patent law. With the growth of Silicon Fen over the last few years, their business had expanded.

'A night or two in London?' I asked.

' 'Fraid not.' He wasn't meeting my eye.

'Well, where then?'

'Los Angeles.'

'Los Angeles!' I was astonished. 'But why? And when are you leaving?'

'I've got to fly out today. A taxi's coming to take me to the airport in half an hour.'

Stephen placed a neatly folded pile of white shirts in the top of the suitcase which was lying open on the bed.

'But – Los Angeles!' I said for at least the fifth time. A new thought occurred to me. 'But why can't Rod go?'

'He's in court tomorrow with that breach of copyright case.'

So that was that. They were a two-man firm. If Stephen's partner couldn't go, there was no one else to send.

'In any case it's me they want,' Stephen went on. 'I've got more experience in this area than Rod. Cass, it'll mean a lot to the firm if they start putting business our way. I won't be away long.'

11

'There couldn't be a worse time. The play opens in a week. The next few days are going to be frantic!'

'I know, I know. But now that Grace is getting settled in the nursery, it should make things a bit easier. She's not a tiny baby any more, after all.' He picked up a handful of socks and stuffed them down inside the case. 'Look, why don't you have your mother to stay, if she can get the time off work?'

'She's going away herself. You know that perfectly well. She's leaving in a couple of days to visit that friend of hers in Hong Kong.' I found myself close to tears.

Stephen bit his lip. 'Oh Lord. I hadn't realized that it was quite so soon.'

We looked at each other across the bed.

'I am sorry, love,' he said, 'but you'll be all right, won't you? I mean, I'd feel differently if you were completely on your own out here, but Melissa and Kevin are only just across the way. . . .'

To give myself time to calm down, I went over to the window and looked out. There wasn't a cloud in sight, just a huge expanse of empty sky. On this side of the house the long, flat vista of the fens stretched out to the horizon, a flat line punctuated by an occasional tree. About half a mile across the fields I could see the cottage which our new friends had rented, or at least the little clump of trees that surrounded it.

Grace gave a little cry of discovery. I turned to look. I'd propped her among the pillows and she'd managed to get hold of Stephen's deodorant. When she saw that she had our attention, she gave a big gummy smile. Stephen uncurled her fingers and took the deodorant from her. She wailed and gestured wildly at him. He rummaged around on the bed and found Woolly Bear, her favourite toy. When she saw it her face brightened. Stephen sat down on the bed and put her on his knee. She leaned against him, closed her eyes, and sucked on the ear of her bear.

Stephen looked tired. Fatherhood at forty was taking it out of him. He put up a hand and pushed back the thick dark hair that had flopped over his forehead. For the first time I noticed a few grey hairs. I felt a rush of affection for him. I was just opening my mouth to say something conciliatory when the phone on the bedside table rang. We both looked at it.

'Shall I?' I said.

'Please. It might be Geraldine from the office.'

But when I picked up the receiver, the voice on the end of the line was male and had a slight Birmingham accent.

'You – or your partner – filled in a questionnaire about holidays and if your details are correct, you have won a holiday . . .' There was a slight reverberation and a buzz of background noise.

Stephen gave me a look of enquiry. I shook my head.

'I didn't fill in a form,' I told the man on the phone.

'Your partner then.'

'I don't think so.'

'If you could just answer some questions. Have you and your partner been together more than a year?'

'Who *is* this?'

'Mainline Promotions. It *is* Mr James and Ms Cassandra at this address?'

James is my surname. Stephen's is Newley.

'How did you get this number? I'm ex-directory,' I said.

Click. He'd hung up.

'Another cold caller?' Stephen asked.

I nodded. 'We must be on some mailing list.'

We were silent for a moment, then we both spoke at once.

'I'm sorry . . .'

'The thing is . . .'

'You first,' Stephen said.

'Look, I'm sorry I flew off the handle. I can manage for a few days, of course I can. It was just a bit of a shock.'

'I don't want to turn any work away if I can help it. The more secure things are financially, the better. We've got Grace to think of now and then if we . . .' He hesitated.

'Stephen, you earn plenty. And there's still my job,' I reminded him. 'My maternity leave will be over soon and I'll be back at work.'

'I know, I know, but that's part of it, too.' He joggled Grace up and down. 'It's such a rat-race now, academic life, isn't it? You've often said so. And not very secure. You nearly lost your job last year. You had a terrible time.'

Stephen was right about my job. And it hadn't been all I'd nearly lost. The head of the English department at St Etheldreda's College had died in what at first seemed to be an accident. I had taken over and had struggled to save the department from closure. It wasn't until someone else had died that I finally discovered the truth, and on that same foggy February night six months ago I'd gone into labour. Stephen and the emergency services had struggled to reach me, and Grace had actually been born here in my study at home.

'But that was such an extraordinary one-off event,' I said.

'But the pressures and strains that triggered it all off – they were typical enough, weren't they?'

I was saved from answering by the sound of a car horn. I went over to the window and looked down.

'The taxi's here.'

Stephen put Grace back on the bed and stood up. He looked around the room.

'Oh God, have I got everything?'

'Bathroom things? Razor, toothbrush?'

'Yep.'

'Passport, money, tickets?'

He patted his pockets and nodded. 'And I've left the hotel details on the table by the phone.'

He came round the bed to kiss me. We hugged each other tightly, then pulled back to look into each other's eyes. I really didn't want him to go.

14

'I'll ring you as soon as I get there. And I won't be away long.'

'How long exactly? You didn't say.'

He looked away.

'Stephen? How long?'

'I won't be sure until I see how much there is to do.' He tried to gather me into his arms again.

I stepped back and held him at arm's length. 'But you will be back by the end of the week? For when the play opens?'

'I'll do my best, of course I will. But I can't leave until the contracts are signed. Look, I'm doing it for us, for you and Grace, and we'll need the money even more if . . .' He broke off.

'If what?'

My raised voice disturbed Grace. She looked up at me and frowned. Stephen opened his mouth to speak and closed it again.

'If what?' I repeated.

'Well, if – oh, look, Cass, this really isn't the moment, I've got to go. I'll miss the flight.' He picked up his case.

I grabbed his arm. 'If what, Stephen?'

'Well, if we . . . what if we . . .' Stephen said. I hated the way he did that, the pedantic way he had of hesitating while he looked for the right words before he spoke. I felt a surge of irritation so intense that I wanted to slap him.

'Tell me!'

Grace started to whimper. Outside the car horn sounded again. That seemed to make Stephen's mind up. 'All right then. If we have another baby, we'll need the money. And if we're going to have another baby, we'll have to do it soon, won't we? I mean, you'll be forty in December.'

Grace let out a yell. I lifted her up to comfort her. But it was too late. Her eyes bulged, her mouth opened wide, and she let out howl after howl of misery and protest. I had to raise my voice to be heard over her screams.

If I hadn't been so unnerved by the accident I'd nearly had, I'd probably have kept my mouth shut. I knew it was a mistake even before I'd finished speaking.

'It's about time you got your priorities right. Stuff the money! If you want me to even consider having another baby, you'd bloody well better be back in time for the opening!'

Chapter Two

'HE'S not going to die, is he?' Lady Isabel asked. Her voice faltered and her face was pitifully white in the dim light of the cavernous room. Archibald was sitting beside her on the sofa. He hesitated, and before he could reply there was a sound somewhere behind them.

Isabel gave a start and put her hand on his arm.

'What was that? I thought I heard a noise.'

'There's something flapping at the window!'

They turned and peered into the gloom.

'A bat. I think that's all it is,' Archibald said. 'It must have mistaken its way. There it is again.' He sprang to his feet and moved towards the window.

'I've never seen anything like it,' he said. 'There are hundreds of them!'

Isabel followed him and put her hand on his arm.

'What does it mean?' she cried. 'Perhaps it's an ill omen. Oh, Mr Carlyle. I'm so afraid . . . my dear father. He's all I have in the whole world.'

He took her hands in his. 'It's all right. Look, they're leaving now.'

They stood together in silence. There was the sound of footsteps approaching. A stout middle-aged woman appeared.

'Mrs Mason!' Isabel's face lit up. 'How is he? Can I go to him now?'

The woman didn't speak. Her eyes sought Archibald's and a look passed between them.

'Oh, no!' Isabel took a step back. She stretched out her hands imploringly. Her eyes turned up, the whites glistening in the dim light. Archibald caught her as she fainted and lowered her to the sofa.

'Go and get her maid,' he told the housekeeper.

The woman didn't move. She simply stood there staring at him.

'What are you waiting for?' he said sharply.

'Oh, sir, I hardly know how to tell you. Lord Mount Severn's dead, but that's not the worst of it, sir. There's two men, coarse-looking brutes, they tricked the kitchen-maid to letting them into the house. . . .'

'Bailiffs, I suppose,' he said with a sigh. He sat back on the sofa, took one of Isabel's hands in his and gently rubbed it. 'Poor child. They might at least have waited until after the funeral. I'll come and deal with them presently.'

Still she stood staring at him with huge eyes.

'What's the matter, woman?'

'Oh, sir, they say they've . . . there isn't going to be a funeral!'

Archibald stared at her. 'No funeral?'

'No, sir.'

'But why ever not?'

'Oh, sir, they've come to arrest the corpse!'

Tring, tring! There was a sharp, tinny sound which resolved itself into a jaunty rendition of the first lines of *Für Elise*.

Archibald froze. A moment later, Isabel sat up. Only they weren't Archibald and Isabel any more. It was like one of those trick drawings which you can see as an old crone or a beautiful young woman. One moment the figure on the stage was handsome Archibald Carlyle, mid-Victorian sex symbol, the next he was Clive Ashton, slightly creased middle-aged actor. He was wearing jeans and a black frock-coat so old that it was almost green. Isabel, who was now Melissa Meadow, also seemed to have got suddenly older, though she remained slender and blonde. She was wearing a white T-shirt over which a corset was laced and black cotton trousers. Slung around her waist was a rehearsal crinoline, a contraption like a kind of flexible bird cage, made of a series of metal hoops attached to each other by tapes. Mrs Mason had changed, too. She had become the dear old character actress Celia Durant, familiar from dozens of TV costume dramas. All three of them were staring at me.

I was still so caught up in the drama of the scene that for a moment I couldn't understand what was happening. As soon as I did, the blood rushed to my face. A mobile phone was ringing. My mobile phone.

'Cass!' Stan hissed. She was the deputy stage-manager and was sitting next to me in the stalls with the script open on her lap. Kevin, the director, who in real life was married to Lady Isabel, or rather, Melissa, was sitting next to her. He got to his feet.

'Just what the fuck is going on, Cassandra?' he said pleasantly.

I groaned aloud. 'Sorry, sorry.'

I rummaged around in my bag. Where the hell was it? The maddening sound trilled on and on. In desperation, I tipped everything out on to my lap. I grabbed the phone and cut off the ringing without answering the call.

'You know the rule, Cassandra. No mobile phones at rehearsals,' Kevin said.

'I know, I know. I'm so sorry. Stephen's got stuck at the airport. That's why I had it on and then I forgot to switch it off . . .' After all the rush the day before Stephen had rung me from the airport to tell me that there was a problem with air traffic control and the flight had been cancelled. He had spent the night at an airport hotel.

'OK, OK, it was virtually the end of the scene anyway,' Kevin said. He turned to the actors. 'Pretty good, you guys. Just one or two points.' He ran up the temporary steps to the stage two at a

19

time. He was one of those men with a low centre of gravity: a longish body but short legs so that he didn't look as tall as you expected when he stood up. He certainly made the most of what he did have. He was thickset and muscular, good-looking in a piratical way with that heavy black hair which goes straight from being glossy to oily. The old-fashioned swept-back hairstyle and the sideburns had been adopted for the role of the villainous Captain Levison, but they suited him.

Clive and Melissa came forwards and the three of them conferred.

Stan tapped me on the arm. 'So, have you decided?'

'Decided what?'

'What you're going to wear, of course. You can't arrive at the first-night party looking like something the cat brought in. You are The Writer, after all.'

'Well . . . adapter rather than writer.'

'Whatever.' She waved her hand impatiently. 'You've got to look the part.'

I groaned. 'I've gone through everything in my wardrobe. Nothing's really right. And nothing really fits, either, since I had Grace.'

'Nothing for it, you'll have to have something new.'

'I hate shopping.'

'That's abundantly clear, if you don't mind me saying so.'

I glanced down at what I was wearing. My black T-shirt had a small but unmistakable milk-stain on the shoulder and it had been washed so many times that it wasn't really black any more. My skirt had been smart five years ago. I looked at what Stan was wearing. She was about the same age as me, fortyish, with a tribe of children and an understanding husband somewhere in the background. Her real name was Constantia. She'd explained to me that she'd had to choose between Stan and Connie as a nickname and 'I ask you, do I look like a Connie?' Today she was wearing cropped black trousers and a black T-shirt that made no concessions to her spare tyre. Her dark hair was

hennaed an improbable red and piled up on top of her head. She
always wore scarlet lipstick and when she leaned back and
stretched out her legs I saw that she had nail varnish on her toes
to match. She looked great.

'Less than a week to go,' she said. 'You don't seem to be
looking forward to it very much.'

'Oh, I am really, it's just – oh, well, Stephen's buggered off to
LA on business and I don't think he's going to be back in time.'

'Oh dear dear, you're not going to let that cramp your style,
are you? Come on,' she said, taking pity on me, 'I'll come shopping with you at lunch-time and help you choose something.'

'You shall go to the ball, Cinders . . .'

She grinned. 'Damn right. Are we on?'

'I won't have all that long. I've got to pick Grace up from the
nursery at two o'clock. Oh, well, go on, then. Let's do it.'

The conclave on the stage was breaking up. Kevin was
nodding in satisfaction.

'OK,' I heard him say. 'We'll leave the proposal scene for
now. We'll go on to the scene where the first cloud appears on
the horizon. Celia, I won't need you any more this morning.' He
ran down the steps into the auditorium and took a seat on the end
of the third row.

I yawned and stretched. As I settled back in my seat, a curious sensation came over me, a kind of pressure between the
shoulder blades. It was the conviction that someone was watching me. I turned and looked back. The light from the stage where
the rehearsal was in progress accentuated the dimness. Rows of
seats covered in dustsheets stretched back like frozen waves and
darkness gathered under the overhang of the dress-circle. The
only faces discernible in the gloom belonged to the cherubs and
caryatids that were part of the exuberant Edwardian decoration.
Had I heard some sound without consciously registering it? Or
was it simply that I just wasn't used to having so much empty
space at my back? This was the first time we'd been able to use
the theatre for rehearsals, and the chemical smell of paint and

21

new carpets still hung in the air.

I turned my attention back to the stage.

'Isabel, you must believe me,' Archibald was saying,' You are my own dear wife and you have as much cause to be jealous of my sister as of Barbara Hare. I have never loved her, I swear to you, either before I married you or after.'

'I will believe you, Archibald, it was just a foolish thought.'

Archibald stood looking down at her, his face full of tenderness. Isabel lifted her arms to him. He moved closer, he bent his face towards her. The slightly hooded eyelids drooped, his lips parted.

'My darling,' he murmured, and then, 'Hang on. This isn't quite right.' He turned to face the auditorium. 'It's the crinoline. I can't get close enough.'

'It doesn't seem to be properly attached to my corset,' Melissa said.

Kevin turned to Stan. 'Give me a hand, would you?'

'Sure.'

They went up on to the stage together and fiddled about with the laces of Melissa's corset.

'Look,' Kevin said to Clive. 'You take her by the waist? Like this. OK?' He demonstrated. 'You pull her towards you, and Melissa, darling, you lean forward . . .'

The hoops swung back so that the bottom one touched the ground in front.

'You've been married long enough to have three children and you're both perfectly used to this contraption, this crinoline,' Kevin said, 'so you do it quite naturally, but Clive, I don't want you to look too much at your ease, OK? Remember that you do have a secret, even though it's not the one that Isabel thinks it is.'

Clive nodded.

'Let's run through that a few times.'

On stage Clive gathered Melissa into his arms again and again while Kevin and Stan looked on. There was another pause, a further readjustment of the crinoline.

The play was shaping up well. There had been doubts about the choice of an old-fashioned Victorian melodrama like *East Lynne*. But it was the first play that had been performed when the Everyman had opened a hundred years ago, and it seemed a fitting choice for its reopening. More than that: to me it still seemed astonishingly contemporary: murder, adultery, divorce, a dysfunctional stepfamily, a decadent aristocracy, even a train crash. What could be more up to the moment than that?

Kevin and Stan returned to their seats and the rehearsal trundled on. Again Archibald embraced Isabel. She left the stage and on came Barbara Hare, to ask Archibald's advice: her brother, Dick, who is on the run, is hiding nearby, disguised as a stable-hand. Could Archibald, the family lawyer, advance her some money to give to him? Barbara was played by Belinda Roy, a young actress just beginning to make a name for herself. She was a robust creamy-skinned brunette, whose looks were a good foil to Melissa's more fragile blondness. At the end of the scene Clive and Belinda moved downstage and mimed talking quietly together.

Kevin stood up and took from the seat next to him a frock-coat even more ancient than Clive's. As he shrugged it on, his whole demeanour seemed to change. It was as if Captain Francis Levison had materialized in front of me. He swaggered up the steps on to the stage and I almost seemed to see shiny leather knee-boots, the flick of a riding-crop.

Melissa came on from the right as Isabel.

'What did I tell you, Lady Isabel?' Levison said. 'Even from here you can see how he whispers in her ear, how close his lips are to hers, speaking the loving words that should belong to you alone.'

'I didn't believe you and even now – surely it can't be true . . .'

'Alas, all too true. I overheard them arranging this tête-à-tête. How can you endure the sight of it, and not seek revenge? Never forget that there is one who has always loved you, has loved you constantly, and has suffered the pain of seeing you wronged and deceived.'

Lady Isabel's face was white and set, her shoulders rigid with tension.

Levison gestured downstage. As they watched, Barbara laid a hand on Archibald's arm. He inclined his head so that she could whisper in his ear.

'Come with me,' Levison urged Lady Isobel. 'Come to a life of happiness with one who will devote his life to you. My carriage and horses are waiting.'

I was surprised to see the gleam of a tear on Melissa's face. I didn't remember this from the last rehearsal. The silence stretched out. Had Melissa dried up?

Stan clearly thought so. She looked up from the script.

'Only prove this,' she said in a low but distinct voice.

'Sorry,' Melissa said, in her own voice. 'Sorry.'

Stan got to her feet.

'What the fuck . . .' Kevin said.

Tears were pouring down Melissa's lace. For a couple of seconds she stood there, plucking at her breast. She gave a huge hiccuping sob. Then she turned and ran off the stage. For a few moments no one said a word. Kevin seemed too taken aback to respond. He hesitated, seemed about to speak, seemed to change his mind. Then he ran off the stage after Melissa, leaving the rest of us gaping.

'I bet it's that bloody corset.' Stan said, getting to her feet. She ran up the steps on to the stage. On her way across she collided with someone who was rushing in from the wings.

'For God's sake, Jake!' she said, 'Can't you look where you are going?'

What was it about Jake that reminded me of the White Rabbit in *Alice in Wonderland*? Nothing as obvious as protruding teeth or bulbous eyes. No, it was more to do with his air of quivering, whisker-twitching alertness. Behind him trailed a man who was so different from him in appearance that the two of them looked like a comedy double act. Jake and Geoff: the eager young documentary-maker and his older, more jaundiced cameraman. While Jake was short and stocky, Geoff was tall and thin with hips so narrow that you wondered how his trousers stayed up. He was supporting a camera the size and shape of a ghetto-blaster on his shoulder.

'What's happened?' Jake asked. 'Have I missed something? I have, haven't I?' He looked from Stan to Clive to Belinda and back again. The camera on Geoff's shoulder swivelled round as if it were attached to Jake by a string.

'Yes,' Belinda said.

'No,' Clive said.

Stan overrode them both.

'It was nothing, just a temporary glitch,' she said firmly, 'just a costume problem. Wait here, all of you. And that means you, too, Jake,' she added as he made to follow her off the stage.

Jake rolled his eyes in a parody of frustration. He turned back and began to interrogate Clive and Belinda.

I didn't want to get involved with this. I sunk down in my seat and got out my mobile phone to see who had rung me earlier. The call had been from a Cambridge number, not one that I recognized. If it was important, no doubt they'd ring back, but at least I knew it wasn't Stephen. I looked at my watch. Twelve o'clock. He must surely be airborne by now. If only we'd had a chance to make things up properly . . .

I thought about what he'd said about another baby. I loved Grace and I didn't regret having her, not for a single moment, but the fact remained that she had been conceived by accident. We had accepted the pregnancy and made the best of it. To plan a second child was a very different thing. We weren't even married, and Stephen still had his flat in Cambridge. True, I couldn't remember when he had last spent a night there, but . . .

Jake came clattering down the steps and flung himself into the seat next to me. Geoff followed him more slowly, camera on his shoulder. Clive and Belinda retreated upstage, where they sat

25

down on the *chaise-longue* and chatted quietly to each other.

'Oh, why did I choose this morning to interview the designer, Cassandra? I never seem to be in the right place at the right time.' Jake gazed into my face. He had dark hair worn almost shoulder-length in tight corkscrew curls and unusually long eyelashes for a man. He was only about ten years younger than me but he was from a different generation, more like one of the students I taught at St Etheldreda's College than one of my contemporaries. I found myself relenting and dropping into understanding tutor mode.

'It must be difficult,' I murmured.

'Difficult!' He heaved a sigh.

Geoff had settled himself in the seat in front of Jake. He pulled out a paperback and started to read. Whereas Jake only stopped talking when the camera was running, Geoff rarely opened his mouth. Had I ever heard him say anything at all, I wondered? I shifted in my seat, trying to catch a glimpse of the title of his book. I'm always fascinated by other people's reading habits. I'm shrewd at guessing what their tastes might be, but with Geoff it could be the latest Wilbur Smith or it could be Schopenhauer. I simply had no idea. Though the book didn't look fat enough to be the latest blockbuster . . .

'The first of six,' Jake said.

I realized that I'd missed something.

'And the others?' I prompted, hoping that this would give me a clue.

'Not completely settled yet, but I'm hoping one of them will be set in a fertility clinic, and another one in a monastery. That one was very difficult to set up, I'm really excited about it.'

'And when. . . ?'

Geoff turned over a page. I caught the glint of a wedding ring on his hand. Funny that I hadn't registered that before. Even now it was something I automatically noted when I first met a man. What *was* he reading? I craned my neck.

'That's just what I was saying, Cassandra. They won't happen *at all* if this one isn't a success. This is the *pilot.*'

The camp way he had of emphasizing his words had made me wonder when I first met him if he was gay, but mention of a girl-friend on a traineeship with a TV company in the north had dispelled that notion.

'It's my big break. If I can't pull this off . . . I know Kevin was reluctant to let me into the theatre, but he needs me as much as I need him. He'd better remember that. You did know that his career's on the skids . . .'

'What?' He'd got my attention now all right. I turned to look at him. 'You're not serious?'

'But yes.'

'Jake! He's a household name!'

'*Used* to be a household name. Can you think of anything he's been in lately? He's yesterday's man, sweetie. What is he now, mid-forties? Forty-five, forty-six? He's looking to directing for a fresh start and he's got Melissa to thank for that. Management were very keen to get her and she and Kevin came as a package.'

I thought this over. Kevin had starred in one of those cosy long-running TV dramas that people slump in front of on Friday evenings. He had played a minor fifties rock star who gets involved in solving murders: Agatha Christie meets Billy Fury. *Half-Way to Paradise*, it had been called. It had ended about five years ago and it was true that I couldn't offhand remember anything he'd done since. Could Jake be right? Geoff shifted in his seat, and turned another page of his book. I saw just enough to identify it as a black Penguin classic, but as to which one . . .

Jake leaned towards me confidentially. 'Rumour is, there's a health problem, too. Something serious.'

I hadn't heard anything and I was taken aback. Surely Melissa would have let something slip to me? We'd got on pretty close terms when we'd been together with our babies in the premature baby unit. That was where I had first met Melissa – and Kevin, too. When he had discovered that I taught nineteenth-century literature at St Etheldreda's College, he'd asked me to talk to the cast about the historical background to the play. One thing led to another and I'd got involved with rewriting the parts of the nineteenth-century dramatization that seemed especially stagey and artificial. In the end I'd rewritten the whole thing. I thought back over the last few months. It was hard to imagine that the ebullient Kevin was in anything but the best of health. He threw off energy like a wet dog throws off water.

'I really can't believe there's anything seriously wrong,' I told Jake.

'He was taken very ill sometime last year. Nearly died. I know that for certain. I know someone who was there when he collapsed and was rushed to hospital.'

It dawned on me what Jake must be talking about.

'Kevin does not have a serious illness!' I said. 'He has a nut allergy. That's quite different. Melissa told me about it. He was at a party and ate something that had traces of nut in it. But he did not collapse and he was not rushed to hospital. He's fine as long as he takes his adrenaline, and he always carries it with him. If you're going to be a half-decent documentary-maker, you'll need to have more respect for the truth.'

'Oh.' It was Jake's turn to be taken aback.

'And I hope you haven't been spreading this around,' I continued.

'Of course not,' he said hastily.

I didn't believe him. Neither of us spoke for a while, then Jake sighed and looked at his watch.

'I bet they won't be starting the rehearsal again. What are you doing for the rest of the day, Cass?'

'Stan's taking me to buy a new dress for the opening night.'

Jake's face lit up, 'She's giving you a *make-over*? Great, can I. . . ?'

'Oh, no, no, no. Certainly not.'

His face fell. 'Oh, please!'

'You really think your viewers would enjoying seeing a middle-aged, out-of-shape academic struggling in and out of

28

clothes in a cramped changing-room?'

He nodded fervently. 'Of course . . . human interest . . .'

'Out of the question, Jake. It's a treat they'll just have to forgo.'

He looked at me with spaniel eyes. 'OK, OK, but how about this? We don't see you *inside* the shop, but we shoot you going in and then we shoot you coming out with a whole load of carrier bags.'

All too soon, when *East Lynne* had opened and my maternity leave was over, I'd have to go back to my real life as head of English in a Cambridge college, and I could just imagine what the response among my colleagues and students would be. And anyway, I wasn't at all sure that I could trust Jake not to make me look a fool.

'Sorry, Jake. I have my academic credibility to maintain. I'd never hear the last of it.'

'Oh, well, it was worth a try.'

I looked at Geoff's shoulders. For a moment I'd had the impression that they were shaking ever so slightly, but he still appeared to be engrossed in his book – whatever it was. I tilted my head to get a better view. Yes! I could see the first line of the title. It was *Thus—*

'That's all for today, folks,' Stan said. I jerked my head up. I hadn't noticed that she'd reappeared on the stage. 'You'll remember that we weren't going to rehearse this afternoon anyway. Kevin's got to go to London. The next call is 9.30 tomorrow.'

'How's Melissa?' I asked.

'She's OK now. But Kevin and I think she needs a bit of rest, poor lamb. I'm rejigging the rehearsal schedules so that she doesn't have to come in until after lunch. So please check the board, everyone.'

'Can I go up and see her?' This was Jake.

'Certainly not. But, Cassandra, she'd like you to pop up, if you wouldn't mind.'

Jake gave an ostentatious sigh and tapped Geoff on the shoulder. 'Come on, let's see what's going on with wardrobe and set design.'

Geoff closed his book and slid it back into his jacket pocket, allowing me to glimpse the title at last.

I don't know what I was expecting, but it certainly wasn't *Thus Spake Zarathustra* by Friedrich Nietzsche.

Chapter Three

THE bare lightbulb shed a dim light on the brick walls painted in peeling cream paint and the narrow concrete staircase. There was something familiar about the echoing quality of the uncarpeted floors and the smell of cheap pine disinfectant mixed with a whiff of sweatiness. I realized what it was. It was like the changing-rooms in the dilapidated comprehensive school where I'd been educated, and in the college where I now worked.

I made my way up past the public telephone on the first floor, glancing at the board next to it, which was covered in announcements of flats to let, B&Bs, and train timetables. On this floor there were rooms for storing and ironing costumes. Another flight of stairs led to the dressing-rooms, and here some natural light filtered down from the top floor where there was a light well that opened on to the fly gallery. There were only three dressing-rooms. No.1 was for the leading lady, No.2 was for all the other women, No.3 was for the men. It certainly wasn't glamorous backstage: in fact, it was scarcely even comfortable. The Everyman theatre is squashed on to a such narrow site on the Newmarket Road, that the workshops and offices have to be housed in an office block down the street.

I paused on the landing outside Melissa's door. It was half open and she was lying back in the only easy-chair in the room. She didn't seem to be aware of her surroundings. Her face was undefended and sad. The fine lines incised round her eyes and the little marks like parentheses on either side of her mouth seemed deeper than usual. She looked all of her thirty-three years. She had changed out of her rehearsal clothes into a red silk kimono. I hadn't seen that since our days in hospital together.

I knocked at the door. Melissa started and looked round. When she smiled at me, the sadness vanished and the years fell away. And she'd managed to cry without getting red eyes. Perhaps that's a trick of the trade.

I've read somewhere that actors can be divided into two types, personalities and chameleons. Melissa was definitely a chameleon. She wasn't one of those actors who seem larger than life off stage, and she wasn't quite beautiful. It was that not-quite beauty which drew the eye back to her again and again to work out exactly how she fell short. It also made her a very versatile actress. The long, rather wispy blonde hair framed a face that might have been insipidly pretty if it hadn't been for the stronger modelling of her lower face: the firm mouth and rather square jaw.

'Come in, why don't you?' she said, sitting up and pushing her glasses up her nose. The narrow black frames reminded me of those photos of Marilyn Monroe reading James Joyce when she was married to Arthur Miller. Though Melissa wasn't just pretending to be smart. And, come to think of it, maybe Marilyn Monroe wasn't pretending either . . .

As I stepped over the threshold, I caught a whiff of scent, something very familiar to which I couldn't quite put a name. I sat down next to her in the fold-up plastic chair which was the only other seat in the room.

'Are you feeling better now?' I asked.

'Much better thanks. Shouldn't have had that corset so tight. Not when I'm still breastfeeding.'

I winced sympathetically. 'Ouch!'

'How on earth did women manage in those days?'

'They had wet nurses.'

'The other thing is that I'm just so tired.'

'Me, too. Grace hasn't slept through once yet.'

'Agnes is the same.' She yawned.

That set me off, as it so often does. I yawned so widely that my jaw clicked. Melissa laughed ruefully.

'What a pair we are.' She reached over and squeezed my arm.

I caught again a whiff of scent.

'What's that perfume? No, don't tell me. It's so familiar. Something old-fashioned . . .'

'Oh, do you think so? Good. It's lavender-water. Will it do?'

'How do you mean?'

'For Lady Isabel.'

'Oh, for your character. Let me think . . .'

'I know you said that a respectable Victorian woman wouldn't have been wearing perfume, but I thought lavender-water . . . Wouldn't that be OK? I always like to choose a perfume for my character and wear it right through the production. Not always possible of course, if it's someone who just wouldn't. But you can usually come up with something.'

'It's *quite* good. But I suppose I've always thought of it as a little old lady scent, and Isabella is so young and fresh and innocent when the play starts, isn't she?'

'Yes, she is. Hang on.' Melissa delved about at the side of her chair and brought up a book bound in red and bristling with paper markers.

I rummaged about in my bag and brought out one exactly the same, except that it was even more densely packed with strips of paper.

'Snap,' I said.

Melissa grinned and opened her copy at the first marker.

'A light, graceful, girlish form,' she read aloud, 'neck and shoulders smooth as a child's . . .' She flipped over the pages to another marker. 'She looked so young, so innocent, so childlike in her pretty morning dress, her fair face shaded by falling curls.'

'You *are* doing your homework.'

'It's helping me to fill out my idea of her. There's so much more in the novel than you could possibly have got into in the script.' She shot a shrewd glance at me. 'Some people might think this is a lot of trouble to go to over someone who doesn't really exist.'

I thought about this. 'Well, I don't. Because, for just a few hours every evening, in a way she *will* exist, won't she? At least for the audience.'

'Yes, that's it. That's exactly it.' She sat back in her chair and closed her eyes as if there was nothing more to be said.

A thought popped into my head. 'How about rose-water? She wouldn't wear scent as such but something as light and simple as that . . .'

Melissa opened her eyes. 'Perfect. Yes, rose-water. Just right.'

'Melissa . . '

'Mm?'

'Was that all it was? At the rehearsal, I mean. Tiredness and sore tits?'

'What do you mean?'

'Oh, I don't know. I just wondered – I didn't find it easy to write, maybe it's not an easy part to play,' I said.

'You're right,' she said slowly. 'It's really taking it out of me. Of course you have to identify with your role to some extent. You have to try to – well,' she hesitated, 'it's not easy to explain but you have to kind of . . . squeeze the gap, I suppose. The gap between yourself and the part you're playing. You never close it completely, because then you'd start thinking that you really were Lady Macbeth, or Cleopatra, or whoever. But you have to get as close as you can.'

'And that's difficult with Lady Isabel?'

'It's tough.' She fumbled in the pocket of her kimono and brought out a packet of cigarettes. She tapped one out, looked at it and grimaced. She put it back in the packet and chucked the packet in the wastepaper basket. 'And it's worse when I'm playing Madame Vine. That scene with the dying child! My God!'

In the second half of *East Lynne*, after being disfigured and left for dead in a railway accident, Lady Isabel returns to her old home disguised as Madame Vine to be governess to her own children in the household of her former husband and his new wife.

'I found myself in tears when I was writing that,' I admitted. 'I've got a completely different take on the novel now that I'm a mother myself.'

'Me, too. Sometimes I just want to howl at the thought of it all! Raging hormones, I suppose. On the other hand, that could add something to my performance. If I can keep it under control. No good whingeing, is it? Fancy a cup of tea?'

I nodded.

Melissa squatted down, shook the kettle to see if there was enough water in it, and plugged it into a socket near the skirting-board. The kettle was virtually her only gesture towards making her dressing-room more homely. The tools of her trade – make-up box, wig stand, magnifying mirror on a stand, were neatly aligned on the dressing-table, but there was little of the clutter of the other dressing-rooms. The only personal thing was a collage of photographs, overlapping each other in a silver picture-frame: there was Agnes, a few hours old – she'd been born the same day as Grace, Kevin, looking very dashing in a doublet with slashed sleeves, a holiday snap of a middle-aged couple standing in front of a pâtisserie – Melissa's parents, I guessed.

Melissa was rocking back on her heels and frowning.

'There's something I want to ask you,' she said.

'About the play?'

'No, not the play. Now where . . . oh yes.' She reached over for a sheet of paper and an envelope that lay on the dressing-table. 'Have a read and tell me what you think.'

I looked at the envelope. It had a first-class stamp and an

35

address label typed with Melissa's name and the address of their cottage. It looked innocuous enough.

I read what was on the sheet of paper:

So, we'll go no more a-roving
So late into the night,
Though the heart be still as loving,
And the moon be still as bright.

For the sword outwears its sheath,
And the soul wears out the breast,
And the heart must pause to breathe,
And love itself have rest.

Though the night was made for loving,
And the day returns too soon,
Yet we'll go no more a-roving
By the light of the moon.

from The King of Cups

The signature had been printed upside down. The poem had obviously been word-processed and I recognized the font in which the signature had been written: Old English Text. It's quite common and I'd got it on my own computer. I turned the sheet of paper over to see if there was anything on the back.

There wasn't.

'Do you recognize the poem?' she asked. 'I get the feeling it's written by someone well-known. It rings a faint bell.'

'Sure I recognize it. I mean, it's my job to recognize it. I do teach nineteenth-century poetry, after all.'

'Let me guess. I thought, maybe, Thomas Hardy?'

I shook my head.

'Masefield?'

'Getting colder.'

'Colder? Oh, I see. Further back, then. One of the romantic poets? Wordsworth?'

'Close. It's Byron actually. In a rare mood of sexual restraint. It's a strange thing to send to someone. It doesn't mean anything to you?'

'Nothing at all.'

'And the signature? And why is it upside down? Who is the King of Cups?'

She shook her head. 'No idea. I get quite a lot of fan letters and it's not unusual for fans to come to all your performances and get a bit hung up on you. We seem rather glamorous,' she gestured ironically at her surroundings and made a droll face, 'but the letters aren't usually like this.'

It struck me that it was the kind of thing someone might write at the end of an affair. But in that case, Melissa would surely have guessed the identity of the sender and she wouldn't have shown the letter to me. I stole a glance at her. She was crouching by the kettle putting a tea-bag in each of the mugs.

'Could it be someone from the past?' I said. 'An old boyfriend?'

'I don't think so.' She poured hot water into the mugs. 'I've racked my brains. I can't think of anyone. But you're right, I do get the feeling that whoever it is expects me to understand the significance of it.'

'It's not really sinister, is it? I mean, nothing you'd report to the police. What does Kevin think?'

'I haven't mentioned it to him. He's absolutely at full stretch with this production. He's already got too much on his plate.' Melissa poured some milk into one of the mugs and handed it to me. 'And there's probably nothing to worry about.'

'But you *are* worried.'

'Well, you see, what I can't understand . . .'

The door of the dressing-room swung open and hit the wall with a bang.

'Sorry, sweetie,' Kevin said to Melissa. 'Didn't mean that to happen.' He made a pantomime of closing the door quietly behind him.

Melissa caught my eye and gave me the tiniest possible shake of the head. I slipped the letter out of sight. Melissa and I were occupying the only two chairs. Kevin crossed to the dressing-table and leaned on it. I wondered what it was that Melissa had been going to say about the letter – and why she hadn't told Kevin about it.

If Melissa was the chameleon type of actor, Kevin was definitely the personality type. He seemed to stretch the little room at the seams by simply stepping into it. I found myself wanting to push my chair back. When he spoke it was recognizably in an actor's voice, deep, flexible, and slightly ironic as though he was never a hundred per cent committed to what he was saying.

'Feeling better, sweetie?' He looked fondly into Melissa's face.

She nodded. 'Much.'

He leaned over and stroked the hair back from her forehead.

'All the same, I don't feel happy about leaving you tonight. I don't have to stay in London. I can get a late train back.'

She smiled up at him. 'I'll be fine, honestly, darling. You stay over at the flat. I don't mind, really I don't. I shall just go home and get as much sleep as Agnes will let me.'

'I'm only just across the fields if she wants me,' I said. 'Just give me a ring if you need anything, Melissa.'

'Well, if you're sure . . .' Kevin said.

'Quite sure,' Melissa said.

Kevin turned to me. 'Cass, while you're here, can I have a word about the opening scene – the one we rehearsed this morning? Can we make it a bit more, oh . . . a bit more . . .' He gestured vaguely.

'A bit more what?'

'A bit more sexy?'

'Sexy?'

'Archibald might embrace Lady Isabel, put an arm round her

waist, that sort of thing?'

'But they're not even engaged,' I said, realizing that I sounded like a Victorian chaperon. 'And anyway, there's also the class thing. He only feels he can dare to approach her when he finds out she's been left without a penny.'

Kevin leaned back, bracing himself by grasping the dressing-table. He nodded thoughtfully.

'Look, we've agreed that the play absolutely seethes with repressed sexuality, haven't we?'

'Well, yes, but that's the whole point, it *is* repressed, so it's that much more shocking when it finally erupts and Isabel runs off with Levison.'

'But we don't want to underplay it too much, do we? I know *East Lynne*'s a classic of its kind, but we don't want to be too reverential. I'm thinking of some of the telly adaptations. . . .'

'*Pride and Prejudice* . . . Colin Firth . . . a wet shirt . . . a glimpse of manly chest?'

He grinned. 'Well, maybe we don't want to go as far as that. But if you could spice the dialogue up a bit . . .'

'Well . . .'

There was a crackling of static from the Tannoy. A gravelly disembodied voice said, 'Dr James. Dr James. Your fairy godmother is waiting for you at the stage door.'

'Oh Lord, I've got to go!'

'But, Cass, you will think about it?'

'Yes, yes!'

Chapter Four

THE shoes were slingbacks made of a very soft, supple black leather. They had a cut-away toe and a slender heel much higher than I was used to wearing. Putting them on changed everything. The shoes seemed to alter my centre of gravity and realign my whole body. The black skirt and the jacket with its mother-of-pearl buttons had looked dowdy a moment ago. Now they looked stunning. The cut of the jacket accentuated my waist and showed off the cleavage that I'd acquired since the birth of Grace. The bulge of my stomach had disappeared. I didn't look flabby any more. I looked voluptuous. I gazed at myself in the mirror, really seeing myself for the first time for months. I ran my hands through my hair. It was so short that it didn't need any more than that. I turned my head to one side; the outline of my chin wasn't quite as sharp as it had once been. I would be forty soon. I didn't think I looked my age, but then who does? And what was it Gloria Steinem had said when she was told she didn't look like forty? 'This is what forty looks like now.'

There was a knocking on the door of the cubicle. Stan's voice said:

'How are you getting on?'

I pushed open the swing-door of the changing-room and stepped out.

A big smile spread across Stan's face.

'Wow,' she said. 'You look like the *femme fatale* in a film noir. I think it's the shoes.'

The assistant nodded eagerly.

'How much are they?' I asked the assistant.

'Ninety-five pounds.'

It took me a moment to absorb the shock. I'd never paid that much for a pair of shoes before.

'They're a very good leather and they're made in Italy,' the assistant said.

'You've got to have them,' Stan said. 'Put them on your credit card.'

I couldn't make up my mind. It seemed an awful lot of money. Since I'd had Grace I'd found vivid memories of my own childhood coming back to me, and often now I saw those episodes through my mother's eyes. My father had left when I was seven and my mother had struggled to train as an accountant. There hadn't been a lot of money. I'd had one pair of shoes for everyday, one for best, and boots for winter. I saw myself, a small child trying on shoes with my mother kneeling beside me, pressing her thumb on the toe to see if there was enough room. The memory of her face, anxious and intent, hurt me in a way that it never had before. The shoes had to be right. She couldn't afford another pair if they weren't. Having more shoes than was strictly necessary still seemed to me extravagant, profligate even. Sometimes it wasn't until a pair of shoes were falling apart that I forced myself to buy some new ones. Those days were long gone. My mother worked for a firm of accountants in the city now. She had a terrific sense of style and loved to see me well-dressed. She was all too often disappointed. I knew exactly what she'd say: *Go on, darling, treat yourself, or better still, let me treat you.*

Still I hesitated.

'I don't know what Stephen would think,' I heard myself saying feebly.

'Ah, but Stephen's not here,' Stan said.

41

'That's right. He isn't, is he?'

Our eyes met and Stan winked.

'Burn the receipt. That's what I do,' she said.

Comfort shopping? Revenge? Who cared?

'Sod it,' I said. 'I'll take them.'

'Bravo. Buy them before you change your mind, and I'll treat you to lunch.'

As I turned to go into the changing-room, Stan said:

'There is just one thing, though. . .'

I looked back. Her face was serious.

'Yes?'

'I ought to warn you. . .' She shook her head.

'What?'

'If you're not home by midnight, you'll turn into a pumpkin.'

The assistant was just beginning the credit card ritual when them was a little fanfare followed by a tinny rendering of the opening bars of *Lillibullero*.

'I must get that bloody tune changed,' Stan said. She rummaged around in her capacious handbag and fished her mobile out.

'Yep, yep, OK,' I heard her say as I scribbled my signature on the credit-card slip.

'See you soon then. 'Bye.' She clicked the off button, pushed the aerial back and dropped the phone into her bag.

'Gotta go, Cassandra, we'll have to take a raincheck on lunch. They want me back at the theatre. Belinda's throwing a wobbly over something. Apparently she's in a right old state.'

The green room was just a sliver of a room, reached by a little corridor to the right of the stage door, not nearly big enough to hold all the cast and company at once. There was a little refrigerator, a small scratched table with a few back numbers of *The Stage* on it, several fold-up wooden chairs and a couple of scuffed leatherette armchairs. As Stan and I approached the open door, the group of figures inside seemed frozen into a tableau.

Belinda was slumped in one of the armchairs. She was very white and it was obvious that she was only just holding back tears. Her strong emphatic eyebrows, beautifully plucked and shaped, stood out against the pallor of her face. It was like one of those Victorian problem pictures, *The Last Day in the Old Home* or *When Did You Last See Your Father*? Had she gambled away the family fortune, been discovered in adultery, confessed to an illegitimate child? Clive was sitting next to her, holding her hand. Jake was hovering with a white plastic cup of water in his hand. Geoff was standing off to one side with his camera running.

The next moment the tableau broke up. The instant Belinda saw Stan she began to cry in earnest. Clive stood up and looked at Stan as if appealing for help. Jake stood back against the wall to allow us into the room.

Stan took charge immediately. She headed for Belinda and Clive stepped aside to allow her to take his seat. Belinda twisted sideways and put her head on Stan's shoulder.

'There, there, sweetie. It's all right,' Stan said. She stroked Belinda's hair. 'Jake, go and get some brandy, please.'

He hesitated, obviously afraid that he was going to miss something.

'I don't know where...'

'The stage door. Fred'll have some.'

He dashed off and returned with a glass and a bottle of Courvoisier. Stan poured out a generous measure. After a few sips of it, some of the colour came back to Belinda's cheeks.

'Now, what's all this about?' Stan asked.

Clive said. 'Belinda's had a bit of a shock, poor love.'

I thought for a moment that she was going to start crying again. She pressed her lips together tightly.

'She wanted to check her moves in the first act,' Clive went on, 'so she thought she'd have a quiet half an hour on the stage, and then. . .'

Belinda took up the story. 'After a bit I got the feeling that someone was watching me. . . I went to the front of the stage and peered in the stalls. It was dark, of course, but when my eyes had adjusted a bit, I could see that there wasn't anyone there. And I was just going to get back to work, when I heard a slight noise. It seemed to come from higher up and when I looked at the dress-circle, I could see that there was someone there after all, sitting in the back row. I called out to them. Asked them what they were doing there. And they didn't reply. They didn't say anything at all. It was horrible. There was just this really heavy silence.'

I wondered how frightened she'd really been. It seemed to me that she was enjoying being the centre of attention. But then I remembered the frisson of unease I had felt earlier. An empty theatre is a creepy place, and a theatre that's supposed to be empty and isn't . . . well, it was no wonder Belinda had got the wind up.

'Where exactly was this person sitting?' Stan asked. 'At the side? Towards the middle?'

'He was in the seat on the right of the centre aisle.'

'You're sure it was a man?'

'Well, I thought it was, but I don't know for sure. Like I said, he didn't speak.'

'And then what happened?'

'He stood up. He was wearing a long black cloak with a hood, and I could see this really white face. It just seemed to kind of float in the dark and then. . .' Her voice trailed off.

'Yes,' Stan prompted.

'And then the lights went out. I was in pitch dark. I've never been so scared in my life! I was feeling my way off stage on to the dock when I ran into Clive, but of course I didn't know it was Clive.' She dabbed at her face with a paper tissue.

'I got a helluva shock, too,' Clive said. 'She screamed her head off! I'd come back for my script. Couldn't find it in the dressing-room and thought I must have left it in the auditorium. I was half-way across the dock when the lights went off. After fumbling about for a bit, we managed to find the lights and put them back on. We found Jake and Geoff in the green room. I left Belinda with them and had a quick look in the auditorium. Nobody there, that I could see. But then I couldn't see much. Didn't have a key to the lighting box, so I couldn't put the house lights on.'

'Wait a minute,' I said. Every head swivelled in my direction. 'Who was actually in the theatre while all this was happening?' I asked.

'Good question,' Stan said.

'Ain't nobody here but us chickens,' Clive said. 'Just the four of us left as far we could make out: me and Belinda, and Jake and Geoff. And Fred on the stage door, of course.' He exchanged a glance with Stan. 'You don't think. . .?'

She gave her head the kind of quick shake that means 'not in front of the children'. Clive gave a little concurring nod. They both glanced at Belinda as if to see whether she'd registered the interchange. Belinda was too busy looking at her face in a little mirror to have noticed anything.

'How about some lunch?' Clive asked her. 'Come on, I'll take you somewhere nice. My treat, all right?'

Belinda's face brightened at this prospect. She got to her feet.

'That'd be lovely. I'll just go and tidy myself up.'

She headed for the door.

'And I'll pop up to my dressing-room and get my jacket,' Clive said.

He was about to follow her out, when Stan said, 'Thanks, Clive.'

He winked. 'My pleasure.'

'Ah, the resilience of youth,' I said.

'Nothing gets them down for long at that age, does it?' Stan said, smiling. Then she frowned. 'All the same it's not very nice, is it? Hope this isn't someone's idea of a joke.'

'Could someone have wandered in off the street?' I asked.

'It's been known to happen,' she admitted, 'but usually the

doors of the auditorium are kept locked. So they'd have to have come in by the stage door and Fred would have seen them. I'd better check, I suppose.'

We made our way down to the dock, Jake and Geoff following behind. Geoff was still filming. The dock is a big, cavernous space where the scenery is brought in. One side opened on to the stage and on the other I could see a narrow line of light from under the double doors that opened on to the street.

'Wait here,' Stan told Jake. He opened his mouth to protest but shut it again when he saw the expression on her face. She selected a key from a large bunch fastened on to a belt slung round her hips. At the far end of the dock was a door that led to some stairs into the auditorium. We went up them and Stan opened the door of the first box. Stan stepped inside. I followed her. There was a series of clicks as she flicked switch after switch. Section after section of the auditorium leapt forward out of the darkness: the boxes, the proscenium arch, the stalls, the dress circle, the gallery, and finally a blaze of light burst from the chandeliers on the ceiling. We stood there blinking in the bright light. The whole theatre lay spread out before us, a dazzling confection of blue, cream and gold. Cherubs with puffed-out cheeks and trumpets in their mouths balanced insecurely on the proscenium arch; caryatids with beaming faces supported baskets of fruit and flowers; the dress-circle and the gallery were slung with gilded swags and garlands. I hadn't seen the auditorium properly since the restoration, and I forgot our mission as I craned my neck to look at the ceiling; the huge gasolier was flanked by two exuberant paintings of the Comic and the Tragic Muse. Up there the mode was more rococo: all frothy pink clouds, rosy bottoms and floating limbs. It was bold, it was vulgar, it was unashamedly over the top.

Also, it was completely empty.

'No one here now,' remarked Stan. 'A real little gem, isn't it? Designed by Frank Matcham. I love his theatres. And it's not just that it looks wonderful, it works as well. The sightlines –

there isn't a single seat where you can't get a decent view of the stage. And the acoustics . . . well. . .'

'You don't seem very worried. First Melissa, now Belinda. . .'

'Oh, it'll all come right. In every production there always a moment when Murphy's law goes into overdrive and everything starts to unravel. People who were word-perfect fluff their lines. Props fall apart in people's hands. Someone bangs a door and the set falls down. There's always a point where you simply can't imagine how everything's going to come together.'

'But it always does?'

'Oh, yes.'

I wasn't totally convinced, and I didn't think Stan was either. But it was her job to sound confident and optimistic, so I left it at that.

'What was Clive about to say when you shut him up?' I asked.

Stan looked at me appraisingly as if she was deciding whether or not to tell me. Then she said: 'He was suggesting that the theatre might be haunted.'

'He really thought that?'

'Oh, well, lots of these old theatres are.' She spoke as casually as if she was talking about an infestation of mice. 'They're usually completely harmless. To tell the truth, I'm more worried about the electrics. You see, there's a working light that's separate from the stage lights, and I can't understand them both going off. I'll have to have a word with the electrician. And there's something else I'm a bit curious about. What was Clive still doing here? There isn't another rehearsal until tomorrow morning.'

'You mean?'

'Clive and Belinda.'

'Oh, no, surely not. Not Clive, I mean, uxorious isn't the word. He never stops talking about – what's her name? Roberta?'

'Yeah, you're right – she's lovely, actually, and so are those daughters of his. And it's different now. In the old days before

47

Aids, everyone used to be at it like rabbits, but that's all changed. In fact, I've never known a production with so little social life attached to it as this one. At the first opportunity everyone's off home like a shot. Even Jake and Geoff. Jake heads north to that girl in Leeds, Geoff is off in that Jeep to his wife in Wales.'

'Oh, Geoff's married, is he?'

'Very devoted, I gather. He and wife run a smallholding together. He showed me a photograph the other day. His wife looked really sweet. And it's an idyllic place. Tucked away in a valley in Snowdonia.'

She leaned over and with a few clicks the auditorium disappeared. For a moment or two the after-image of the lights blazed on my retina, then they too were extinguished. It was as if Stan had conjured up the whole glorious confection out of nothing and then dissolved it again into darkness. I could almost believe that it really wasn't there.

We made our way back down to the dock. When Jake was agitated he had a habit of rising up and down on the balls of his feet as if he was trying to compensate for his lack of height. He was doing that now.

'Well,' he said eagerly, 'Is there someone lurking there?'

Stan shook her head.

Jake's face fell. 'Are you sure?'

'Quite sure.'

'They might be hiding?' he persisted.

'More likely Belinda imagined it. Trick of the light or something.'

Jake was gazing at Stan intently. 'Wouldn't it be worth going out front and having a proper look? After all, Belinda didn't imagine the lights going off. And shouldn't we have a look under the stage? They could be there – waiting until we've gone. . .'

Stan considered. 'Perhaps it would be just as well,' she said at last. 'I'll have to go back and put the house lights on. I'd better get a torch as well. We'll go under the stage and round the other side of the auditorium. If there is anyone there, we'll flush them out. If I ask Fred to come and wait in the dock, we'll have all the exits covered.'

There are dressing rooms and the green room on one side of the stage, but on the other there's only a corridor. To reach it during a performance there's a passage that runs along the back wall under the stage. We went in single file down a narrow flight of stairs. Stan went first, I followed, with Geoff behind me, still filming, and Jake at the rear. Where the light from the naked lightbulbs touched the wall beads of water stood out on the surface as if it were sweating. The space behind the orchestra pit was used to store props and the path behind them was narrow.

We were half-way through, when Jake said, 'Jesus, what's that? I thought I heard something.'

Stan stopped and swung her torch round. The beam of light picked out a jumble of objects in surreal juxtapositions: a hip-bath with an old Singer sewing-machine balanced across it, a rocking-horse, a dressmaker's dummy draped in a dustsheet. Jake elbowed his way past Geoff, so that he was standing next to me.

'There's someone there,' he said. 'I know there is.'

'Don't be silly,' Stan said, raking the floor with the torch beam. 'Look at the dust.' There was an intricate pattern of paw prints. 'No one's been in there for months except the theatre cat. Come on, let's get on with it.'

We emerged at stage level. This side was really only used for actors to make exits and entrances. The gloom was made more intense by the way that everything – walls, radiators, woodwork, pipes – was painted in a dark, reddish brown that was almost maroon. There was a typed notice stuck on the wall announcing that insecticide spraying had taken place. DO NOT BRING FOOD INTO THIS AREA, it warned. It was dated 2 September 1978: over twenty years ago.

Stan saw what I was looking at and grinned.

49

'The land that time forgot. Hopefully they'll do something about all this when the next stage of the grant comes through.'

We followed her up some stairs and through a door into the dress-circle. It was like stepping into a different world. The brick walls with their peeling paint were replaced by red-and-gold striped wallpaper. Our footsteps had been loud on the concrete floor. Now they were muffled by a thick, brand-new, red carpet. We walked up the side aisle to the back. Even with all the house lights on it was darker here under the overhang of the gallery than it was at the front of the stalls.

'No one here now,' I said.

'If there ever was,' Stan said. She peered down the row. 'Hey, what's that?'

'What?'

'There!' She pointed down the row.

I still couldn't see anything.

'What is this? The ghost scene from *Hamlet*?' I only realized how much on edge I was when I heard myself snap that out.

Stan didn't say anything. She took my arm and pulled me closer so that I could share her line of vision. Jake and Geoff crowded up behind us. Stan leaned forward and gathered up the dustsheet. With a flourish, like a magician pulling the cloth off a fully laden table, she jerked it towards us.

The dustsheet came flowing down the row and I saw what it was she had been pointing at.

Chapter Five

I drove home in a very different mood from the day before. The weather was uncomfortably hot and muggy. Grace was feeling the heat, too. She cried as I negotiated my way out of Cambridge, and she didn't fall asleep until I turned off on to the A10. I'd gone only a couple of miles, when a lorry carrying a huge tower of hay bales pulled out in front of me. Specks and stalks of chaff and wheat dust eddied and darted about in front of me like sparks in the draught of a bonfire. I slowed right down and closed the car window. The heat was sweltering. On a day like this, the flatness of the fens and the huge empty sky were oppressive. I felt like a fly crawling across a table.

When I'd finally seen what Stan was pointing at in the theatre, I'd felt a shiver of unease. It hadn't been Belinda's imagination after all. There was a seat stuck down at the aisle end of the row. Someone had been sitting there. We had searched the theatre and hadn't found any more signs of an intruder. But we had found, right up at the back of the gallery, an unlocked door to a flight of steps that ran down to the foyer. The decorators were coming and going all the time. It wouldn't have been too difficult for someone to slip in and out unnoticed if they'd timed it right.

I didn't like the way things were going at the theatre. Up to now, it had seemed to me that we'd all been one happy family – a cliché, but that was how I'd felt. I'd been surprised at how smoothly everything had gone and how different it was from the academic world, where there is so often an edge of competition in even the friendliest of exchanges. But probably Stan was right, and we'd just hit the doldrums. If only I could talk things over with Stephen . . . if only we hadn't parted on such bad terms.

Ahead of me the tower of hay bales wobbled as the lorry went round a tight bend in the road. I slowed down even more and let the distance between us increase. It was impossible to overtake: there was a constant stream of traffic coming the other way. But I'd soon be home anyway. I turned off down the track to the Old Granary with a sense of relief. Look on the bright side, I told myself. There was nearly a week to go before we opened and as for Stephen, he wasn't the kind to bear a grudge. Generally speaking he was an easy-going sort of bloke. Probably he'd have rung from the airport and left a message on the machine. If not he'd certainly ring when he landed.

I slowed right down when I got to the gate. This time no black-and-white shape came hurtling out. I parked and got out of the car, plucking the shirt from my body. It was damp with sweat. Grace woke up and began to complain as I got her out of the car. I went up the path with her in my arms and sat down on a bench by the house to cool off. It was warm enough for Grace to be wearing just her nappy and T-shirt and her small body was hot against mine. Bill Bailey, my long-haired cat, came round the corner of the house. Grace stopped crying when she saw him. He stretched out on the grass at a discreet distance while Grace murmured nonsense and waved her hands at him. He blinked and yawned. He didn't object to her as long as she kept her distance; the little grasping hands were apt to fasten round his tail or to grab a handful of fur. I drank in the scent of the summer garden: honeysuckle on the wall nearby, a bed of sweet peas. The only sound was the gentle sigh of running water. I calculated the least I could get away with doing this evening. I could tuck Grace up in our bed and get in beside her with a sandwich and a peach, perhaps even a glass of wine, though not more than one. Then sleep, possibly even six or seven hours of it, if I was very, very lucky. Getting between those sheets would be like diving into a cool pool on a suffocating hot day. I could hardly wait. I gave a yawn, the kind that makes your eyes water.

I stood up and hoisted Grace on to my shoulder. Inside the house the phone began to ring. It was awkward holding Grace with one hand and fumbling in my bag for my key with the other. The thought that it might be Stephen made me even more butter-fingered and when I did find my key I immediately dropped it and had to grope around in the laurel bush by the front door. I finally got the door open, and rushed into the kitchen.

I grabbed the receiver, afraid that I'd be a split second too late. 'Yes, hello?'

There was silence on the other end of the line – then an exhalation of breath and with a quiet click the caller hung up.

Almost immediately the phone began to ring again. I snatched it up.

'Who is this?' I snapped.

'I beg your pardon?' The voice on the end of the line was a woman's, unfamiliar and rather husky. 'Is this Dr James?'

'Yes?'

'You've been selected for a complete make-over of the façade of your house.'

'I'm really not interested – look, did you ring me just now and hang up?'

'Just now? No, but if I could just tell you about our offer: completely free, I assure you, no strings attached. We ask only that you allow us to take before and after photographs and—'

'I'm sorry,' I said. 'I live in a beautiful old weather-boarded house and there is nothing that you could do to it that wouldn't make it *less* attractive!'

'You could save pounds on your fuel bills. May I ask, do you have double-glazing—'

'Double-glazing! You must be joking! It's a Grade II listed building!' I slammed the phone down.

Grace had got bored and was beginning to cry again.

'Oh, hell,' I muttered.

Perhaps if I put her in her cot, she'd settle down, and then I could have a nap myself. I toiled up the stairs. As I passed through my study, the little red light on the answering machine winked at me from my desk. I picked my way over the piles of books and papers on the floor, resolving for the hundredth time to clear up and deciding for the hundredth time that it would have to wait until the play had opened.

I pressed rewind. There was one call. It was from Cathy, my departmental secretary in college. She sounded worried.

'Cass. I'm so sorry. There's this young girl in the office on work experience. She was only trying to be helpful, but she answered the phone to someone yesterday and I've only just found out that she gave them your mobile number. Apparently this chap said he was a visiting fellow at St John's and he sounded very disappointed when he heard that you weren't likely to be back in college until September. The name was Baldassarre. Professor Baldassarre. I hope you do know him. It's not the kind of name you'd be likely to forget, is it? See you soon. 'Bye.'

I sat down abruptly on the swivel chair by my desk.

No, indeed, I thought, it certainly wasn't a name I'd easily forget.

Not when it belonged to a man who had once been my husband.

Grace wasn't asleep by eight o'clock, nor by nine. Neither was I. I was pacing up and down my bedroom with Grace against my chest, her cheek on my shoulder. She had a clean nappy, she was full of milk, and as long as I was walking up and down or rocking her, she was a happy gurgling baby. But the instant she stopped moving she began a thin, high wail. There was something about it that reminded me of the cat on a car journey, something obdurate and measured about it. There didn't seem to be any reason why she should ever stop. Probably my own state of mind had something to do with it. My brain was seething and I couldn't settle to anything. It was so long since I'd seen Joe – since I'd thought of him, even. We'd completely lost touch after the divorce. And when had that been? Fourteen years ago? fifteen? We'd been so young when we got married. How had he tracked me down? It wouldn't have been difficult. I'd resumed my maiden name. I'd kept that through my second marriage. And with Stephen, well – I hadn't got round to tying the knot yet. It was a case of twice bitten . . .

And why hadn't Stephen rung yet?

I paused at the window and looked out towards Ely. The sky seemed too light for the darkening landscape, it was like one of those trick paintings by Magritte where a blue noon-day sky is matched with a dark, lamp-lit street. There was a prickling of little lights where Ely stood up from the plain. As I watched, automatically rocking Grace against my shoulder, the flood-lights around the cathedral came on. The single tower at the west end and the elegant octagonal crossing tower sprang into relief. It was a sight I never tired of.

It was strange to think that where Stephen was the sun would be setting eight hours later. I pictured the plane high in the sky racing westward ahead of the night. It made him seem terribly far away. My own day seemed to have been going on for ever too. Having a small child is like having permanent jet lag. Time slows down and the boundaries between day and night become blurred. I tried to work out what time it was in Los Angeles. About 1.30 in the afternoon. And what time was his flight due in? I couldn't quite remember. I tried counting from the other end. The flight was leaving at ten o'clock and Stephen had said it was an eight-hour flight, so he must have landed hours ago.

On the bedside table Stephen had left details of the hotel where he was staying.

I punched in the number. The phone was picked up on the third ring.

55

'The Four Seasons Hotel. How may I help you?' said a sing-song female voice.

'Oh, hello. I wonder if I could speak to Mr Newley.'

'Mr Newley. Certainly, madam.'

I heard the rapid pattering of fingers running over a keyboard. The voice returned.

'I'm sorry. Mr Newley isn't here.'

'He probably hasn't checked in yet. Can I leave a message for him, please?'

'We're not expecting him. He rang a short time ago and cancelled his reservation.'

Of course there had to be a perfectly straightforward explanation. I was still trying to work out what it was when a minute or two later the phone rang. At first I couldn't make out who it was at the other end of the line. There was a sound of – what was it – gasping, sobbing?

'Who is this?' I said sharply.

'Cass?' The voice was high and quavering.

'Melissa?'

'I think there's someone prowling around the house. I heard a clattering noise outside.'

'Oh God.' The hairs were standing up on my arms. 'What can I do? Shall I call the police? No, hang on, I know. I can see your house from here. Go round and switch on all the lights. You have locked all the doors, haven't you?'

'Yes.'

'I'm putting the phone down now, while I go and look through the binoculars, OK?'

I put Grace down on the middle of the bed and put Woolly Bear in her arms. Stephen's bird-watching binoculars were lying on the sill. I lifted them to my eyes and fiddled with the focus. I saw a clump of tussocky grass hugely magnified and realized that I was looking at the bottom of my garden, then I swung the binoculars too high and caught a pylon on the horizon. I pulled them down and at last I was looking at the cottage. It was surrounded by a windbreak of trees. The upper windows were fully visible, every one of them glowing with light, but lower down I could see only shreds of light through the trees. I scanned the lane by the house and this time I saw something – or thought I did: a patch of white near the ground which disappeared into the hedge as soon as I focused on it. Of course! Why hadn't I thought of that?

I went back to the phone.

'Melissa? Could that noise have been the dustbin going over? There was a dog hanging around here yesterday. I nearly ran over it.'

'Hang on a minute. I can see the dustbin if I go to one of the upstairs windows.'

Grace might have been momentarily diverted by all this activity, but now it struck her that she was being neglected. She began to cry.

'Oh, Lord!' I picked her up and joggled her on my hip.

When Melissa came back, her voice was full of relief. 'That's what it must have been. There's stuff strewn all over the patio. Silly of me. I don't know why I got the wind up so much.'

'Are you all right now?'

'Yes, yes.' But she didn't sound it.

Grace was pumping up the volume again and her face was going red. I made up my mind.

'Look, why don't I come over for an hour or two.'

'Oh, I couldn't let you . . .' she said hesitantly.

'It's OK. Really. I'm having trouble settling Grace. A drive in the car is sometimes the only thing that will send her off. And I could do with a bit of company myself.'

It was only when I'd hung up that I realized that I might miss Stephen's call. A watched phone never rings, I told myself, and it would be better to distract myself by going over to Melissa's than to sit here brooding. I switched the answer-machine on. I wrapped Grace up in a shawl and took her out to the car. I left the lights on in the house and double-checked that I'd locked the door properly. The evening air was unexpectedly cool and a few stars had appeared now over towards Ely.

The Fens are so flat and level, the huge fields so precisely squared off that it's like driving across a giant chessboard. The *Alice in Wonderland* sensation was increased by the way that I first had to drive a couple of miles in the opposite direction and then double back. A railway line and a couple of drainage channels, one of them several feet deep, lay between the Old Granary and Journey's End. Melissa and Kevin's cottage was the only house beyond the railway line and the barrier was operated manually by a pump. By the time I'd slowed down for the red light Grace was already asleep. This was the Ely to Cambridge line, so it was busy. Far away, towards Cambridge, a light appeared. There's something fascinating about watching a train go by. I could hear a thrumming now as it rushed towards me. As it went past it pushed a gust of wind through the open window of the car. I caught a glimpse of people sitting by the lighted windows. Then the train was gone. The thrumming receded. The red light on the crossing turned to green. I got out and raised the barrier. I looked carefully both ways before I drove over the track. I never felt at ease doing this, especially with Grace in the car.

A rutted track led from the cottage to the level crossing. As I drove up to Journey's End, the door opened and Melissa appeared, outlined against the light. She came out to meet me. It was almost dark now, a rich soft blue August darkness. She was wearing a pale dress of some soft, filmy material and her face seemed luminous in the dusk. She looked spectral, almost wraithlike. I remembered how Belinda had described the stranger whose face had seemed to float in the dark. No point in telling Melissa about that when she was already feeling jittery.

I got out of the car and she gave me a hug and a kiss. The scent of roses enveloped me. It seemed like an emanation of the night air, and then I realized. 'You've managed to get hold of some rose-water.'

'Not exactly. I remembered I'd already got one of those rose-based scents. Tea-rose, it's called.'

'Mm. It's lovely.'

I followed Melissa into the cottage. It was a converted agricultural labourer's cottage and had just one main room downstairs into which the front door opened. There wasn't much furniture, just a wicker sofa and chairs with cushions of a coral-red that toned in with a brightly coloured kilim and the terracotta tiles of the floor. The house belonged to a couple of anthropologists who had let it while they were away on a field trip. The few ornaments, a tribal mask, a sculpture of a mother and child in some dark, unfamiliar-looking wood were theirs. Kevin and Melissa hadn't left much of a mark, but then they weren't here very much. When they did have a day or two off from rehearsals, they drove down to London and stayed in their flat there.

When Melissa turned back towards me I saw that it wasn't just the dimness of the light in the garden that had made her face seem white. She really was very pale.

'You look tired,' I said.

'Oh, I'm all right. It's so sweet of you to come over. Fancy a cup of tea?'

'Please.'

'Why don't you pop Grace in with Agnes?'

'Good idea.'

Melissa headed for the kitchen. I climbed the steep staircase to the first floor. There were just two bedrooms and a little bathroom. In the smaller bedroom Agnes was asleep in her cot. I tucked Grace in at the other end, arranging the cellular blanket so that it covered Agnes's feet, but left Grace's face clear.

I strolled over to the window and looked out. Light was spilling from the house, illuminating the garden like a stage set. Beyond the pool of light was darkness, but across the fields I could see the tall narrow shape of the Old Granary. Knowing that I'd be returning in the dark I'd left some lights on, one of them in my bedroom window. The house stood out like a beacon in the landscape. And suddenly I had the strangest feeling that if I could look in through those windows I'd see myself there, in bed maybe, or sitting at my desk. And Grace would be there, too, asleep in her cot. It was as if I was standing outside my own life looking in. . . .

'Cass?'

I gave a start and turned to see Melissa was standing by the cot.

'Are you OK?' she asked.

'Oh, yes, yes, I'm fine.'

I went over to join her by the cot and we stood looking down at the children.

'This is like old times,' she said.

I nodded. It was. During the long days and nights in hospital attached to drips ourselves, leaning over the incubators containing our babies, we'd become very close. Perhaps inevitably some of that intimacy had ebbed away. It had been a special time, like being on board ship together or meeting on holiday, a special time, and a wonderful time, but not an easy one. I remembered how it had been, listening to the sigh of the ventilator, scarcely daring to take my eyes off the little chest as it rose up and down, the feeling of that tiny curled hand closing round my finger. I couldn't risk going through that again, I thought, not yet anyway.

'It kind of gives the lie to astrology, doesn't it?' I said. 'Being born so close together you'd expect their personalities to be similar, wouldn't you? But they're not at all, really, are they?'

'I think it's a bit more complicated than that. I didn't tell you, did I, that I looked up their Chinese horoscopes? They were born in the year of the tiger but they have companion animals according to when exactly they were born. Agnes's companion is the pig. It's nicer than it sounds. It means she's easy-going and well-balanced.' She leaned down and stroked Agnes's cheek with one finger.

'What about Grace?'

'Her companion animal is the rooster.'

'That figures!'

'The rooster and the pig get on well together. Maybe they'll be friends when they grow up.'

I don't believe in astrology, or even destiny, not really. I go along with Cassius: 'The fault, dear Brutus, is not in our stars but in ourselves, that we are underlings.' And yet we can never really know the consequences of our actions. Things so rarely turn out as we expect and always they could so easily have been different. The road forks all the time and every decision leaves behind a trail of unrealized possibilities. What if I had stuck with Joe? Grace wouldn't exist, but I might have had other children with Joe, and their existence would have seemed just as inevitable as Grace's did now. . . .

Melissa broke in on my thoughts.

'Are you all right, Cass?' She was looking concerned. 'You seem miles away. Is there something wrong?'

'No, no, I'm OK. Someone who was once very important to me is trying to get in touch. I don't know what to do.'

'Come on, let's have that cup of tea and you can tell me all about it.'

And sitting together on the sofa downstairs with Mozart playing on the hi-fi I did tell her about it. Joe was twenty-five, I was only twenty-one and we'd met at Birmingham University where I'd just started my PhD. We'd only known each other a few months when we got married. Joe had come over from the States on a post-doctoral fellowship in computer science. When it was over he went back to the States and took a job with a small firm in the midwest. I stayed in England to finish my PhD and then I'd been offered my first academic job in Sheffield. That was when the trouble started. Joe hit the roof when he realized that I wasn't going to join him in Colorado.

'I couldn't face living there,' I told Melissa. 'If it had been New York or the West Coast, things might have been different. And Joe wouldn't come back to Britain.'

'So it was stalemate,' Melissa said. 'You weren't tempted to give in?'

'Tempted, yes. But in the end, too stubborn. And so was Joe. Neither of us would back down. Oh, well, who knows, maybe it wouldn't have worked anyway. Perhaps as time went on we'd have found we didn't have that much in common. That's what I tried to tell myself.'

'So what was he like?'

I reached for my bag, rummaged in it and brought out a photograph. 'I dug this out of an old photo album.'

We looked at it together. It had been taken on the beach after a friend's wedding in Jersey. Joe was wearing tails and I was wearing a brightly coloured cotton dress, decorated with big, splashy flowers and pulled in tightly at the waist. Joe had pulled his tie loose and I was barefoot with a pair of white sandals swinging from one hand. We were walking hand in hand on a path between gorse bushes and sand dunes. Even with my shoes off, it was clear that Joe was an inch or two shorter than me.

'It looks so romantic . . . like a scene from an arty French movie.'

'I know. *Jules et Jim* . . . it was just magical, that day. I haven't thought about it for years.'

'When you said Joe was American, I imagined someone tall and blond and athletic. The beach-boy type. But I suppose – what's his surname? Baldassarre? – is that Italian?'

'American–Italian, yes. More Dustin Hoffman than Paul Newman.'

'Dustin Hoffman without the nose. More like Robert De Niro, really. He is handsome.'

'I certainly thought so,' I said, looking at the sallow skin and the brown eyes under dark, arched eyebrows. 'Of course this was – what? Sixteen years ago? Seventeen?'

'You didn't stay in touch after the divorce!'

I shook my head. 'I don't know anything at all about what's happened to him. Except that he's here in Cambridge right now.'

'Aren't you dying to know what he's like now? You are going to meet him, aren't you?'

As soon as the words were out of her mouth, I knew that of course I would. Had I ever really doubted it? I looked at my watch.

'I'll ring him now. It's not too late. I'll only be jumping every time the phone rings if I don't. Might as well get it over with.'

A look of surprise passed over Melissa's face. Then she said:

'Go for it. Why not? The phone directory's over there. I'll leave you to it. I'll go up and check on the kids.'

The porter at St John's told me that Professor Baldassarre was staying in a college flat in Thompson's Lane and gave me the number. I punched it in quickly before I could change my mind. It was answered almost immediately.

'Hi there,' said a brisk familiar voice.

I wouldn't have been able to describe it beforehand, but as soon as I heard it, I felt I would have known it anywhere. My stomach flopped over and for a moment or two I couldn't speak.

The voice went on. 'This is Joe Baldassarre. Can't come to the phone right now. Leave a message.'

An answering machine. Thank God. I took a deep breath.

'Joe? It's, mm, it's Cassandra. Er, well, give me a call, why don't you?' Oh, God, what was my phone number. I simply could not remember. 'Er, you've got my mobile number, haven't you?'

I managed to hang up before I started laughing. I was still sitting there, giggling, the phone in my hand, when Melissa came downstairs.

'Well?' she said, looking at me expectantly.

'Got the answer machine. Wouldn't you just know it? And my mind went a complete blank. I couldn't remember my own phone number.'

'Nerves?'

'Partly that and partly sheer exhaustion. I find numbers are the first thing to go. I can never remember my PIN number these days – and as for my mobile number, forget it.'

'Tell me about it. I'm building up a serious sleep deficit. I never knew it was possible to manage on so little.'

She put up a hand to conceal a yawn. It triggered off a chain reaction. I yawned so widely that my eyes watered.

Upstairs a baby began to cry.

'I don't think that's Agnes,' Melissa said.

'No, I think it's Grace. Thought all this peace and quiet was too good to be true.'

I went upstairs. I'd just got Grace's dirty nappy off when I heard the muffled sound of my mobile phone ringing in my handbag downstairs. I went to the door and called down to ask Melissa to get it for me. A moment or two later the sound stopped and I heard the murmur of her voice.

Then she called up the stairs.

'It's Joe.'

'I'll be down in a moment.'

Of course, I was all fingers and thumbs. I accidentally pinched Grace and she yelled blue murder. I thought I would never be through, but at last I went downstairs with the grumbling baby in my arms. I heard Melissa saying:

'Yes, we open next week. You must come.'

I raised my eyebrows. She grinned and winked. I handed Grace to her. She gave me the phone, took Grace out of my arms, and headed off to the kitchen.

'Cassandra! Is that really Cassandra? Well, by all that's—'

'How are you?'

'I'm good. And you?'

'I'm fine, just fine. Wow, it's great to hear your voice.'

Neither of us spoke for a bit, then I said:

'I just don't know what to say . . .'

'I know, I know . . .'

'How long are you over for?'

'Just a semester. Till Christmas. Cass, I can't get over this, hearing your voice . . . after all this time.'

'How did you know I was in Cambridge?'

'Nothing easier. Did a search on the net. You're on your university's website.'

It's one thing to wonder, to dream even, about what an encounter with the past would be like, but the impact is quite different. Perhaps in the silence that followed Joe was thinking the same thing.

'So,' he said. 'You married?' Right out with it. That was just like Joe.

'Not married, no, but I am with someone, yes, Stephen's a lawyer, works in Cambridge. We've got a little girl, Grace, six months old.'

'That's just great.' His voice was warm.

'How about you?'

'Two sons. Daniel's eight. Josh is six. They're great kids.'

There was a short silence. Joe said, 'Hey, sounds like we've got a lot to catch up on. How about lunch?'

When I'd closed up the phone and put it back in my bag, Melissa emerged from the kitchen.

'Well?' she asked.

'Lunch tomorrow. He's meeting me at the theatre.'

'Fast work!'

'That's Joe all over. He sounds just the same. And now I think I really must go home. I know it's not far, but I'll be in danger of falling asleep at the wheel if I don't go soon.'

Melissa came to see us off. I'd put the car into gear and was about to drive off, when she tapped on the window. I wound it down. She bent down to speak to me and I caught a whiff of rose-water. She frowned. Her eyes met mine and I thought she was going to say something important. But all she said was:

'I'll want to hear all about that lunch.'

She smiled and stepped back. She blew a kiss. Then I was reversing away. I turned the car and drove out on the track. In my wing mirror I could see her outlined against the golden rectangle of the doorway, her arm raised in farewell. I remembered that I'd meant to ask her something. What was the other thing she had thought was strange about the anonymous letter? It really wasn't worth going back just for that, I thought. I could ask her tomorrow. A turn of the track whisked her out of sight.

Chapter Six

I dried my face on a paper towel and stood staring into the mirror. I was alone in the female dressing-room getting ready for my lunch with Joe. I still hadn't heard anything from Stephen. My thoughts ran round what was now a well-worn track. There had probably been some misunderstanding with the clients over which hotel he was booked into, and then it might have been too late to ring me. It was now nearly half past twelve so that meant it was the middle of the night in LA. I'd probably hear from him this evening. And after all, what could have happened? I knew there hadn't been an air crash – it would have been all over the news. But all the same the fact remained that I didn't know where he was or how to contact him. And what would I do if he didn't ring? I told myself to get a grip. I'd ring his office of course, speak to his secretary. I'd feel a fool but. . . .

There was a spluttering like the sound of something being thrown into hot fat. I came to myself with a start. It was the Tannoy.

'Dr James to the stage door, please. Professor Baldassarre for you.'

Oh Lord. My stomach turned over. I looked at myself in the mirror, seeing myself now as Joe would see me. Lack of sleep had taken its toll. I'd been up with Grace in the early hours of the morning. I'd got so worried by her persistent crying that I'd rung the National Health Direct Line. Twice. And Grace had at last fallen asleep during the second phone call. Teething had been the verdict. I rubbed some colour into my cheeks. Lipstick would help. My hand wobbled and I smeared it over the edge of my lower lip. I had to scrub it off and start again.

The Tannoy seemed to clear its throat. 'Dr James . . .'

I couldn't put it off any longer. I grabbed my bag and ran down the stairs.

Joe was waiting for me outside the front of the theatre. He was looking up at the façade. He must have heard my footsteps on the pavement. When he turned towards me, my first thought was that he had been made up for the stage. Those lines, the wrinkles round the eyes, the fuller cheeks, must be paint and latex, and the thickness round his waist was padding. The next moment I understood. Joe was middle aged. The skinny youth I'd known was now a roly-poly, teddy-bear of a man with a thick waist. The abundant hair had receded, was cut close and was generously salted with grey.

My surprise must have shown on my face. Joe laughed.

'Not quite what you were expecting, huh? Guess I've changed a little over the years. You look great, though. It suits you, having your hair short.'

'It's only been like that for a few months, actually.'

We stood looking at each other.

'Interesting place you've got here,' Joe said, gesturing towards the theatre.

We stood looking up at the stone exterior with its first floor balcony and twin leaded domes. It wasn't as spectacular as the auditorium, but the balustrades and swags and turrets were still impressive.

'I could show you round after lunch,' I offered.

'Terrific. I've booked a table at a neat little Italian restaurant down near Magdalene Bridge. It's a bit of a ways from here, I hope you don't mind a walk. I fixed it for one o'clock, so there's no hurry.'

'That's fine.'

We set off down the street in silence. Has this been a terrible mistake? I thought. It's been too long: we're strangers now. How could I break the ice . . .

As we passed the Racquet Kings, Joe slowed down to look in the window.

'A shop entirely devoted to selling and restringing racquets. Only in Cambridge,' he said.

I caught his eye in the reflection in the glass. He grinned at me.

'What am I thinking of?' he said. 'Come here.'

He turned to me and pulled me into a hug. There was a smell of aftershave, something sharp and tangy, and the pressure of his solid chest and belly against me. He squeezed me hard and then stood holding me at arm's length. Our shared past had lived on in my mind like a series of stills from an old movie, drained of life and power. The feel of Joe's arms, the smell of him that lay beneath the aftershave, brought it vividly to life. I remembered how much I'd liked this when we first met: his confidence and lack of physical inhibition, his readiness to hug and hold hands, were so unlike the other boyfriends I'd had.

We started to laugh.

'Gee,' Joe said. 'I almost felt shy there for a minute.'

'But only for a minute!' I said.

He took my hand and tucked it under his arm, anchoring me to his side. The theatre is on Newmarket Road, at the point just before it turns into Maid's Causeway. It's about a ten-minute walk to the river.

Cambridge is surprisingly quiet in August. The undergraduates and many of their teachers have drained away, and the place is left to locals and to tourists. Infected by the relaxed atmosphere, we dawdled along in the sun. Joe had a question about everything we passed. In his company I saw the familiar city with fresh eyes. We stopped to admire a fine row of elegant Georgian houses in Doll's Close and as we passed Jesus College, I said:

'You should have a look round here sometime.'

Joe looked at his watch. 'No time like the present.'

'Oh, OK.' For a moment, I was taken aback, then I thought, why not?

We walked down the entrance known as the chimney: it's a long path flanked by high brick walls that conceal the Fellows' and the Master's gardens. We passed through the Tudor gatehouse into First Court. The college was built on the site of a medieval priory and one side of the court remained from that building. The two other sides were Tudor. But it wasn't just the buildings that made me feel that I was stepping back in time. The court was as secluded and cloistered as the nunnery it had once been. The noise of the traffic on Jesus Lane was scarcely audible and there wasn't a soul in sight. The only evidence of the twentieth century was a wonderful Elizabeth Frink statue of a horse on the striped lawn in the centre of the court. Off to the left was a vista of shaved lawns and mature trees in full bloom. As we wandered in that direction, we saw one or two people – a gardener trimming the edge of a lawn, a secretary walking between two buildings – but no one took any notice of us.

'This is just great,' Joe said. 'I want to see all the colleges while I'm here.'

'That's more than I've done,' I admitted. 'I have been here, but only once, and that was at night. I was a guest at High Table. They had grace in Latin.'

'Tell me three things to do in Cambridge that I might not think of, things that aren't in the guide books.'

'It's hard to choose . . .'

'Come on. Off the top of your head.'

'OK. Visit the Oxfam book shop on Sydney Street, you find all sorts of things there: it's especially good on American editions. Visiting students and fellows, like you, leave them behind. Eat a cheese scone in the University Library tea-room, and – this isn't original, but never mind – go to choral evensong in King's College Chapel, but it must be a winter afternoon, and preferably raining to get the full experience.'

'No problem. I'm here all fall.'

'Oh, and another thing.' I was warming to my task now. 'Read the ghost stories of M.R. James. You might be able to kill two birds with one stone and pick up a copy in the Oxfam book shop. And then there's Kettle's Yard, that's just about my favourite museum anywhere, and the Scott Polar Research Institute, where they've got the relics of Scott's expeditions and—'

'Enough, enough!' Joe was laughing. 'Time for lunch.'

He steered me back the way we had come. We walked on down Jesus Lane and Bridge Street, always busy with shoppers, whatever the season. We paused on Magdalene Bridge for a few moments to watch the sun glinting off the water and the punts drifting beneath us. Joe told me about his return to academic life, how he'd grown tired of managing huge numbers of people and of always having to worry about the bottom line.

'When the offer of a chair at Columbia came up a couple of years ago, it was too good to turn down. I wanted to get back to research. And there were other reasons. . . .

'You must have taken quite a drop in salary,' I remarked.

He shrugged. 'Who cares? It's only money. And, anyway, I've got plenty stashed away from all those years in business. I could afford to please myself.'

We walked on to the restaurant. When we were given the menus, Joe fumbled in his jacket pocket and got out a pair of half-rimmed glasses on a chain. He saw me looking at them and grinned.

'Used to think these were the epitome of middle age,' he said, 'but I had to give in to it a couple of years ago.'

He scanned the menu. 'What shall we have to drink?'

'I'll stick to mineral water. I've got to pick Grace up fron nursery later.'

'Oh, a glass of wine won't do you any harm.'

That was something else I'd forgotten: how bossy Joe could be.

I ordered tagliatelle and wild mushrooms and Joe ordered

penne with chorizo and chilli. A wine conversation followed and Joe ended by ordering a half-bottle of Soave and a half-bottle of Valpolicella. I smiled to myself. The old Joe would have been satisfied with beer or coca-cola.

Joe slipped his glasses back in the breast pocket of his linen jacket.

'Know when I *really* began to feel middle aged?' he asked. 'When I realized that I'd overtaken Elvis.'

'Overtaken Elvis?'

'He was forty-two when he died. That was always a kind of benchmark for me somehow.'

'I'm closing on it fast.'

'Comes to us all.'

'You've still got your collection of fifties and sixties singles?'

'You bet.'

A waiter arrived with the wine and mineral water. When he'd gone, I said:

'Do you remember when John Lennon died?'

'Yeah.' His face grew thoughtful.

In my mind's eye I saw a tiny kitchen in a flat in Birmingham; I was washing up, Joe drying. The radio was on the windowsill. I reached over and switched it on just in time for us to hear the news. I could see Joe now, standing stock-still, the tea towel in his hand, his mouth open in surprise and dismay.

'December 1980,' he said. He poured out two glasses of wine. 'You know, I don't live far from the Dakota Building. Just a few blocks away. Riverside Drive.'

'You must have done all right for yourself.'

He grinned. 'I've done OK. But so have you. You're head of department, aren't you? Plenty of hits when I looked you up on the web. Books, conference papers, articles. Short-listed for an award a couple of years ago. You're a big noise in nineteenth-century fiction.'

We chatted about academic life. The waiter brought our main courses.

'How are you settling into St John's?' I asked.

'Oh, OK. But it's awfully quiet. Hardly anyone about.'

'Cambridge *is* quiet in August. Virtually all of my colleagues at St Etheldreda's are away.'

'And the academics I do bump into seem a little on the reserved side – even to me – and I'm from Boston. I'm finding it kind of lonely.'

'They're funny places, Cambridge colleges. Do you know the limerick about St John's?'

He shook his head.

'There was a young man of St John's, Who wanted to roger the swans, "Oh, no", said the porter, "Make free with my daughter, But the swans are reserved for the dons." '

Joe laughed.

'They don't take deference quite so far these days,' I added.

Joe gestured towards the wine, I shook my head and he poured another glass for himself.

'So you haven't brought your family with you?' I said.

The pause was just long enough for me to realize that this might have been a tactless question.

'Amy's taken the kids to her parents in Florida. Her folks retired there.' He hesitated. 'Actually, we're, well, we're separated.'

From the way he said it, I guessed that this was recent.

'I'm sorry.'

He shrugged. 'Ah, well.'

An awkward silence was broken by my mobile phone ringing.

'I'm sorry,' I said, delving inside my handbag, 'I hate it when people do this, but I think I'd better get it. I'm expecting to hear from Stephen. He's in LA—'

'LA?' Joe's eyebrows shot up.

But it wasn't Stephen. It was Stan.

'Cass, we've got a problem. It's Melissa. There was a one-thirty call for a run-through of Act Two. She hasn't turned up. We've tried ringing the cottage but there's no reply.'

'Her mobile?'

'Switched off.'

'What about the nursery?'

'Kevin's tried there. She was supposed to drop Agnes off at one o'clock but she didn't show.' I heard a murmur of voices in the background. 'Look, Kevin wants to have a word with you.'

There a moment's pause while the phone was handed over. Then I heard Kevin's voice.

'Hi, Cass. I don't suppose that there's anything to worry about. Perhaps she went back to bed and fell asleep ... she might have unplugged the phone so as not to disturb Agnes. But the thing is I wasn't able to contact her earlier on either.'

I thought he was trying to sound unconcerned, but he couldn't conceal the anxiety in his voice. I began to feel uneasy, too. Melissa was a professional down to her fingertips. Being late for rehearsal was so unlike her.

'I was wondering,' he said. 'Could you possibly pop over and see if she's all right?'

'Pop over?' Across the table from me Joe was pouring himself another glass of wine. Then I understood what Kevin meant. 'But Kevin, I'm not at home. I'm still in Cambridge. I'm having lunch with a friend.'

'Oh, I see.' He sounded downcast.

I looked at my watch. 'Look, I've got to pick Grace up from the nursery soon anyway. I can be back there in, oh, say three quarters of an hour.'

'You angel. You're sure? I mean, more than likely, she'll turn up here before long, but if you're going home anyway ...'

'I'll ring you when I get there, OK?'

I put the phone away. Joe was looking at me sympathetically. 'Trouble back at the ranch?' he said.

I screwed up my napkin and put it on the table. 'It's probably nothing, but Melissa, she's taking the leading role in *East Lynne*, she hasn't turned up at the rehearsal and she lives near me, she's got a baby the same age—'

'Hey, you don't have to explain. You need to check it out. You go right ahead.'

'You don't mind? I'll have to show you the theatre another time.'

'We're old friends, aren't we? Of course I don't mind. I'll have a coffee and read the paper.'

I gathered my things together and got up from the table. Still I hesitated.

'You're sure?'

He spread his hands. 'Of course. There's plenty of time. I'm here until Christmas. And my diary isn't exactly full.'

'You must come over and have a meal.'

'I'd really like that.'

As I pushed past his chair, he took hold of my hand to delay me for a moment. 'It's been great seeing you, Cass.'

'You, too.' We smiled at each other.

With a little sigh he released me.

The crunch of my tyres on the gravel was loud through the open window. I pulled up outside Melissa's cottage and got out of the car, leaving Grace asleep in the back. I rang the door bell and listened to the sound reverberating inside the house. No one came. I tried the door. It was locked. There was only one small window on this side of the house and the curtains were closed; the glass panel in the front door was covered by a blind.

I walked back along the drive and through a gate into the garden. I crossed the lawn to the french windows. Putting my hand up to shade my eyes, I peered in through a crack in the curtains. I couldn't see much. I went further on round the corner of the house and tried the back door. That was locked too. The dustbin was lying on its side and rubbish was strewn around: coffee grounds, tea-bags, potato peelings. Odd that Melissa hadn't cleared that up.

I went back to the car. Grace had fallen asleep on the drive over, but she was stirring now and she would soon want feeding.

I picked the phone off the passenger seat and rang the theatre.
'She's not here,' I told Kevin.
'She hasn't shown up here, either – and her mobile's still off.
Oh God, where can she be? Has her car gone?'
'Well, it's not in the drive.'
'Have you checked the garage?'
'I'll do that now.'
I made my way along the drive, my feet sinking into the
gravel. The garage was a few feet beyond the end of the house.
It was the old-fashioned sort with a corrugated iron roof and
double doors. I turned the handle and pulled one of the doors
open. There was a fresh oil-stain in the middle of the concrete
floor and there was a shelf on which rested a set of spanners and
a petrol can. But that was all.
'It's empty.' I told Kevin. 'What now?'
'I don't know what to think . . .'
'Perhaps she's had an accident on the way into work.'
'I'll ring the hospital . . .'
'Wait a minute. I thought I heard something.' I held the phone
away from my ear and turned my head towards the house. The
house and the garden and the car with Grace in the back lay
silent in the heat. A single fluffy white cloud drifted across the
vault of the sky. There wasn't a soul in sight, but it's never
completely quiet in the country. The rustle of the breeze in the
beech hedge and the distant rumble of a train served simply to
emphasize the cottage's isolation.
'It's nothing,' I said.
And then I heard the sound that made the hairs on the back of
my neck stand on end.
It was the thin, high wail of a baby. And it was coming from
inside the house. For a few seconds I just stood and listened,
waiting for the crying to change and subside, somehow expecting that someone would go to her. From the phone close to my
ear Kevin was saying:
'Cassandra, what's happening? What is it?'

The crying continued; it settled into a rhythmic bawling, as if Agnes was pausing only to catch her breath.

'There's something wrong,' I said. 'It's Agnes. She's inside the house and she's shrieking her head off.'

'Agnes is in the house? On her own?'

'Can't you hear her?'

'But where's Melissa? She must have been taken ill or something, she'd never leave Agnes—'

'Is there a spare key somewhere?'

'Oh, God, oh, God, yes, there is. Let me see ... where exactly? Yes, go into the garden shed. There's a row of jamjars on a shelf. One of them is full of nails. Look in the third or fourth along. There's a key to the back door buried in it.'

'I'll ring you when I'm in the house.' I closed up the phone.

Grace was beginning to grizzle. I thought of leaving her alone in the car, but I didn't want to do that. The crying baby, the lonely countryside, the locked house: it was all giving me the jitters. I wanted Grace with me. I unbuckled the car seat – it was heavy but at a pinch it could be used as a carrier – and went back through the garden, past the french windows and round the corner of the house.

The shed was opposite the back door and shared a paved area with it. It was cool and dim inside and very neat: implements hung on the wall, plant-pots were arranged according to size. I tipped the nails out of the jamjar on to the floor and spread them out. The key was one of those old-fashioned ones with a long shank.

I stepped out into the sunshine, squinting in the glare. I struggled for a few moments with the key. There was a click, but even then the door didn't open. I shook it. It rattled but held firm. Bolted from the inside, I guessed. I didn't bother ringing Kevin. I went back into the garden shed and looked around for something to wrap round my arm. There weren't any sacks, so I made do with half a dozen black plastic bin-liners. I put Grace in the middle of the lawn well out of the way, and pulled the wooden garden-bench up to the kitchen window. When I broke the glass, the sound startled me – and Grace, too. She let out an indignant yell. I opened the window and climbed through. There was the sound of breaking glass again as my foot caught a tumbler on the draining board and knocked it on to the tiled floor. Ten seconds later I was standing in the middle of the kitchen floor, breathing heavily. I brushed myself down and looked around.

The washing-up from the night before hadn't been done and the kitchen smelt stale. I went to the back door and unbolted it. Grace was crying now and my breasts were aching in sympathy. I'd have to feed her soon. I collected her from the lawn and went through the house into the sitting-room. The sight of our tea mugs still on the coffee table in front of the sofa added to my sense of unease.

Over my head Agnes paused for a moment in her wailing. She resumed it on a slightly different note.

I put Grace in her carrier in the middle of the floor. When she realized that I was leaving her there, her face crumpled up and she began to yell. The stairs were steep and dark, lit only by a shaft of sunlight that came from the partly open door of the main bedroom. I was half-way up when my telephone rang. I nearly jumped out of my skin. I fished it out of the pocket of my shirt and answered it. It was Kevin.

'Cass, what's happening? Are you in the house? Is Agnes all right?'

'Oh, Christ, Kevin. I've only just got in. I had to break the window. Hang on.'

I went into Agnes's room. When she saw me the yells subsided into hiccuping sobs. She was red in the face. She lifted up her arms and whimpered. I went over and lifted her out of her cot. She grabbed my shirt with both hands and nuzzled into me. Holding the hot little body close against my shoulder, I went into Melissa and Kevin's bedroom. The duvet had been thrown back as if Melissa had just got out of bed. A faint scent of roses hung in the air. I went back on to the landing and opened the bathroom door. That room was empty, too. I put my hand on a bath towel that trailed down from the towel-rail. It was dry.

I went back into the larger bedroom and sat down on the bed. I got out the phone again.

'Kevin. I've got Agnes. I think she's OK. But Melissa's not here.'

'You mean – she's left Agnes on her own?' Kevin sounded incredulous. 'She wouldn't do that! She must be there somewhere. Have you looked?'

'Of course I have!' Agnes had got hold of a fold of my shirt and was mumbling it in her mouth. Downstairs Grace was bellowing with rage.

'But where is she?' Kevin persisted.

'Stop asking me that! I don't know where she is! It's like the *Marie Celeste*. You'd better get over here.'

Chapter Seven

I was sitting on the sofa in the sitting-room with Grace at my breast and Agnes propped up beside me asleep, when Stan's car drew up. A door slammed and a moment later Kevin erupted into the room. Stan followed more slowly.

'She hasn't come back,' Kevin said.

It was more of a statement than a question, but I shook my head anyway.

He stared past me through the open kitchen door.

'She hasn't done the washing up.' In other circumstances the look of astonishment on his face would have been comical.

The next moment he was heading for the stairs. I heard him running up them and the floorboards overhead creaking as he went from room to room. Stan and I looked at each other.

'Is Agnes all right?' she asked.

'I had to change her nappy. She was sopping wet. I found some formula in the kitchen and gave her a bottle. Then she fell asleep.'

Overhead we heard the sound of drawers being pulled open, then footsteps, the creak of a wardrobe door. Stan sat down heavily in one of the cane chairs.

'I don't like the look of this,' she said. 'Not one little bit.' Her hennaed hair was pulled up and fastened with a rubber band on top of her head, making her look like an anxious Pekinese.

Kevin came back down the stairs more slowly than he had

gone up. He flung himself into the other armchair. His slicked-back hair was untidy and a heavy lock was hanging over his eyes. He brushed it back, mussing up his hair even more.

'Her handbag's gone,' he said. 'But everything's still there in the bathroom. Toothbrush and so on. She hasn't taken her make-up.'

'I keep thinking there must be some straightforward explanation that we haven't thought off,' I said.

'Is her diary here?' Stan asked.

'That would be in her handbag,' Kevin said. 'But there's a calendar with appointments on it. In the kitchen.' He got to his feet. He was back a few moments later, shaking his head. 'There's nothing on it. And anyway I know what she was supposed to be doing this afternoon. She was supposed to be rehearsing.'

'And the baby,' I said. 'Even if she did have an appointment I just can't believe she'd go off and leave Agnes like this.'

We looked at her. She had slumped sideways and her mouth had fallen open. She was sleeping with that total abandon that you only see in babies and small children.

'OK,' Stan said. 'What if Melissa needed something from the shops and just popped out to the nearest one, thinking Agnes would be OK for half an hour.'

'But she's been a lot longer that. Why hasn't she come back?' Kevin objected.

'I don't know . . .' Stan shrugged. 'A flat tyre? An accident?'

'But wouldn't she have rung us on her mobile?' Kevin said.

'If she had it with her,' I said. *And if she was capable of using it.* I had a momentary vision of a car bonnet buckled against a tree or the boot of a car sticking out of a ditch – or even worse – out of the water. The drainage ditch. . . .

Stan's eyes met mine and I wondered if she was thinking the same thing.

'Why don't you go and check it out? Take my car,' Stan said. She reached for her bag, pulled out the keys and tossed them to Kevin.

When he'd gone, Stan said, 'I suppose it's better for him to feel he's actually doing something.'

'But you don't think that's what happened?'

'Well, do you?'

I busied myself with Grace. She had dropped off my breast and had fallen asleep with her head back and her arms hanging down. I wiped her mouth and settled her down in her carrier. I didn't really want to think about what might have happened to Melissa. I was concentrating on the present, going with the flow. Any moment Melissa might turn up safe and sound and I would just have wasted time and energy worrying about her. And if she didn't, well. . . .

I buckled Grace into the carrier and got to my feet.

'How about a cup of tea?' I said.

'Couldn't hurt.'

Agnes had woken up and was making little mewing noises. Stan picked her up and took her into kitchen.

'What a mess!' I heard her say, as I followed her. 'And what a stink!'

The stale atmosphere had sharpened into something that was nose-wrinklingly fishy. A couple of flies were buzzing around a dirty plate. There was broken glass on the window sill, the draining-board and the floor. Stan fastened Agnes into her highchair at the table. She found a dust-pan and brush and began to clear up the broken glass. I began slotting cups and glasses into the dish-washer. I was scraping a gluey conglomeration of fish-skin and bones into the bin, when the telephone rang in the sitting-room.

Stan and I looked at each other. I was closest.

'I'll get it,' I said. I went into the sitting-room, my heart beating fast. Please, I thought, let it be Melissa – or Kevin saying that he's found her. . . .

I picked up the phone. 'Hello.'

'Cass?'

'Stephen?'

'Are you all right? I've been trying you everywhere. I rang home and then the theatre. Fred told me you were here.'

Stan had appeared at the kitchen door. *Stephen*, I mouthed. She nodded and turned away.

'Why haven't you been in touch,' I said. 'And where have you been? I rang the hotel and they said you'd cancelled your room.'

'Oh, God, I'm sorry. It's just been one thing after another. There were problems landing, we were circling for ages. Then when Bob met me at the airport, he insisted that I stay at his place. He's got a guest-house attached to his home and he's putting me up there. And there was a pile-up on the freeway, we were stuck in this jam, and then it was so late . . .'

'It's OK. As long as you're all right.'

'A bit jet-lagged, but I'm fine otherwise. You should see this place, Cass, it's up in the hills, there's an enormous swimming-pool. You and Grace will have to come next time.'

'Next time!'

He laughed. 'Are you both OK?'

I glanced over to where Grace was tilted to one side in her carrier fast asleep.

'We're fine.'

'I gathered from Fred that there's a bit of a panic on.'

'You could say that. Melissa seems to have disappeared.'

'How do you mean?'

'She didn't turn up for rehearsal and she's not at the cottage. Agnes was here on her own, crying. I had to break in through the kitchen window.'

It took a moment or two for him to take this in.

'But what's happened? Has she done a bunk, do you think? I can't believe it. Not Melissa.'

On the other end of the line I heard something in the background, perhaps a door opening, then the murmur of a voice. Stephen said, 'Just a moment' to someone and then he turned back to the phone.

'Are you sure you're OK?' he asked me.

'Yes, really, Stan's here now and Kevin.'

'Bob's waiting to drive me into the office. Look, I'll ring you very soon, OK?'

'Yes, please.' There was a pause. Then Stephen said in a different tone of voice:

'We'll be all right, won't we?'

' 'Course we will.'

'Love you.'

'And you.'

'Give Grace a kiss for me. I'm sure Melissa will turn up soon.'

It wasn't until he had hung up that I realized that I still didn't have a phone number for him. And there was no point ringing 1471 for an overseas number.

In the kitchen, Stan was filling the teapot with hot water. Agnes was banging the tray of the highchair with a plastic spoon. When I went in, she paused and fixed her eyes on my face. Her gaze slid past me to the open door. She was looking for Melissa. Her face creased into a frown and I felt a pang of sympathy. I brought my face down to hers and nuzzled her cheek. She grabbed my hair and rubbed her face against mine. Stan put the teapot on the scrubbed pine kitchen table and set out mugs. I lifted Agnes out of the highchair and joggled her up and down. She grinned and blew a raspberry at me; I blew one back. Stan was just about to pour out the tea when we heard a car drawing up. She froze with the teapot in her hand. All three of us looked towards the kitchen door, and Agnes began to wriggle in anticipation. From where I sat, I could see through the sitting-room to the front door. As soon as Kevin came in I could tell from the set of his shoulders that he hadn't found Melissa. He looked at me with a mute appeal in his eyes: please, please, tell me that she rang while I was out, tell me that this nightmare is over.

I shook my head. 'I'm sorry.'

His face fell. He came into the kitchen and, with a groan, sank into a chair opposite me.

'No sign of her?' Stan asked.

Kevin shook his head. 'Nothing. They didn't remember seeing her in any of the shops she might have gone to. And I didn't see any sign of the car. I've kept on trying her mobile. It's still switched off.'

Stan put the teapot down with the tea still unpoured.

'Well, then, it's obvious what we've got to do next,' she said.

Forty-five minutes later, Constable Tim Fisher was listening to Kevin's account of how Melissa had failed to turn up for rehearsal.

'I was worried right away,' Kevin said. 'She's never late.'

We were ranged around the coffee table in the sitting-room, Fisher and Kevin in the two cane chairs, Stan and I on the sofa opposite. Mercifully, both babies were asleep now and we'd put them upstairs in the cot.

I'd expected someone young, but Fisher was around my own age, forty or so, and his brown hair, cut short, was evenly flecked with grey. He was leaning forward now, head a little on one side, nodding from time to time, occasionally glancing at Stan and me to see if we agreed with what Kevin was saying. For a moment I saw us all through his eyes. Kevin was wearing a tightish white T-shirt that showed off his muscular body, and jeans with a heavy belt with a big buckle. He was too olive-skinned to look pale, but his face was sallow and there were dark shadows under his eyes. Stan was wearing a dress like a long black T-shirt, which went down to her calves. Over it she wore a vivid fuchsia shirt with the ends knotted under her breasts; it should have clashed horribly with the scarlet of her lipstick – a little smudged now – and the henna of her hair, but somehow it didn't. She was fidgeting in a way that I knew meant she wanted a cigarette. They both looked larger than life, appropriately theatrical. And what about me? I was suddenly conscious of my own dishev-elled hair and damp armpits. That morning I'd put on a smart white linen shirt in honour of my lunch with Joe. It was creased now and there was a long narrow smudge of dirt down the sleeve. That must have happened when I climbed in through the window.

I looked at Fisher. He was wearing dark-blue trousers and a pale-blue short-sleeved shirt that showed off tanned forearms. It was a uniform, I suppose, but a discreet one. He was like an envoy from another world, somewhere slower and calmer – and, I realized, he was looking at me. Kevin had reached the point where he had rung me and asked me to check up on Melissa. I took up the story.

When I'd finished, Fisher said;

'I'll need to take some details.' He picked up his clipboard from the coffee table and took a biro out of his shirt pocket.

'Her full name. . . ?'

'Melissa Meadow,' Kevin said.

'Is that her real name or her stage name?'

'Her stage name. She was originally Melissa Godwin.'

No reason why I should have known that, I suppose, but I was mildly surprised all the same.

'Age?' Fisher continued.

'Thirty-three.'

'Description? Height? Hair? Eyes?'

'She's about five-foot eight inches, has shoulder-length blonde hair and blue eyes. I can give you one of her publicity shots if that would help.'

'Yes, it would. Any distinguishing feature? Birthmarks? Scars? That kind of thing?'

Kevin thought for a moment and shook his head. 'Don't think so.'

'What about her arm?' Stan said. 'There was something. I noticed it yesterday when I was helping her out of her costume. A red mark. Looked like a burn.'

'Oh that,' Kevin said. 'Yes, she did that a few days ago. Getting something out of the oven.' He looked at Fisher. 'I thought you meant something permanent.'

'I'll make a note of it all the same.' Fisher was scribbling on the form. 'Right or left arm. And whereabouts on the arm?'

'Now let me think. Right arm?' Stan said, looking at Kevin. He nodded and she went on, 'Yes, just below the elbow. On the inside.'

I found myself thinking that it was the kind of detail you'd need to identify a body. I pushed the thought away.

'So: she took her handbag,' Fisher went on. 'And mobile phone, yes? But it's switched off whenever you try to ring her. I'll need the number and details of her car.'

'It's a red Renault Clio,' Kevin said.

'Fairly distinctive. Good. OK. Number plate?'

Kevin told him.

'And Dr James here was the last person to see or speak to Miss Meadow?'

'Sorry, no, that's *not* right. Didn't I say? She rang me at the flat in London. It must have been just after Cass left. About quarter to eleven, something like that.'

'Tell me a bit more about the flat in London.'

'The flat? Well, it's in Camberwell Grove—'

'Is that your permanent home, would you say?'

'Well, yes, it gives us a base and it's convenient for the West End. I had a meeting with my agent – and I needed to go to the flat to collect our post. It seemed easiest to stay overnight.'

'Could your wife have gone there?'

Kevin stared at him. 'But surely . . . I mean, I was there myself . . .'

'What time did you leave the flat to come up to Cambridge?'

'About seven.'

'I'd like you just to check that she isn't there.'

Kevin got up and went over to the phone. He punched in a number. The three of us sat in silence.

Kevin shook his head.

'It just rings,' he said. 'I must have forgotten to put the answering machine on.'

87

He sat down again.

'Any relatives she might have gone to?'

'Her parents are dead – oh, not recently,' Kevin said, answering the question on Fisher's face. 'There's a sister, but she's in Australia.'

'A close friend she might have gone to?'

Kevin hesitated. 'I can't think of anyone in particular. She has friends, of course, but . . . no, I can't think who . . .' His voice trailed off.

'To go back to that phone call. What did she say?' Fisher asked.

'Nothing special, really. She wanted to know how I'd got on with my agent. She said Cassandra had been over and that she was tired and about to go to bed.'

'She wasn't angry or upset?'

Kevin frowned. 'We didn't have an argument, if that's what you mean. She seemed just as usual.'

'And was that your impression, Dr James?' Fisher turned to me. 'Any sign of depression, would you say?'

I thought back to the previous evening. I saw Melissa's pale face, the weary way she had brushed her hair back.

'Not depressed, exactly, but she did look tired. She found the play a bit of a strain. I know that.'

'She did get a bit upset earlier in the day,' Stan said. 'She was having problems with her costume, nothing that couldn't be sorted, but she did get a bit emotional.'

'Any post-natal depression?' Fisher was looking at Kevin now.

Kevin pursed his lips and shook his head. 'Not really. It was a worrying time, of course, Agnes was six weeks premature. Had to spend a week or two in an incubator. But she's fine now. Melissa was coping all right.' He appealed to me. 'Don't you think so, Cass.'

'Better than me to tell you the truth. She was much better organized.' I wondered why I was speaking in the past tense. I hoped Kevin hadn't noticed.

'So, nothing else out of the ordinary in the last day or two? Apart from the upset over the costume?'

'Well,' I said, 'there was something.' I told him about the anonymous letter. The expression on Fisher's face, sympathetic, concerned, didn't change, but still I got the impression that his interest had been aroused.

'An anonymous letter containing a poem by Byron,' he said thoughtfully. 'What did you make of it, Mr Kingleigh?'

Kevin shrugged. 'Not much, really. Actors get a lot of letters from cranks and people with a screw loose. There's nothing in it, usually.'

So Melissa had told him after all? Kevin glanced at me and quite suddenly I knew that she hadn't. I saw the four of us as people sitting down at a game of poker, each wondering what cards the others held. And Kevin, I thought, was bluffing, though I couldn't imagine why.

The telephone rang. We looked at each other, then Kevin sprang up. He snatched up the receiver.

'Yes?'

We watched the hope die in his face.

'Oh, Richard. No,' he said. 'She's not back yet. I'm talking to the police at the moment, can I ring you back? Yes, yes, Stan's here.' He held the phone out to her.

'Tell him I'll ring him back on my mobile.' She looked at Fisher. 'Do you mind? It's the theatre manager, I think I'd better . . .'

Fisher nodded and Stan disappeared into the kitchen. Kevin sat down wearily.

'I need to know what Miss Meadow was wearing last night,' Fisher said.

I thought for a moment. 'A long, floaty dress. Pale yellow, I think.'

'Ghost,' Kevin said. Fisher and I stared at him. 'Ghost,' he said again. 'It's the name of the designer. She never wore the same thing two days running, so she won't have been wearing that. Unless . . .'

His voice trailed off. He leaned forward and put his head in his hands.

Unless she never took it off, and that would mean that she had been gone for – how long? It was nearly six o'clock now, so it was around nineteen hours since anyone had seen or spoken to her. How long had Agnes been alone here?

Stan came quietly back into the room and sat down next to me.

'And you're sure you can't think of a friend she might be with?' Fisher asked Kevin. 'There's usually someone—'

'No! No! No! What have I just told you! I can't think of anyone. Don't you think I'd have already rung them if I had any idea who she might be with! I can't believe she's done this!' He was half-rising from his seat. The force of his anger was such that I found myself leaning back. He clenched his fists and I thought for a moment he was going to jump up and grab Fisher by his shirt.

'Kevin!' Stan spoke sharply.

He looked at her as though he didn't know who she was. Then the anger left his face. He sat down again.

No one spoke for a few seconds. Then Kevin said:

'I'm sorry. I'm beside myself with worry. I can't imagine what can have happened. It's so unlike my wife, leaving Agnes like this. And there's the play as well. I just don't know how we're going to manage.'

Fisher had stopped writing, but his pen was still poised over the form. 'That's all right, sir.' He spoke with equanimity, but he didn't look up from his clipboard. 'However I will still need whatever names you can give me. And I think it's time I had a look round. Mr Kingleigh, I'd like you to look in the wardrobe and see if the dress is there. And perhaps, you will be able to tell if anything appears to be missing.'

'I always helped Melissa choose her clothes so I've got a

pretty good idea what should be there.' Kevin stood up. His shoulders were drooping. Now that his anger had subsided, he seemed meek and anxious to please.

The two men went upstairs together. In silence Stan and I collected the teapot and cups and took them into the kitchen. We sat down on either side of the kitchen table.

'I thought Kevin was going to lose it there completely,' I said. 'I've never seen him like that before.'

'It's no wonder, is it. It's not just his wife that's missing, it's his leading lady as well. It's Wednesday today and we open on Monday!'

'What's going to happen?' I asked.

'That's what Richard rang up about. And why I didn't want to take the call in front of Kevin. You see, if Melissa doesn't come back, we'll have to ring round the agents, see who's available to take her place.'

She saw the expression on my face.

'Sweetie, I'm just as worried as you are, really, I am,' she said. 'It seems hard, I know, but . . .' she shrugged.

'The show must go on?'

'Just think about it, Cass. How many actors are there in the production? A dozen or so? And then there's all the technical crew, there's the big opening that's already been publicized, the sponsors, the tickets sold. We have to open next Monday, come hell or high water. It's a cast-iron rule. Everyone accepts that. Melissa knows that as well as anyone.'

'But what if she's had some sort of crisis and she comes back in a day or two?'

Stan shook her head. 'We can't wait on the off-chance. We'll have to act soon. Richard said that if she's not back by nine o'clock tomorrow morning, he'll be ringing round the agents to find a replacement.'

'Will he find someone at such short notice?'

'Oh, he'll find someone. But who? That's the question. We'll be lucky if we can get anyone a tenth as good as Melissa – and it's such a big part. Will they be able to learn it in time?'

At 6.30 Stan went into the garden and smoked a cigarette. At seven o'clock she made cheese sandwiches. At ten past seven Jake rang to find out what was happening. At seven I fed Grace. At 7.30 I gave Agnes another bottle and put her to bed. At 7.45 Tim Fisher rang to say that the police had gone round to the flat in Camberwell. There were no signs of Melissa. And there were no reports of an accident involving her car. Stan went out into the garden for another cigarette. At eight o'clock Clive rang to find out what was happening. At 8.30, Richard rang to find out what was happening. At nine Stan rang home and told her husband she'd be staying the night at Kevin's. At 9.15 she had another cigarette. At 9.30 she told me to go home and get some rest. I didn't need much urging. My head was buzzing with fatigue. Kevin had spent the whole evening by the phone. I was exhausted by the strain of watching him pace up and down, by the adrenaline rush every time the phone rang, and by trying and failing to think of reassuring things to say.

I drove slowly home. I brought Grace in from the car. The unusual day had worn her out and she didn't wake up. I went up to my bedroom and put her in the bed with a pillow next to her to stop her falling out. I was so tired that as I undressed the floor seemed to rise up to meet me. I dropped my jeans and shirt on the floor and fell into bed.

Almost instantly it seemed I was on the stage of the Everyman theatre. Stephen was explaining to me that he would have to be back for the opening of the play, because he was going to take the part of Lady Isabel. Of course I'd have to rewrite it – and could I please be quick about it, because the play was going to start in half an hour.

I woke with a jerk. The red numbers on the digital clock told me that it was ten. I'd been asleep for ten minutes. I was wide awake. Without putting the light on I padded over to the window and opened it. The cool night air made me shiver. It was a clear, cloudless night. The sky was the colour of slate, but soft like flannel. Far across the fields I could see that the lights were still on at Journey's End.

Twenty-four hours ago I'd been saying goodbye to Melissa. Was there anything that could have warned me about what was going to happen? I saw her as I'd seen her the night before, leaning over the cot, brooding lovingly over her baby. Had she been too anxious, perhaps, had it all got too much for her? Somehow I didn't believe it. But what was the alternative? I was too tired to think it all through, and yet I couldn't stop the events of the day going round and round in my head. If only I could talk things over with Stephen. But it was mid-afternoon on the West coast. He was somewhere in the bowels of the huge organization that was employing him – and I couldn't even remember what it was called.

I got back into bed beside Grace. Sometimes having the radio low in the background helps me to sleep. I switched it on. Grace must have grabbed it earlier and shifted the tuning knob. It was always happening. Instead of *A Book at Bedtime*, there was a blast of music. Even before I consciously recognized the voice and the song, my stomach flipped over. Elvis Costello singing 'My Funny Valentine'. I hadn't heard it for years. Perhaps it was because I was so tired, so strung out, but the memory it brought back was so vivid that I could see the little flat in Birmingham as if it were yesterday: the bed on a metal frame that came down from the wall, the narrow galley kitchen full of flecked fifties Formica, the surprisingly large and very cold bathroom. I saw the books on the floor, the cheap, spindly furniture, the absurd jungle-pattern wallpaper, the windows misty with condensation.

The barrier between past and present wavered and dissolved. It almost seemed possible that if I caught the bus from New Street station, as I'd so often done all those years ago, and walked in through the door of that flat, my old life would be waiting for me there. Joe was in the kitchen, making spaghetti and meatballs. Elvis Costello was on the hi-fi. We knew that LP – *Armed Forces* – by heart. He'd hold his floury hands apart and

I'd walk into his arms. I felt the pressure of his wrists as he crossed them in the small of my back and locked my body into his.

His hips moved against mine in time to the music. We fumbled for each other's mouths. Without taking his lips off mine, Joe walked me backwards to the kitchen door. The flat was so small that it was only a few steps to the bed. . . .

The telephone rang, slamming me back into the present. My heart was beating fast as I picked up the receiver.

'Cass?'

'Joe!' It was as if I had conjured him up.

'I hope this isn't too late to ring? I rang a little earlier . . . didn't want to leave a message.'

'Oh, no, it's fine.'

'You sure? You sound as if I've woken you up.'

'No, no, it's not that. It's just that . . .' I cast around for something to say and what I came up with was the truth, even if it wasn't the whole truth. 'I'm so worried about Melissa.' And I told him what had happened.

'Jeez, you've had quite a day, haven't you? But the most likely thing: it's all got too much for her and she's gone off somewhere to get her head together.'

'But leaving her baby like this?'

'It does happen.'

'Joe, I can't help thinking that something awful might have happened to her. To have done that – perhaps she was feeling really desperate, perhaps she's . . .'

'Don't let's even go there,' he said firmly. 'Hey, now listen, shall I tell you what happened to me one time? Amy once did something much the same.'

'She did?'

'That's right. She went off, booked herself into a motel for the weekend. I didn't have a clue where she'd gone. Left me holding the baby. Literally. Josh must have been – oh, about nine months? Yeah, that's right and Daniel was about three.'

'But why?' I found myself relaxing back on to the pillow, like a child listening to a bedtime story.

'We had a row. She thought I wasn't helping enough with the kids. She wanted to teach me a lesson. She did that all right.'

'But Kevin would have said if it had been something like that.'

'Well, now, would he? People are funny, you know? Might be too embarrassed or ashamed.'

'You're right.'

'You're on your own out there, aren't you? When does that man of yours get back?'

'Stephen? Not sure. Maybe not for another week at least.'

'If you want to talk, give me a ring. Any time. And you know what? Things'll look better in the morning. She'll probably have shown up by then. Let me know what happens, OK?'

'OK.'

'Better now?'

'Yep.'

I did feel better, more ready to believe that Melissa hadn't come to any harm. Joe had always been able to talk me down when I got into a state. When we'd first met he had seemed so much older, more worldly wise. Four years is a big gap when you're only twenty-one. Of course there was no earthly reason now to think that Joe knew better than I did – maybe there never really had been. But I couldn't help being comforted all the same.

That feeling evaporated the next morning when Stan rang me up to say that there was still no news of Melissa.

Chapter Eight

'YOU never intended to be back in time,' I said.

Kevin didn't reply immediately. I glanced up from my script. His face had a yellowish tinge and his slicked-back hair was greasy.

But when he did at last speak, his voice was firm enough.

'Well, my dear, you've rather put yourself beyond the pale, haven't you?'

'For myself I am past caring – I no longer even wish to marry you – but why should my child – our child – have to suffer for our sin?'

It was eleven o'clock the following morning and we were on stage at the Everyman. Over in his office Richard was busy on the phone trying to track down a substitute for Melissa. Kevin had asked me to read the part of Lady Isabel so that rehearsals could continue. It was strange to hear myself reading Melissa's lines, lines I'd written myself. Stranger still to realize that I was so used to hearing her speak them that I was using exactly her own intonation.

'Hard lines, I agree,' Kevin drawled. 'You can't suppose I'm pleased that my first son's been born a bastard. But you must see that it's quite impossible for me to marry a divorced woman—'

'Kevin. Cradle,' Stan said in a low voice.

'What?'

'You were supposed to go over and look in the cradle during that speech.'

'Oh Christ.' He thumped his forehead with his clasped fist. 'But no, hold on, we changed that. It was too awkward getting back across the stage. We decided to move the cradle instead.'

There was silence.

'So why *haven't* we moved the fucking cradle?' he enquired. 'It's still on the other side of the stage.'

'Sorry, Kevin. Can't think how that happened.'

I couldn't see Stan clearly, because I was wearing my reading-glasses, but I could tell from her voice that she was flustered. It wasn't like her to make this kind of mistake.

There was another silence. Then Kevin said:

'I'm sorry I snapped. The situation's getting to me.' He walked across the stage and picked up the cardboard box that was standing in for the cradle. 'OK, then. Cradle over here. I walk over to it, I pick up the baby . . .'

As Kevin moved back and forth across the stage, I let my mind wander. In my reading-glasses, everything more than a foot or two away was blurry, adding to the feeling of unreality induced by lack of sleep and anxiety. Kevin looked even more villainous as Captain Levison when he wasn't in focus. I took my glasses off and rubbed my eyes. The theatre was empty except for a smattering of people in the stalls. Stan, still wearing yesterday's clothes, was in the front row. A little further along Clive and Belinda were sitting next to each other. Clive had stretched his long legs out and had his eyes closed. Belinda was reading her script, her lips moving – going over her lines, I guessed.

I found my eyes straying up to the spot in the dress-circle where Belinda had seen the strange figure and Stan and I had found the seat down. There was no one up there today.

'We'd better take it from the top,' Kevin decided.

I turned my attention back to my script. I was about to put my glasses back on when something flickered on the edge of my vision. I looked back into the auditorium. At first, I couldn't see anything. The contrast between the light on the stage and the dimness at the back of the auditorium was too great. I thought I'd imagined it, then just as I was about to turn away again, there was another movement. I could see now that there was someone standing next to the double doors at the back of the stalls.

I gave an involuntary gasp.

'Cass?' Kevin was staring at me. Then he turned to follow my gaze down the centre aisle. The people sitting in the front rows of the stalls were also looking round.

'Who's that?' Kevin said.

His voice was gentle, hopeful almost. He didn't sound as if he was challenging an intruder. Then I understood: he thought it was Melissa. Could it be? But no, the figure was advancing down the aisle now and it was too tall.

Then it spoke.

'I do beg your pardon. The chap on the stage door said you'd be breaking in five minutes or so. He thought it would be OK if I slipped in the back.'

It was Tim Fisher. I'd been holding my breath. I let it out in a sigh.

Fisher reached the front of the stalls. Kevin stared down at him. 'I thought for a moment,' then, his voice quickening, 'You haven't. . . ?'

'I'm sorry, no, we haven't found her. Not yet. I'm afraid there are a few more questions I need to ask you. Perhaps we could have a word in private? And I'd like to see Miss Meadow's dressing-room.'

'Of course.' Kevin hesitated. 'I'll take you up there. We can talk there, too. There's only one thing. Richard's going to be here in a few minutes, and the rest of the cast and the crew. We've got to explain what's happening.'

'No problem. I'll just wait here, shall I?' Fisher took a seat in the front row.

Kevin went over and sat down on the sofa at the side of the

stage. I went down the stairs and sat next to Stan. She gave me a conspiratorial grimace. No one spoke. Soon people began to drift in. They were a scruffy lot: cast and crew alike wore washed-out T-shirts, badly cut jeans and baggy cardigans. And yet one could immediately tell which were the actors; there was something in the way they dropped into their seats or perched on the edge of the stage, in the way that they frowned and murmured to one another. Their concern was genuine, but they were always acting just a tiny little bit, I thought, always projecting themselves even when they were at their most sincere.

Richard appeared on the stage. He was a big, heavy man, with a high-domed forehead which he was now mopping with a large white handkerchief. Jake and Geoff were close on his heels. All this excitement and drama: it must be money from home for Jake, I thought. Richard headed for Kevin. He seemed suddenly to realize that Jake was right behind him, and flapped his handkerchief at him like a man shooing away a wasp. With evident reluctance Jake backed off and signalled to Geoff. They retreated to the side of the stage.

Richard sat down next to Kevin and spoke quietly in his ear. Kevin nodded. He got up and went to the front of the stage. There was an immediate hush.

Kevin cleared his throat.

'All of you will know by now that Melissa has gone missing. I won't need to tell you how desperately worried I am. I'm hanging on to the hope that it's all been too much for her and she's gone away somewhere for a few days to rest and recuperate.' There was a murmur of sympathy. 'In the meantime,' he paused, 'we're going to carry on as best we can. Richard has arranged for Phyllida Haddon to come up from London to take over as Isabel.'

The faces around me registered mingled concern and relief.

'We didn't expect to get someone like her at such short notice, but she just happens to be free,' Kevin went on. 'Something to do with a change in a filming schedule. We've got some bloody hard work ahead of us. But I know I can rely on you. This afternoon I want the entire cast here. We'll have a complete read through with Philly, and then we'll go through the blocking with her. I'm breaking now for . . .' Kevin looked at Fisher. 'Twenty minutes?' he asked.

Fisher nodded. It was oddly as though their roles were reversed, and it was Fisher who was the director, Kevin merely an actor.

'OK, twenty minutes,' Kevin went on. He looked at his watch. 'Then we'll go on rehearsing Act Three, Scene One. Everyone else back here at two o'clock sharp, OK? But before we break, Richard wants a word . . .'

Richard joined Kevin at the front of the stage.

'The press,' he said. 'There's no way we're going to keep them off our backs. We've already had the *Sun* on the phone. I don't want them to get hold of a lot of idle gossip. That's not going to help Melissa – or Kevin. I'm not suggesting that we keep it quiet – couldn't do that if we tried, actually, but I want everything, and I mean everything, to go through the press office. Understood?' Everyone nodded. 'OK, that's it, folks.'

'Phyllida Haddon,' I said to Stan. 'The name rings a bell.'

'She's done a lot of period stuff. There was one of those Henry James adaptations. *The Spoils of Poynton*, was it? And that movie version of *Our Mutual Friend*.'

I remembered her now. 'Oh, yes, of course, she played Bella. Blonde hair, one of those rather bland, doll-like faces.'

'Kevin was right. We're lucky to get her at such short notice.'

I detected a reservation in her voice. 'You don't sound very sure.'

Stan heaved herself to her feet. Her hair, which had been screwed into a rough bun, was listing to one side. She rolled it up and skewered it into place with a pencil.

'Well, between you and me she has a reputation for being difficult to work with. And that's the last thing we need at the moment. As long as she turns up on time, says her lines and doesn't bump into the furniture, that's all I ask.' Stan yawned. 'I'm gagging for a cup of coffee. Come on.'

We made for the green room.

'Are you going to go home at lunch-time?' I asked.

'Probably not. I'm OK actually. Brushed my teeth and changed my knickers. Those are the main things. I always keep a bag with a few spare things in the car. You just never know in this job. I once had a technical rehearsal that went on all night. Don knows to expect me when he sees me.'

'I'd offer to collect Agnes from the nursery, but I've only got one car-seat.'

'All sorted. Don't worry. They'll keep her until six and we'll bring her back to the theatre. I'm going to get my eldest, that's Tilly, to come and baby-sit. Kevin'll be here until God knows when. It's going to be all hands to the pumps.

'That reminds me,' she went on. 'I'll have to go over to the car-hire place – sort out a car with a baby-seat, otherwise Kevin won't be able to take Agnes home. Will you be a love and drive me over to Mill Road later on, so that I can drive it back here?'

' 'Course I will.' I looked at her with affection – and a touch of envy, too. Was there anything she couldn't cope with?

'Have you ever thought of running for prime minister?' I asked.

She grinned. 'Nah, wouldn't be enough of a challenge.'

There was no one in the green room. I filled the kettle and Stan dropped into one of the leatherette chairs. There was a knock on the door. Without waiting for an answer, Jake poked his head into the room.

'OK if we come in?'

Stan looked at me and rolled her eyes.

'If you must,' she said.

Jake slipped into the room, followed by the silent Geoff. He propped his bum on the edge of the table and began leafing through the latest copy of the *Stage*. Geoff leant against the wall, his camera resting on his chest. He was wearing beige trousers and an off-white shirt. With his tow-coloured hair, he was almost camouflaged against the cream-painted brickwork. I realized that I'd almost stopped noticing him. He had a talent for effacing himself.

I made the tea and sat down in the other armchair. I flipped over the pages of my scripts, looking ahead to the next scene I'd be rehearsing. Stan heaved a sigh and wrapped her hands round her mug.

No one said a word.

Jake tossed the *Stage* on to the table. 'This is about as interesting as watching paint dry,' he said.

'I'm not feeling very chatty,' Stan said.

'Me neither,' I agreed without looking up from my place.

'Of course, I know everyone's upset,' Jake said. 'I hardly slept last night myself.' His voice was full of emotion. I looked up in surprise. It was true: there were shadows like bruises under his eyes. Perhaps I'd misjudged him.

'It could have meant the end of everything,' he continued. 'I haven't got nearly enough in the can. And worse than that: if the play doesn't actually open, the company'll pull the plug on the documentary.'

'And goodbye, to Jake's dream of being the brightest star in the documentary firmament,' Stan said. Her voice was rich with contempt.

'A woman goes missing, leaving her baby behind, and that's all you care about?' I said incredulously.

Jake flushed. 'Well, no, I'm worried about Melissa, of course I am.'

Stan got up. She went over to Geoff and put the palm of her hand over the lens of his camera.

Geoff prised himself off the wall. 'Careful,' he muttered, 'you'll scratch the lens.' It was the first time I'd heard him speak. He had a Scottish accent of the soft, West Coast variety.

'Turn it off,' Jake said.

'No, on second thoughts,' Stan said. 'Let's have this on tape.'

She put a hand on the camera and swivelled it towards Jake. 'Can I point out, Jake, that there's more than one way of looking at this? An injection of drama is just what you need to make your documentary go with a swing. So don't be surprised if you find the police taking a long, hard look at you!'

Now it was Jake's turn to look outraged. His eyebrows shot up. His mouth fell open.

'No one could think ... I wouldn't ...' He turned to me. 'Cassandra, you don't think I had anything to do with this?'

I couldn't help laughing in spite of the seriousness of the situation.

'Of course I don't and neither does Stan. She's trying to wind you up, that's all. I should try to disguise that naked ambition if I were you. It's not very attractive.'

But he wasn't looking at me any more. And a moment later I realized why. The door behind me was creaking open.

'What's going on here?' Kevin said.

Everyone looked at him. Stan was still standing next to Geoff with her hand on the camera. Kevin scanned our faces. 'What's going on?' he asked again, looking at me.

'It's nothing,' I said. 'Really.'

'Have you been causing trouble, Jake?' Kevin spoke quietly but there was something in his voice that made me glad the question wasn't addressed to me.

'I haven't done anything, really I haven't.'

'I hope that's true. Don't forget that I have a veto on this documentary. I'm not sure that I want you here at all now, not sure that it's still appropriate. But certainly if I hear so much as a whisper that you've been upsetting any of the cast, you are dead meat. Understand?'

To my relief Jake had enough sense not to say anything. He nodded and slipped out of the door. Geoff followed.

'Are you really going to boot him out?' Stan asked. 'I know he's a tiresome little bugger, but he'll be screwed if you do.'

'Oh, Christ. I don't know. I'll have to think about it.' Kevin lifted a hand wearily to his head. 'I'd almost forgotten what I came down for. Cass, could you go and see Fisher? He's up in Melissa's dressing-room. He wants to talk to you.'

I felt a nostalgic longing for a past that was only two days old. The dressing-room looked as if Melissa might walk in at any moment to take up the reins of her life. The make-up box was there and the small mirror on its stand. The same old pink cardigan with a frayed sleeve was hanging on the back of the door. Only one thing had changed: Fisher was now sitting where Melissa had sat. And yet as I looked around the room I wondered: *was* that the only thing that was different? I wasn't quite sure that everything was just as I had last seen it.

'I wanted to ask you a bit more about that letter Miss Meadow showed you,' Fisher said.

'Yes, of course.' I was still scanning the dressing-room. There was something, but what was it? Something missing or just something out of place?

'What's the matter?' he asked.

'What? Oh, nothing, sorry.' I gave him my full attention. 'You wanted to know more about the letter?'

'Mr Kingleigh hasn't been able to put his hand on it. It's not at the cottage. And it's not here either. We've just looked through the drawers. Mr Kingleigh says that his wife told him about the letter when he spoke to her the night before last on the phone. He didn't actually see it.'

I remembered my certainty that Kevin had first heard of the letter only when I mentioned it. I wondered if I should say something, but after all it was only an impression. Perhaps Melissa had told him about it. But why had she concealed it from him in the first place? I wondered again if the letter was from someone in Melissa's past.

'You did actually read it yourself?' Fisher continued.

'Yes, here in this very room.'

'You said it was typed?'

'Word-processed, yes. The font was unusual. Gothic script. And the signature, "The King of Cups" – well, it wasn't a signature, exactly – it was printed – did I mention that it was upside down?'

He frowned. 'Wouldn't that be rather difficult to do?'

'Not really, You could print out the letter without the signature, then turn the sheet of paper round and send it through the printer again to add the signature. You'd have to fiddle about a bit to get the spacing right, but it wouldn't be all that hard. I could do it on my own printer.'

'OK. What did you make of the content of the letter?'

'About the signature, I had no idea. But I did recognize the poem and I've found out a bit more about it since then. It was written in eighteen seventeen in Venice, where Byron was leading a pretty riotous life – and he'd also just heard of the birth of an illegitimate daughter, Allegra, by a mistress he'd already discarded. And he'd left England under a cloud the year before – his marriage had failed and there were rumours of incest with his half-sister.'

'But the poem didn't seem to mean anything to Miss Meadow?'

'She seemed mystified by it. Didn't even know that it was by Byron. And I got the impression that there was something else – apart from the content – that Melissa found disturbing. But I didn't get a chance to ask her what it was.'

'You can't hazard a guess?'

I shook my head.

'What did she do with the letter after you'd read it? Did she put it in her handbag perhaps? That would explain why we haven't found it.'

'Just let me think.' I closed my eyes and tried to visualize what had happened. I saw the letter in my hand. We'd still been talking about it when Kevin came in. I heard the sound of the door hitting the wall and felt again the force of Kevin's presence like a gust of wind through the room. I saw his face smiling and apologizing. And what had I done with the letter? It was infuriating. I simply could not remember. But I *did* remember that Melissa hadn't wanted Kevin to see the letter. So had I perhaps slipped it into my handbag? And then what? Had I handed it back to Melissa later? No, I couldn't have done that, because I'd left the room before Kevin. Could it be that it was still in my handbag?

'I might still have it. I think I'd better just check,' I said.

Feeling self-conscious, I tipped the contents of my handbag out on to my lap: mobile phone, purse, lipstick, a book, a small knitted rabbit that belonged to Grace, biros and pencils, an electricity bill, screwed-up paper handkerchiefs, a little black leather-bound notebook. There were also several letters, but Melissa's wasn't among them.

'Sorry, no, it's not here,' I told Fisher, as I stuffed everything back in. 'I'm afraid I can't quite remember what happened to it.'

'Pity,' he said. 'Let me know if you do remember.'

He sat back and stretched out his legs thoughtfully. He smoothed back the grey-flecked hair, which was cropped short like the coat of a dog.

'Tell me about the play,' he said.

'The play?' I was surprised.

He sat up and leaned forward. 'It's a Victorian melodrama, isn't it? But Mr Kingleigh also said that you'd had a hand in it.'

'Oh, yes, I see. Kevin thought it needed updating a bit in terms of language and so on. That's where I came in. *East Lynne* actually started off as a novel.'

'Oh, that much I do know,' he said. 'Written in the 1860s, by Mrs Henry Wood. And would I be right in saying that it was one of the novels of sensation, the successors to the Silver Fork novels of the 1840s? *East Lynne* could be said to combine their interest in high society with elements common to the sensation novel, such as – let me see – sexual transgression, moral retribution?'

I stared at him with my mouth open.

He was enjoying my surprise.

'The most famous line, "Dead, and never called me mother," appeared not in the novel, but in the stage version and was parodied in the music hall. Now, was *East Lynne* published after Mrs Braddon's *Lady Audley's Secret* or before?' he mused.

I got a grip on myself. 'Before, actually. Eighteen sixty-one. *Lady Audley's Secret* was eighteen sixty-two. But I'm surprised you don't know that.'

'Touché. Couldn't resist showing off,' he said, smiling. 'Actually, that really is about all I know. I'm doing an Open University degree and I did a credit on the nineteenth-century novel a couple of years ago. I looked up *East Lynne* last night. I've never actually read it. Could you run it by me, tell me what happens? And about the part Miss Meadow was playing?'

'Yes. Of course. Let me see.' I thought for a moment, getting it clear in my mind. The interview was developing the reassuring give-and-take of a tutorial. I was on my home ground here. It was only later that I realized how skilfully Fisher had put me at my ease.

'Well, you were right about the aristocratic element,' I told him. 'Melissa was playing Lady Isabel. Her father gambles away all their money, and when he dies, the family lawyer, Archibald Carlyle, buys East Lynne, the ancestral home. He asks Lady Isabel to marry him. He's a long way below her socially, but he's a gentleman and a good, honest man. He's played by Clive Ashton. Isabel not only accepts his proposal, but falls passionately in love with him. They get married and have three children. But then everything starts to unravel. Isabel finds out that Archibald is having clandestine meetings with Barbara Hare, a young woman who used to be in love with him. The meetings are actually about Barbara's brother, who is on the run for a murder he didn't commit, but Isabel doesn't know that.'

Fisher was nodding and fingering the magnifying mirror, tilting it this way and that on its stand. The feeling that I'd had earlier came back to me. There *was* something missing. What had been on the dressing-table before? Wig stand? Yes, that was still there . . .

'What happens next?' Fisher had stopped playing with the mirror and was looking at me.

'Oh, yes. sorry. Well, there's a villain of course, the real moustache-twirling thing. That's Captain Levison, who's played by Kevin. Levison works on Isabel's jealousy and seduces her. She runs off abroad with him and of course she's absolutely ruined. Archibald divorces her. There's an illegitimate baby and she's abandoned by Levison. It was all very topical: the novel was written only four years after the eighteen fifty-seven Divorce Act. Anyway, then she's nearly killed in a railway accident and the baby dies. Back in England they think she's dead, too. She returns in disguise as Madame Vine and is employed as governess to her own children.'

Fisher's eyes were fixed on me. He seemed about to say something. I waited for him to speak but he nodded for me to continue.

'By now Archibald is happily married to Barbara Hare, and Isabel suffers torments seeing them together.'

'So she's punished for leaving her husband and children?'

'Oh, yes. She suffers terribly. It's agony for her, especially being apart from her children. Maternal love: that's a real driving force in the novel. I think that was one reason for its popularity. And of course it's terrifically sentimental. We've had to tone that down. It'd be too much for a present-day audience.'

'And what happens to the seducer?'

'Oh, don't worry, he doesn't get off scot free, far from it. He turns out to be the real murderer. There's a really grisly courtroom scene where the judge puts on a black cap and Levison faints in the dock. In the end the sentence is commuted to penal servitude for life, but it's pretty dramatic all the same.'

Fisher said, 'That last rehearsal, the one where Miss Meadow broke down. Which part of the play was it?'

'It was the scene when Levison persuades Isabel to leave her husband.'

'And the next day Miss Meadow disappears, too. Maybe that's more than a coincidence.'

When he put it into words, I could hardly believe that I hadn't made that connection myself. I was just too close to it all, I suppose that's what it was.

'That hadn't occurred to you before?' Fisher said, seeing the expression on my face.

I shook my head. 'No, but now that you've mentioned it, yes, life does seems to be mirroring art in a rather disturbing way.'

'It sounds to me as though she had a very demanding part, especially for a woman who'd just recently become a mother herself. In the play her baby dies, and then the older child. That's right, isn't it?'

'She *was* finding it demanding,' I said slowly. What had she said to me in this very room about squeezing the gap between herself and the character she was playing? Had it just become too difficult, too painful? I shook my head.

'I just can't see it. I mean, if she was upset about the children in the play, surely that would make it even less likely that she'd go off and leave her own child behind.'

'That's what she seems to have done,' Fisher said.

'Is there any chance – I mean, I'm sure you've thought of it – what if she didn't leave of her own accord?'

'That she was abducted?' He pursed his lips. 'No sign of forced entry – except by you, of course.' He smiled at me. 'She took her handbag. She seems to have left in her own car.'

'Someone could have forced her to drive it away.'

'But how would that person have got to the cottage in the first place if they didn't have their own transport? They'd have had to walk from Ely station – in the dark probably, though that depends on when she left. We won't be in a hurry to rule anything out, don't you worry, but some kind of nervous breakdown is by far the most likely explanation.'

I nodded.

The interview seemed to have reached its end, and I waited for Fisher to indicate that. But he remained seated, looking down at his notebook. There was more to come. He raised his eyes to mine.

'I have to ask you this,' he said. 'Could there be another man involved?'

'I don't think so. I have wondered,' I admitted. 'But I never got the slightest hint of anything like that. Apart from anything else, how would she have found the time – or the energy? She had a six-month-old baby and was in rehearsal for a play that opens next Monday.'

Fisher nodded. 'Was the marriage in good shape, would you say? It can be a difficult time, when a baby comes along. Some men don't take kindly to not being the centre of attention any more ... perhaps Mr Kingleigh ...' Fisher shrugged. 'He's an attractive man, after all. ...'

Yes, Kevin *was* attractive: that easy charm, that energy. There would be no lack of opportunity. He seemed devoted to Melissa, but how well did I really know him?

Fisher picked up on my hesitation. 'Well?'

'Things seemed OK.'

Fisher nodded. He didn't speak. Neither did I. I recognized this technique. In fact, I used it myself in tutorials. If the silence stretched out for long enough, someone would usually feel impelled to break it. Now I knew what it felt like to be on the receiving end.

I sighed. 'I don't know what I can tell you. Melissa didn't talk very much about her marriage. But then, women don't usually, I mean, in terms of complaining. Not much point in bad-mouthing a guy if you have to go on living with him. It's better to make the best of it.'

Fisher tapped his pen on his notebook. He said, 'I got the impression that Mr Kingleigh could be a little, well, shall we say, demanding? Does he tend to make a fuss if things aren't exactly as he likes them?'

I saw again the expression on Kevin's face when he realized that Melissa hadn't done the washing-up.

'He does like things to be just so,' I admitted.

Fisher went on. 'What I'm getting at is this: if Miss Meadow was already under pressure, it could have added to the strain if a lot was also expected of her domestically.'

As he spoke, a memory came to me of an evening that Stephen and I had spent over at Journey's End. I saw Kevin and Melissa in the kitchen there. He was clowning about in an apron, tossing pancakes with one hand, his other arm round Melissa's waist.

'I thought they were happy,' I said, with more conviction. 'Kevin *is* a bit fussy, especially about what he eats, but then he has to be. He's got a serious food allergy, he can't eat nuts. He does most of the cooking, actually.'

'OK.' He didn't sound altogether convinced. Nevertheless he leaned back in his chair and put his notebook away in his breast pocket.

'What will you do next?' I asked.

'Appeal through the press. There'll be a lot of coverage anyway. I'm afraid you're in for a pretty rough time. Everyone here at the theatre will be pestered, including you. In fact, especially you. You were the one who broke into the house to rescue the baby. That's the down side. The plus side is that when someone well known like Miss Meadow goes missing, they generally don't stay missing for long. Her photo will be everywhere and someone will remember seeing her.'

Her photo? Something snagged in my memory and that was it: I knew now what had been nagging at me since the beginning of the interview.

'There's something missing,' I said. 'Something that was here on Tuesday. Melissa's family photos. There was a collage of them – pictures of her family, Kevin, Agnes – in a big silver frame. Right there on the dressing-table. What's happened to it?'

*

'I'm sorry, Cass,' Rose said. 'Stan's just popped out to the chemist. She wanted to get some nappies for Agnes. She said to tell you she won't be long.'

I'd arrived out of breath in the costume department. I'd arranged to meet Stan there to take her over to the car-hire place. The interview with Fisher had taken longer than I'd expected. The department was housed on the third floor at the back of a small office block a couple of hundred yards from the theatre. During working hours, the quickest way in and out is via the fire escape. I had just run up them, only to find that Stan wasn't there.

I sank on to a stool. It was another hot day and sunshine was coming in through the metal-framed windows on to a big dressmaker's table which stretched almost the whole length of the room. Bolts of fabric were heaped up at the far end. At this end Rose was leaning down to jot something in a notebook lying open in front of her. She was an elegant young woman with long blonde hair so straight that it might have been ironed.

'It's awful about Melissa,' she said without looking up. A wing of hair fell forward. She pushed it back behind her ears and added something to her list. 'Do you think it's post-natal depression? My sister had that really badly. I bet that's what it is.'

'Maybe,' I said non-committally.

'Stan told me about Phyllida Haddon,' Rose went on. 'We could do worse. I think she has very much the same sort of figure as Melissa. With any luck I'll be able to get away with a few nips and tucks. Otherwise I just don't know how we'll manage. I mean Lady Isabel wears a different dress virtually every time she comes on, and there's the Madame Vine outfit, too.' She bit her lip and looked sideways at me. 'I expect you think I'm awful worrying about that at a time like this.'

'No, I don't,' I said. 'The dress rehearsal's only two days away: I'm not surprised you're worried.' I was more amused than anything by the way that everyone was seeing the situation from their own point of view: Stan was concerned with reliability and punctuality, Rose with whether the costumes would fit. And was I any better? I'd been wondering whether Phyllida would learn the lines in time. No point in feeling guilty about that. It was natural and it didn't stop me being worried sick about Melissa at the same time.

Rose sighed. 'I'll be working round the clock, and that reminds me, I'd better grab a sandwich before Phyllida arrives and I know the worst. Do you mind if I just pop out? I won't bother to lock up if you're going to wait here for Stan.'

'Off you go.'

'Thanks. I won't be long.'

She grabbed her handbag and pushed open the opaque glass door on to the fire escape. The metal structure shuddered and clanged under her feet and then there was silence.

Normally the costume department is one of the busiest places in the theatre. If it isn't an actor having a fitting, it's one of the technicians dropping in to get a button sewn on. There were often more people in here than there were in the green room. There's somewhere like that in most organizations, a special corner where people tend to gather and gossip. Today there was no one, and I was glad of a few more minutes to myself.

I was rattled by those missing photos. I couldn't think of any reason for anyone except Melissa to take them. I was pretty sure no one else *could* have taken them, because the dressing-room was kept locked. Fred had a spare key and he had opened it for Fisher to use that morning. Melissa's key was presumably in her handbag, and that was, presumably, with her, wherever that was. I could think of only one reason why she would take the photos: she knew she was going to leave home and she wanted to take a memento with her. And if that was the case, then it wasn't a spur of the moment thing. And that in turn meant that when I had seen her that last evening, she must have known that she was going to leave. But surely I would have had some inkling that something was wrong. Or had I been so distracted by the prospect of meeting Joe that I just hadn't noticed? I didn't want to believe that of myself.

I got up and wandered around the room. The door to the costume store was ajar. I pushed it open and breathed in a smell that was compounded of dust, sweat and something a little acrid: dry-cleaning fluid, maybe. It was a large windowless room densely packed with racks of costumes suspended from the ceiling and winched up so that they hung a couple of feet from the floor. The place was like a child's dream come true, the biggest dressing-up box in the world.

I strolled down the aisles, pausing here and there to stroke the fake ermine on an Elizabethan costume or the satin of an Edwardian ball-gown. If I'd been in a carefree mood, I'd have been tempted to try out a new identity as a twenties flapper, or a nun, or the conductor of a brass band. There were big open boxes of shoes jumbled higgledy-piggledy together. I remembered Rose telling me actors were protected by Equity from having to wear other people's shoes. They're the only things that have to be new for every production. Ranged on the shelves all the way round and stacked up on the floor were dozens and dozens of brown cardboard storage boxes. I read the labels: boned bodices, bust supporters, bloomers. There was a kind of poetry about it. The lid was askew on 'Ostrich – primary and secondary'. I put out a hand to press it back down and met resistance. Something made of heavy black material, like felt, had been stuffed in on top. I pulled it out, revealing flattened ostrich-feathers underneath. The garment fell into my arms in heavy folds. I held it at arm's length and shook it out.

I was looking at a long, black hooded cloak lined in a shiny black material like silk. Why hadn't it been hung up? I could think of only one reason.

The rows of hanging costumes muffled sound. That was why I didn't hear someone come into the outer room and why I nearly jumped out of my skin when the dark shape of a figure appeared at the door.

'Cass?'

'Stan!'

'Christ! You nearly gave me heart failure. I didn't realize there was anyone in there. Where's Rose?'

'Went out to get a sandwich. She'll be back any moment.'

Stan came into the room.

'What have you got there?' she asked.

I held it up for her to see. 'I found it stuffed into the top of a box of ostrich-feathers.'

She looked at me then back at the cloak.

'Someone borrowed this, didn't they?' I said. 'And when they brought it back they needed to conceal it in a hurry. It wouldn't be difficult to do that, would it? To take this away and bring it back without anyone knowing?'

Stan was gazing at the cloak through narrowed eyes,

'No, it wouldn't. You know what it's like here. People in and out all the time. You'd have to choose your moment, of course. It's not very likely that anyone would notice it was missing . . .'

'Because of course you wouldn't need it for very long.'

'Oh no, not for very long. Just long enough to hide in the back row of the dress-circle and scare the shit out of an impressionable young woman.'

She took the cloak from me and examined it carefully as if it might yield up a clue to whoever had taken it.

'It's awfully creased, but other than that . . .' She frowned.

'What's the matter?' I asked.

'Can you smell something?'

I sniffed. 'Don't think so.'

She gathered the collar and hood close to her face and buried her nose in them. She gestured to me to come closer. I lowered my own face to the cloth. I caught the faintest possible whiff of something musky, something just on the very edge of being familiar.

'I thought I smelt something, but it's gone,' I said.

We looked at each other and I knew we were thinking the same thing. Whoever had last worn this cloak had left something of themselves behind.

'What was it?' I asked. 'Not cigarette smoke?'

'No,' Stan said. 'But I think I've smelt it before.' She raised the cloak to her face again. She shook her head. 'I can't even smell it now.'

'Would you recognize it again?'

'I think I might.'

Chapter Nine

I put my hands over my ears and closed my eyes. Grace stopped yelling. I kept my eyes shut and my ears covered. After a bit I opened my eyes. Grace was staring up at me from her cot. She was goggle-eyed, her face was scarlet, and a string of saliva was swinging from her jaw. Cautiously I lowered my hands from my ears. She glared at me and took a long deep breath, filling up her lungs. There was a pause that stretched out like the moment before a wave breaks. The noise began again.

I'd gone through her usual routine: a feed, a bath, and I'd put her down to sleep at 7.30. I looked at my watch. It was quarter past nine. She'd been crying off and on for over an hour and a half.

I'd arrived home to find ten separate messages from journalists on the answering machine. I had no idea how they'd got my number and I knew it was only a matter of time before they discovered where I lived. It was a miracle that I hadn't found them camped out round the front door. I thought of driving back to Cambridge and holing up in Stephen's flat, but I wanted to be close to Journey's End in case Melissa came back.

Probably Grace was picking up on my stress but knowing that didn't help. I put my hands under Grace's arms and lifted her up so that her face was level with mine. Her eyes were blurred with tears and she was pumping out scream after scream.

'Are you doing this on purpose?' I said through gritted teeth.

Didn't she know how tired I was – and how anxious I was about Melissa? I couldn't take this a moment longer. I wanted to shake her until she stopped. I shut my eyes and took a deep breath. Then very carefully I put Grace back in her cot. I left the room and closed the door on her. I could hear her still shrieking as I walked out of the front door.

I went round the house into the garden and the noise grew fainter. The evening air was cool on my face. I sat on a wooden bench by the stream. The sky was a dark, rich blue shading to lilac in the west, and a full moon, so improbably huge and yellow that it didn't seem real, hung on the horizon. I breathed in the mingled scents of night-scented stock and tobacco plants that Stephen had planted nearby. Behind that I caught a whiff of something more acrid, redolent of water and decaying vegetation. There was a loud *miaow*. Bill Bailey came threading his way through the long grass, his white paws and face and chest luminous in the dusk. He leapt up lightly on to the bench beside me and pushed his head against me. I stroked him absently. I was shaken by the quickness and fierceness with which my anger had flared. I wondered whether Melissa could have felt like this. Agnes wasn't such a demanding baby as Grace, but could it be that Melissa had found it all too much? Where was Melissa now? Was she watching the same moon? Or was she sitting in some bleak hotel room looking at the photograph of Agnes that had gone from her dressing-room. But maybe the room wasn't bleak? Perhaps she was lying in a luxurious bath somewhere, sipping champagne.

The idea was ludicrous. I just could not see her going down the stairs at Journey's End and walking out of the house with no idea how long she was leaving Agnes to cry unheard, with no one to feed her, to comfort her, or to change her nappy. Every time I tried to picture this I hit a blank in my imagination. I tried not to think of it, and found I was thinking instead of the cloak that I'd found in the costume store. If Stan and I were right, it meant that the figure in the dress-circle had not been some stranger who had wandered in off the street. It was someone in the theatre, someone I knew; they had been playing a silly and cruel joke. It couldn't be anything more than that, could it? I felt again the weight of the cloak and saw its inky blackness, so deep and rich that it had been like clasping a piece of the night.

All of a sudden the evening air was chilly. I realized that Grace had stopped crying. I got up and went into the house. The moment Grace saw me she began to howl again. I'd only been away ten minutes, but I felt calmer now. I reached down into the cot for her. When I was little, I thought that if you concentrated hard on someone, perhaps they would feel the pressure of your thoughts, like a hand on their shoulder, however far away they were. A small part of me must still think that: when the telephone rang, the first thought that shot through my head was, Melissa!

I left Grace in the cot and went into the kitchen. I picked up the receiver.

'Hello?'

'Cassandra?' It was Kevin.

I'd been holding my breath. I let it out in a sigh.

'Oh, hi. Is there any news?'

'No, there's nothing. Cass, I'm really worried. It's Agnes. I think she's ill.' I could hear the strain in his voice.

'Oh God, what's the matter?'

'She's really wailing. I've never heard her like this before. It's been going on for an hour or more.'

'OK, OK, don't panic. Do you think she's in pain?' Grace was bellowing in earnest now and I didn't hear what he said next. 'Sorry, Grace is making such a racket, I didn't catch that. You'll have to speak up.'

'I can't tell if she's in pain or not!'

'It might be colic or something.' I was almost shouting.

'Shall I call the doctor?'

'This is impossible. I can't hear myself think. Hang on a sec.'

I closed the kitchen door. The decibel level dropped a little. I took a deep breath and put the phone back to my ear.

'Cass, Cass, are you there?' Kevin was saying.

'Yes, yes, I am. Does she feel hot?'

'Hot? I don't think so,' he said vaguely.

I sighed. We were getting nowhere fast. 'Look, it's probably not serious. Do you want to bring her over? We can try and sort her out together.'

'She yells even louder when I pick her up. I wonder – I know it's a lot to ask . . .'

'I'll come over.'

'Cass, you're an angel.'

'It's OK. Actually, I've been having trouble getting Grace off. A ride in the car might do it.'

After he'd rung off, I stood rubbing my forehead with the heel of my hand. It occurred to me that perhaps Grace was crying *because* she wanted a ride in the car. Perhaps I'd end up taking her out every night. Oh Lord. What should I take with me to Kevin's? Baby thermometer, yes, and what else? The phone rang. I snatched it up, expecting it to be Kevin again.

'Yes?'

'Cass?' It was Stephen.

'I'm so glad to hear your voice.'

'Same here.'

'Grace is playing me up,' I said. 'She just won't go to sleep, I don't know, maybe she's teething. Listen, can you hear her bellowing?'

'You poor thing. You sound absolutely shattered. I'm sorry I'm not there to help. Can I say hello to her?'

'Hang on.' I went and lifted Grace out of her cot. I hitched her high up on my hip so that she could share the receiver with me.

'Here's Daddy,' I told her. I didn't think she'd recognize his voice, distorted by the phone line, but the tears vanished as if by magic and she started to giggle. Maybe she'd been missing him, too, or maybe she just liked the telephone. When someone's only six months old, it's hard to tell.

'What's the news about Melissa?' Stephen asked, when I'd got him to myself again.

'No news.' I told him about the events of the day. 'And now there seems to he something wrong with Agnes. I'm about to go over.'

'What, now? It must be, what is it, getting on for ten? Are you sure that's a good idea? Cass, you're wearing yourself out.'

'Well, for tonight, at least, I can't leave the poor bloke to struggle on his own.'

'If Melissa doesn't turn up soon, Kevin will just have to make proper arrangements for Agnes to be looked after.'

'You don't sound very sympathetic.'

'I wouldn't be all that surprised if it turned out that Melissa had had enough of Kevin. I've never really taken to him. It's strange her leaving Agnes, though. That's the bit I can't understand.'

'You don't like him? You've never said.'

'Well, Melissa's your friend and anyway it wasn't anything I could put my finger on. The guy's always pleasant enough. Just one of those things. "I do not like thee, Doctor Fell, The reason why I cannot tell, But this I know and know full well, I do not like thee, Doctor Fell." '

'Masculine intuition?'

'Something like that.'

'So how are you getting on?'

'Oh, it's great, just terrific. I'm getting on like a house on fire with Bob. In fact . . .'

He hesitated.

'What is it?'

'Oh, well . . .'

'Stephen! I know there's something! Out with it!'

'Oh, all right, but we can't really discuss it over the phone. We'll have to talk about it when I get back. The thing is: I've been offered a job.'

'A job!'

'It's the clients out here. I think that's part of the reason they got me over.'

'Oh, what! You don't need a job! You've got your own firm!'

'Look, I'm not saying I want to take it, but it's such a good offer, we have to at least consider it. Like I said, we can talk about it when I get back.'

'And what about me and my job! I don't want to move to Los Angeles!'

'Look, I'll have to go. I'm at work. I'll ring you again tomorrow, OK?'

Low-lying mist drifted across the fields. The land between the Old Granary and Journey's End could almost have been covered with water just as it had been for centuries before the fens were drained. The moon was higher now. It seemed strange that it could be so light and yet this was a world drained of colours. I drove to the cottage across a landscape of black and grey and silver, of silhouettes and shadows.

Kevin was standing framed in the doorway. He came hurrying out across the gravel and opened my car door.

'You've been a long time,' were his first words.

'Stephen rang,' I said shortly.

'Sorry: didn't mean to sound – it's just that I'm worried.'

'Of course you are,' I said, relenting. It wasn't his fault that I was in a filthy mood.

I got out of the car and opened the back door. The drive had done the trick. Grace was fast asleep. I unbuckled her and followed Kevin into the house. Something was not as I expected it to be. I looked round. Everything looked much as usual. Kevin must have tidied up. Then I realized what was missing.

'I don't hear Agnes crying,' I said.

Kevin looked surprised. 'You're right. That's funny. She was still at it when you drove up.'

'Let's go up and have a look at her. I'll leave Grace down here.'

I put her on the sofa and Kevin helped me to fence her in with cushions. I took my bag up with me in case I needed the thermometer. In Agnes's room the night-light cast a dim glow. Agnes was lying on her side with her thumb by her cheek as if it had been in her mouth and had fallen away when she fell asleep. I bent down into the cot and put a finger on her cheek. She didn't seem to have a temperature and her breath was coming from her lips in even little puffs.

'She seems fine,' I said. 'It's hard to believe that there's anything wrong with her.'

'And yet she was yelling her head off only a few minutes ago.'

'Hard to believe,' I repeated, shaking my head. And no sooner were the words out of my mouth than I thought, perhaps it's hard to believe *because it isn't true*. This baby had surely been peacefully asleep for more than a few minutes. I looked at Kevin. He was standing at the bedroom door. Light was coming in from the landing, throwing his face into relief. The dark eyes looked darker than ever. His face was impassive, carefully blank, it suddenly seemed to me. The fens were stretching out in darkness all around us. There was no one else for miles. And who knew I was here? Stephen – yes, but Stephen was thousands of miles away, damn him. But if this had been a ruse to get me over here, then why. . . ? Kevin took a step towards me. At that moment my mobile phone rang. Kevin paused. I pulled the phone out of my bag and answered it.

'Cass?'

'Stephen!' I said.

'Look, I was a bit abrupt earlier. Of course, there's no question of us moving if you don't want to—'

'No, no, you're right. We ought to talk about it at least. No harm in seeing what's on the table.' My eyes met Kevin's.

He turned away and switched on the main light.

'That's right,' Stephen said. 'Are you at the cottage?'

'Yes, yes, I am, I'm with Kevin now.'

123

'Is Agnes OK?'

'I think so, yes.'

'Oh. That's good. D'you think I could have a word with Kevin?'

I handed the phone over. From Kevin's reactions I guessed that Stephen was commiserating with him. Then he frowned. 'Well, if you think so,' he said. 'Yes, yes, I'm sure you're right. I'll give you back to her, shall I?'

He handed the phone over.

'I've told Kevin not to let you overdo it.'

'Oh, really!' I felt a familiar flash of irritation, but I couldn't be truly angry. I'd been so relieved to hear his voice.

'Got to go. I'll ring you tomorrow. Love you.'

'Yeah, good. I mean, me too. 'Bye then.'

Kevin was standing on the landing now, his back turned tactfully towards me. I joined him and we went down the stairs in silence. I was longing now to get away.

Kevin said, 'Don't come into the theatre tomorrow. Stay at home. Have a rest.'

'I'm sorry about Stephen. I'll be OK, honestly,' I said, rummaging about in my bag for my car keys.

'No, Stephen's right. And anyway, it's the technical tomorrow. It's not absolutely essential that you're there.'

'You're sure? What about Agnes?' The keys weren't in my bag. What on earth had I done with them? I started patting my pockets.

'I expect I can get Tilly to baby-sit again after the nursery closes,' Kevin said.

'I don't know what I've done with my car keys.' I looked round the sitting-room to see if I'd put them down somewhere.

'Have you looked in there?' Kevin pointed to the zipped compartment on the outside of my bag.

'I don't remember putting them in there but . . . Oh yes, here they are. These days I'd forget my head if it was loose.'

I collected Grace and Kevin walked me to the door.

124

'I'm really sorry I bothered you. I guess I overreacted,' he said, his hand on the latch.

I opened my mouth to reply but I didn't get anything out, because overhead, as abruptly as if someone had pressed a switch, Agnes started to howl.

Kevin winced. 'Spoke too soon.'

I'd never heard her make such a terrible noise before. It was gut-wrenching.

'Is that what she was doing before?'

He nodded. As we went up the stairs together, Grace stirred against my shoulder and whimpered, disturbed by the noise. We looked into the cot. Agnes's face was red and creased and already glossy with tears. Her fists were clenched. I handed Grace to Kevin, and bent over into the cot.

'Shush, shush,' I murmured. I opened one of the little hands and stroked the palm. The fingers closed tightly round mine and the crying stopped. She lay there hiccuping and gazing up at me. I stroked her stomach with my other hand. Her eyes remained fixed on mine.

'*Is* it colic?' Kevin asked.

'No. I don't think it is. Grace had it a month or two back. It wasn't like this. They draw their legs up to their chest. Could she be hungry?'

'I did try her on a bottle but she only had a little bit of it.'

Agnes had started crying again and was lifting her arms imploringly to me.

'Let's try her again.' I said. 'Put Grace in the cot. With any luck she'll stay asleep.'

I picked Agnes up and we went down to the kitchen. I saw that Kevin had somehow found time to have the kitchen window boarded up.

'It's in the fridge. It'll need warming up,' Kevin said.

'I'll do it,' I said, handing Agnes to Kevin. 'And I'll make a cup of tea. Might help to keep me awake.'

I got the bottle out of the fridge and put the kettle on. Kevin sat down at the table and tried to distract Agnes by joggling her up and down.

'There should be some biscuits somewhere,' he said. 'Try that cupboard.'

'This one?' I opened a door on an array of packets and jars and reached for a tin that looked as if it might contain biscuits.

He looked up from trying to entertain Agnes. It wasn't working anyway, she was still sobbing away.

He raised his voice to be heard over her. 'No, no. That's all our landlord's stuff in there. They're coming back in October. Next along. Yes, there's a packet of digestives.'

I got it out, sat down opposite Kevin and watched him handling his baby. What had I been thinking of? There was nothing sinister about this. I was so tired that I was losing my grip on reality. Kevin was just an anxious father, and no wonder, alone here with Agnes. As for how Agnes had looked earlier, well, I knew from my experience with Grace how quickly even a fractious baby could tall asleep.

'Cass?' There was a note of pleading in Kevin's voice. 'You would say, wouldn't you, it you had any idea at all why Melissa's left or where she's gone?'

'Of course I would. But honestly, Kevin, I don't have a clue.'

He said, 'I just thought she might have confided in you.' He looked as if he was about to cry.

I shook my head. 'I wish she had.'

Agnes had stopping crying, and was trying to stick her hand in Kevin's mouth. He took her hand away.

'You know, looking back. I think perhaps she hadn't been herself since the baby was born. I'm blaming myself for not taking more notice. I wasn't always as attentive as I might have been. If I hadn't been so busy with the play . . .'

There were tears in his eyes. I felt tears of sympathy welling up in mine. I didn't know what to say and, God, I was so tired. A wave of fatigue swept over me. I could have put my head on the table and fallen asleep right there and then.

The kettle clicked off. I got up and moved around the kitchen in slow motion. Find jug, yes, water into jug, yes, bottle into jug . . . Agnes began bawling again. I held out my arms for her and Kevin handed her over. I gave her my finger to suck and for a little while there was silence. I leaned back against the work surface. The next moment Agnes was yelling again. My eyelids shot up and I realized that I had actually fallen asleep for a few seconds with the baby in my arms.

'I've got to sit down,' I said. 'I'm falling asleep on my feet. Now I know how they felt in those dance marathons in the twenties.'

Kevin shook out a few drops from the bottle on to the back of his hand. 'It's ready anyway,' he said.

I went into the sitting-room and sat down on the sofa with Agnes in the crook of my arm and offered her the bottle. Kevin sat down in a chair opposite. At first, the baby sucked greedily on the teat, but after a few moments she began to whimper. She pushed the bottle away and started to cry again, this time in a monotonous, hopeless wail, even more nerve-shredding than before. Upstairs Grace had woken up. She began to yell and the two shrill voices wove in and out of each other in a counterpoint of misery.

I got up and put Agnes in Kevin's arms.

'Here, walk up and down with her. Maybe that'll help.'

I went upstairs. As soon as I lifted Grace out of the cot, she clutched me and nuzzled her face into my breast. She wanted feeding again. I looked round for somewhere to sit down. There was just the cot, a chest of drawers and a small table. I took her next door and sat on Kevin and Melissa's bed. The noise downstairs broke off briefly. I unbuttoned my shirt and opened my bra. Grace latched on to my breast. I looked up to see Kevin standing in the doorway. Our eyes met and he looked away. Agnes was still crying, but as soon as she saw me, she stretched her arms out towards me.

He said, 'She wants her mother.'

127

'Give her to me.'

He hesitated. Then taking care not to look directly at me, he placed Agnes by my side. He turned and went downstairs.

I offered Agnes my other breast. She latched on eagerly and started to suck.

Silence settled over the house.

Chapter Ten

JOE leaned towards me and pressed his lips to mine. He drew back a little to allow me to respond. Without hesitating I kissed him back. The kiss was gentle and romantic, scarcely erotic at all. We were somewhere outdoors and it was sunny. I was floating in a haze of warmth and light. And now something wasn't quite right. The light was too strong. I was wincing and blinking. A dazzling shaft of light had fallen over my face. I hadn't quite closed the curtains the night before, that was the problem. I shifted my head on the pillow. I was in bed, and Joe had gone. I wanted to sink back into the dream, but it was too late. Where was I? Not at home. The light was coming from the wrong side. So where was I? At Stephen's flat? At my mother's? I even wondered if I was back in my old childhood home in York. Then the warmth and weight of Grace against my side reminded me that I was a mother myself now. There seemed to be something on the other side as well. Did I have two babies, then? It all came back to me. I was lying fully clothed on Melissa and Kevin's bed. My shirt was undone, but someone – presumably Kevin – had covered me with the duvet and there was a baby tucked in on each side.

I looked at the bedside clock. Seven o'clock. Amazing that they'd both slept through. Grace was making little snuffling noises, clenching and unclenching her fists. Agnes was still sound asleep. When I stroked her face, she didn't stir. I disengaged myself from the pair of them and crawled down the middle of the bed. I pulled the curtains back and looked out of the window. It was another peerless August day.

I had that clammy uncomfortable feeling that comes from sleeping in your clothes and I smelt of sweat and milk. When I ran my hands through my hair it felt sticky. I went into the bathroom, stripped to the waist and had a good wash. I eyed my dirty shirt with distaste. I really didn't want to put it back on. Should I borrow one of Melissa's? It didn't seem quite right somehow, but borrowing one of Kevin's would be even worse. I'd feel like someone in a Whitehall farce. Most of the shirts in her wardrobe were too small for me, but I picked out a baggy candy-striped one that did just fit. Under the circumstances I didn't think Melissa would mind.

Downstairs in the sitting-room, a dented pillow on the sofa told me where Kevin had spent the night. But where was he now? He wouldn't have gone off to the theatre without letting me know. I looked out of the window in the front door. The hire car had gone. I was looking around for a note when I was startled by the phone ringing. I walked over to where it stood on the wooden chest next to the sculpture of the woman and child. I was reluctant to pick it up. I felt like an intruder alone here so early in the morning. *Who's been sleeping in my bed. Who's been wearing my shirt? And now who's answering my phone?* But of course I had to do it. It might be news of Melissa – or even Melissa herself.

'Hello,' I said.

'Hello? Who is that?'

Just for a second, before I caught the slight Australian accent, I thought the woman who replied *was* Melissa, and my heart lurched.

'This is Cassandra James. I'm one of Melissa's friends.'

'Oh, Cassandra. Melissa's told me all about you. I'm Maire, her sister. I'm ringing from Canberra?' She spoke with that rising inflection that makes every statement sound like a question.

'Oh, yes, hello.'

'I've just got in from work. You're ten hours behind us. I guess there's no more news of Melissa or Kevin would have left a message on the machine?'

'I'm afraid there isn't, no.' I heard a sound of a car crunching over the gravel outside.

'Oh, my God, I just can't tell you how worried I am. I just wish I could get on a flight today and come straight over. Guess I'll do that if there's no news soon. How's Agnes? That poor kid's on my mind the whole time.'

There was the slamming of a car door.

'Well, Kevin was worried about her last night. She was missing her mother. Anyway, I stayed to look after her.'

'Bless you. You've a daughter the same age, is that right? Melissa mentioned that.'

'Yes. Look,' I said. 'I know you must be terribly worried, but Stan and I – Stan's the stage-manager – we're keeping an eye on Agnes.'

The front door swung open. Kevin appeared with a sheaf of newspapers in his hand.

'Kevin's just coming in if you want to speak to him. Hold on.' I held out the receiver. 'Melissa's sister.'

Kevin looked rough. His chin was dark with stubble and his hair was lank and stringy. He dumped the papers on the sofa and took the phone from me. A copy of the papers slithered to the floor. As I bent down to pick it up, a huge headline caught my eye. MISSING ACTRESS it screamed.

Behind me, Kevin was saying: 'It's splashed all over the newspapers.'

I sat down on the sofa and skimmed the article: 'Missing since Wednesday . . . acclaimed classical actress . . . married to Kevin Kingleigh, star of *Half-Way to Paradise* . . . blonde 32-year-old . . . has abandoned six-month old Agnes.' There was a highly coloured account of how I had broken into Journey's End.

'Yes, yes, of course, as soon as I hear anything myself,' Kevin snapped. He put the phone down without saying goodbye. He turned to me. 'Could do without her on my case.'

I was surprised by the irritation in his voice.

'She's bound to he worried.'

'Oh, I know,' he said wearily. 'But she made it bloody obvious that she thinks I must be to blame somehow. We've never really got on.' He swept the newspapers off the sofa and sat down next to me. 'These fucking newspapers. That's what has really upset me.'

'But – isn't it a good thing, really?' I said. 'That it's in the papers. Someone might remember seeing her. Or she might see the headlines herself and realize how worried we all are . . .'

Upstairs a baby began to cry. It was Grace. I got to my feet. Agnes began to cry too on a slightly higher note.

'The dawn chorus,' I said. 'Come on, we'd better deal with them.'

Kevin said, 'You're right about the publicity. Of course you are. But somehow this makes it all seem so real, you know? And when it's all over the papers there's no going back, is there.'

I thought about that as I stood by the window in Agnes's room, holding Grace up so that she could look out. It hadn't occurred to me the newspapers might make it harder for Melissa to come home. What had Thomas Wolfe said? *You can never go home again.* And in a way he was right, wasn't he? The home Melissa came back to wouldn't be the one she had left and the newspaper coverage could increase the gulf between the two. Seeing what she had done in cold print might make it seem more final and dramatic. And it would never be forgotten: whenever a journalist turned up the files to do a lazy scissors-and-paste job on Melissa – or Kevin – the story would come up again.

I turned from the window. Kevin fastened the tabs on Agnes's nappy and straightened up.

'She's too young to find this out,' he said.

'How do you mean?'

'What life's really like. That you're never safe, not really. You know, some people manage to get through their entire life and they never realize that. Not until the end anyway.'

I knew exactly what he meant, but all the same . . .

'I don't think Agnes really understands that Melissa has disappeared. They say that babies are about six months old before they realize that it isn't a new mother who appears every day. So if Melissa seemed to disappear every time she left Agnes, this might not be much different.'

Kevin lifted Agnes up and swung her gently with his hands under her arms. She chortled and waved her hands about.

'What about last night?' he said. 'Agnes was missing her mother then, wasn't she?'

'Perhaps she was just missing the breast. She fell asleep when I'd fed her.'

Kevin looked dubious and I wasn't convinced myself. Did Grace really forget about me when I was out of sight? I didn't believe it for a moment. To hell with the baby books.

'Anyway,' I said, 'I'm sure Agnes doesn't know what's happened. And perhaps she won't have to know. Melissa could show up any moment. I mean, thousands of people go missing every year and most of them turn up again, don't they?'

'Tim Fisher told me that two hundred thousand people go missing every year and all except three thousand come home in a few days.'

We contemplated that fact.

Kevin said, 'Somehow, I can't quite get a handle on that.'

I knew what he meant. On the one hand the odds seemed almost to guarantee that Melissa would be back in a day or two. On the other, 3000 seemed an enormous number: it was enough to fill the Everyman theatre three times over. I saw row after row, tier after tier, of blank faces . . .

The doorbell rang.

Kevin froze with Agnes held up in the air and we stared at

each other. The window looked out on the other side from the drive so we hadn't heard anyone driving up.

Then he put Agnes in her cot and made for the stairs.

'I hope that's not the bloody press,' he said.

I followed more slowly with Grace in my arms and was just at the bend in the stairs as Kevin opened the door. I stood and watched. Outside were two strangers: a tall thin man and a woman with fairish gingery hair. I thought Kevin might be right, but then it struck me that the suit the man was wearing and the woman's jacket and skirt weren't quite right for journalists.

The man unfolded his wallet and showed something to Kevin.

'Detective Sergeant Michael Vickers,' he said, 'and this is Constable Wendy Pritchard, from Cambridge CID.'

'What's happened?' Kevin asked.

'Can we come in, Mr Kingleigh?' His voice was slow and deep, making everything he said seem deliberate and considered.

'But why? What is it? What's going on? Where's Tim Fisher?' When Vickers didn't reply, Kevin looked at the woman for a response. She said nothing. My own feeling of foreboding increased.

'If we could come in . . .' Vickers repeated.

Kevin stood back and they filed in past him. They had their backs to the stairs and didn't seem to have noticed me.

Vickers said, 'We've found your wife's car, Mr Kingleigh.'

'You've found the car? But then where's Melissa?' Kevin's voice was hoarse. Was he wondering – like me – if they had come to announce the discovery of a body?

'We're hoping you can help us there,' Vickers went on.

'Me? But – where did you find the car?'

'Oglander Road.'

Kevin looked baffled. 'But – *where*?'

'You don't know?'

Kevin shook his head. 'I've never heard of it.'

'It's in London. East Dulwich. Not all that far from your flat in Camberwell Grove, Mr Kingleigh. Twenty minutes' walk at the most.'

The repeated use of Kevin's surname seemed ominous.

'But does that mean . . . has she gone to the flat?'

'Can you tell me where you were between the hours of eleven o'clock on Tuesday evening and nine o'clock on Wednesday morning?'

'I was at the flat all night until around seven when I left to come up to Cambridge.'

'Can anyone confirm that?'

'I've already told Constable Fisher that I was all alone there.'

'Sure about that?'

'Of course I'm sure!

There was a small silence, then Vickers said:

'I want you to come down the station to answer a few more questions.'

'But what more can I tell you! And I've got the technical rehearsal this morning, it starts at ten.'

'Don't you want to help us find your wife, sir?' said Vickers.

Kevin stared at him. 'Of course I do! But—'

'It won't be necessary for me to arrest you, sir, I'm sure. You'll want to give us every assistance in your power. Won't you, now?'

Chapter Eleven

'THEY haven't actually arrested him?'
'No, but I think they would have done if he hadn't gone of his own accord. They let him drop Agnes off at the nursery first.'

'Oh, God. And Melissa. They really think she might be . . . ?'

'They didn't really say. They're playing their cards very close to their chests.'

'I just don't believe it,' Stan said. 'It's impossible that Kevin could have, well, you know . . .'

'I can't believe it either,' l said. 'I mean, what possible motive could he have?'

Stan was still pursuing her own line of thought.

'Not in the middle of rehearsals. The director murder his leading lady before the opening night?' She shook her head as if words failed her.

I looked sideways at her, wondering if she was serious.

We were sitting in the stalls. Richard had asked Stan to take the technical rehearsal. We had come into the auditorium ahead of time because it was the only place where we could find privacy to talk. She gave me a rueful little smile.

'Though they might have felt like it sometimes. Oh, look, Cass, I know it's nothing to joke about, but honestly, it is ludicrous. You know how important this production is to him. His big break and all that. He'd never have done anything to jeopardize that. Unless . . .'

136

'What?'

'What if he didn't mean to do it?' she said. 'What if he just lost his temper and hit her?'

She saw the problem at the same moment that I did. We both spoke at once.

'No – he wasn't—'

'He wouldn't have—'

I gestured to Stan to continue.

'He was definitely in London that evening,' she said. 'So he'd have had to come back on purpose.'

'It would have had to be planned and premeditated.'

Did the police really think that? That in the middle of the night while Grace and I were asleep less than a mile away, Kevin had arrived at Journey's End, murdered Melissa and driven off with her body in the boot. It was ludicrous. Wasn't it? I remembered his reaction to her disappearance. Surely even Kevin wasn't that good an actor.

'Are you really going to be able to run the technical rehearsal without Kevin?'

'Oh, yes. It's all in here.' She tapped the bulky ring-file on her lap. 'Every detail of every scene. Lighting, sound, everything. And don't forget I'll have to run the production anyway once it's opened.'

'But who's going to be Captain Levison?'

'Rufus can go on.' Rufus was the assistant stage-manager.

'But he doesn't know the part.'

'He'll have to take the script on with him. I've even seen that done on the first night. But, oh God, I hope it doesn't come to that. After all, they'll probably let Kevin go soon. I mean, there can't really be anything in it, can there? He can't really have . . .' Her voice tailed off. We contemplated the unspoken thought in silence. Stan's hand strayed to her mouth and she chewed on a nail. She suddenly realized what she was doing and jerked her hand away.

'Haven't bitten my nails for years.'

137

'What are you going to tell everyone?'

'As little as possible for now. Just that Melissa's car has been found, and so Kevin is talking to the police.'

'Who's not here?' Stan said.

'It's Belinda,' Clive said.

The cast were ranged along the front row of the stalls. Stan was standing on stage in front of the closed curtains.

'Has anyone seen her?' No one spoke. 'Clive? How about you?'

He shook his head. 'Not since the end of yesterday's rehearsal.'

'Well, we'd better go on.'

I found that I was biting my nails, too, or rather, the skin around them. One of my fingers was bleeding. I stuck my hands firmly under my thighs and listened as Stan outlined the situation with skill and economy, putting it in its most unthreatening light. It was an admirable performance, but I wondered if anyone was fooled: not Clive, judging by the glance he darted at me.

'The best thing we can do,' Stan concluded, 'is get on with the technical until Kevin shows up, so let's all give our minds to that, OK?' Her gaze travelled along the front row, eliciting nods of agreement. She looked at her watch and frowned. 'We don't need Belinda right away, so we'd better start. Mike,' she beckoned to one of the stage hands, 'see if you can track her down, will you? OK, everyone, beginners in place, please.'

The curtain rose to a smattering of disorganized clapping from the audience. I had never seen so many people in the auditorium before: all the technical crew, the designer and her assistant and anyone else who had worked on the set. Jake and Geoff were filming from one of the boxes and out of the corner of my eye, I saw Jake clapping energetically. I'd already seen the designs for the drawing-room of East Lynne, of course, and there had been a model. But that had been only one twenty-fifth the size of the actual set; it hadn't prepared me for the impact of the real thing.

There were the usual Victorian artefacts: a display of wax birds under a glass dome, a sofa with lacy antimacassars, oil paintings in ornate gold frames, a grand piano, but there was something strangely off-key about it, something edgy and disconcerting. The lighting gave the wax birds a sinister significance, like something in a Hitchcock movie. The ornate frames were actually painted directly on to the walls, with no attempt at illusion. So were the ancestral portraits. The sofa was a kind of acid green and the walls were a strong pink. I knew these colours were historically accurate – the new chemical dyes that had been developed early in the nineteenth century were both garish and popular – but the effect was unexpectedly strident.

The drawing-room occupied only the front of the stage. French windows opened on to the vista of a long formal garden. Here too there was something askew. A balustrade jutted out at a strange angle. The topiary shapes were hard to read. Was that an eagle or something more sinister . . . a vulture perhaps? There was a vast urn on a plinth and a bust with a draped head, like something out of a cemetery. Again it wasn't clear at first what was illusory. The topiary bushes, yes, those were of flat, painted board . . . but the urn and the bust, they were solid.

Act One began. This was the first time I had seen Phyllida Haddon in the flesh and my heart sank. I tried to tell myself that I was bound to have a less than favourable reaction to whoever took over from Melissa. Melissa *was* Lady Isabel for me. Phyllida had one of those faces where the skin seems to be stretched just a bit too tightly. Her nose was rather sharp and the whole cast of her face was pert and doll-like. I missed the naïveté and innocence that Melissa had managed to convey. I suspected that Phyllida always played the same part, whereas Melissa was a different person in each new role. On the technical side, things went surprisingly smoothly and the first real setback didn't come until half-way through the scene when Archibald proposes to Lady Isabel.

'I would devote my life to making you happy,' he declared.

'Mr Carlisle, you have all my respect. I know – oh fuck, fuck, fuck, what is it that I know?' Phyllida snapped her fingers. 'Prompt.'

' "How noble you are", and it's respect *and* esteem,' Stan said from the side of the stage.

'Mr Carlisle, you have all my respect and esteem. I know how noble you are and I think so very highly of you, but, but . . .' She clicked her fingers again.

'But as for love . . .'

'Yes, yes, as for love . . .'

'Take that speech from the beginning,' Stan said from where she was sitting in the third row of the stalls.

'Mr Carlyle, you have all my respect and esteem. I know . . .'

There was the sound of hurrying footsteps echoing on boards. Belinda appeared at the side of the stage, pale and out of breath.

'So – sorry,' she gasped, holding her hand to her side. 'Stomach – upset.'

Stan nodded curtly. 'Go and get your rehearsal skirt and corset on.'

She didn't need to say anything else. Everyone was well aware that nothing short of cholera or a broken limb – and maybe not even that – was sufficient to excuse being as late as this. I thought Belinda was about to burst into tears. But she bit her lip, and hurried off.

The rehearsal picked up where it had left off. After further declarations of affection Archibald left Lady Isabel to consider his proposal. She stood there for a few moments gazing pensively into the distance. Then she gave a tremulous little smile and walked slowly to the door on the other side of the stage. She opened it and made to go through it. Something seemed to hold her back. She retreated a step or two. I stood up to get a better view and now I could see what the problem was. She tried again to manoeuvre her crinoline through the doorway; it caught on the frame and bounced her back on to the stage. I knew what must have happened. This door had been built to

modern dimensions. It should have been extra wide to accom-
modate the crinoline. Phyllida couldn't get off the stage.

I could see her shoulders quivering with suppressed laughter.
There was a moment's silence. Someone further down the row
from me began to titter. Someone else guffawed, then everyone
was laughing. There was an edge of hysteria to it. Phyllida
turned to face the audience. She was giggling so much by now
that she could hardly stand up. She grabbed hold of the edge of
the door to support herself. I was laughing, too. I couldn't help
myself.

There was a clattering of footsteps coming up the stairs to the
stage and Stan appeared in my line of vision.

'Stop this,' she roared. It was if the headmistress had appeared
in a classroom of unruly children. There was immediate silence.
In a moment or two all that could be heard was an occasional
hiccup from Phyllida.

'Get a grip, all of you,' Stan said. She had lowered her voice
so that one almost had to strain to hear. I couldn't help but
admire her technique. 'Please remember that you are profes-
sionals. This is supposed to be a melodrama, not a bloody farce.'

'I wouldn't be so sure of that, old love,' a voice murmured in
my ear.

I gave a start. With all the commotion on stage, I hadn't
noticed that Clive had dropped into the seat next to me. There
were tears of laughter on his cheeks. He fumbled in his pocket
and brought out a big white cotton hanky to mop his face.

By now the carpenter was running on to the stage. The
designer and her assistant were making their way up from the
stalls.

'She's right about one thing,' Clive went on. 'It's no laughing
matter. Melissa missing. Director in quod. If we lose any one
else, Jake and Geoff won't be filming the bloody show, they'll
he appearing in it. And, frankly, Jake couldn't possibly be worse
than Rufus as Lady Isabel's dastardly seducer. It's more like Mrs
Robinson and the Graduate. Philly could obviously eat him for

141

breakfast. I just hope she does at least manage to learn her lines in time.'

'Have a heart, Clive,' I said, half my mind on what was happening on stage, a pantomime of measuring, head scratching, consulting of designs. 'She only saw the script yesterday.'

'Oh, I know, I know. Mustn't bitch. We're lucky to get her, I know that. But I do so miss Melissa.' His tone was heartfelt. 'It's dreadfully worrying, all this.' He shot a sideways glance at me. 'The police don't seriously think Kevin's got something to do with it, do they?'

'I don't know what they think,' I said, quite truthfully.

Another stage hand appeared. He and the carpenter began dismantling the set.

'Because much the most likely thing is some sort of break-down.'

'Do you really think so?'

'She wasn't her old self at all. Far from it.'

'Really?' He had my full attention now.

'She seemed like a different person. Still very sweet, of course, but much quieter, quite subdued, really.'

'She hasn't always been like that, then?'

'Oh no. Of course you hadn't known her very long, had you? If you'd met her – oh, five or six years ago? – when I was Hamlet to her Ophelia! Darling, she was the least Ophelia-like creature you could imagine. Such fun. Always laughing and joking.'

'Well, she was tired, of course, because of the baby. I mean, I know what that's like,' I said.

'I did wonder too about Kevin. Have you noticed how couples kind of share out qualities between them? Someone timid marries someone even more timid, and the timid one gets bolder and the more timid one gets even more timid. Am I making any sense?'

I thought about this. 'Yes, I think so. You think maybe Kevin got louder and she got quieter?'

The carpenter and his mate took away the wall containing the door.

'I'm on next,' Clive said. He slipped away.

Stan clomped back down the steps to the stalls.

The laughter must have effected some kind of release, because the mood was less tense now. But it was also flatter. The cast were holding back. Not that it mattered too much: this rehearsal was mainly concerned with getting the lights right, making sure that the changes of set went smoothly and that all the props were to hand. There were constant stops and starts and it was 12.30 before we finished the first act.

Stan called everyone up on the stage. Jake and Geoff joined us.

'OK, everybody.' She clapped her hands to get everyone's attention. 'Not bad, not bad at all. We'll break for lunch now. Back here at one-thirty.'

'What are the chances of Kevin being back by then?' Jake asked. 'I mean, they can't keep him at the police station indefinitely, can they?'

Stan glared at him. But now that the question had been asked, it couldn't be ignored. The cast were looking hopefully at her. They, too, wanted to know.

'When Richard last rang the police station, he was still there. Apparently the police can hold him for thirty-six hours if they want to.'

'And then they'd have to charge him, wouldn't they?' Jake said.

There was a little cry. We all turned round to look at Belinda.

'Charge him?' she said. 'But why . . . what's happened?'

There was a moment's silence.

'Oh, Lord,' Clive said. 'No one's told you, have they. Melissa's car has been found in London.'

'Her car? In London?' Belinda looked stunned.

'Not very far from the flat in Camberwell,' I said.

Belinda was struggling to make sense of this. 'But when she

went missing, that was up here – and Kevin was down there, so
. . . I mean, how could he have anything to do with it?'

'Yes, sweetie,' Clive said as patiently as if he was talking to a
child, 'that is what he says and I'm sure it's true.'

'But did anyone see him?' Jake said. 'Can he *prove* it? The
police aren't just going to take his word for it, are they? After all
he *could* have gone back to Cambridge or Ely, couldn't he?
Caught the train or something.'

Belinda's face was dead white. Her eyes looked enormous.

'Oh, God, Jake,' Stan said, 'how can you to be so tactless?'

'Sorry!'

Belinda put her hand to her throat. Her eyelashes fluttered.
Her eyes swivelled up into her head and her knees buckled. Stan
got to her just in time to get an arm round her waist and break
her fall. Between them she and Clive managed to lower her on
to the sofa. Her practice crinoline billowed up around her legs.

'A real Victorian swoon. The most convincing thing I've seen
all day,' Clive remarked. 'Should we give her smelling-salts or
burn feathers under her nose?'

'Stop playing the fool,' Stan snapped. 'Run and get the first-
aid kit and ask Fred to bring the brandy. Get back everybody!
Give her room to breathe. And that means you as well, Jake.
Switch that bloody camera off.'

She knelt by the side of the sofa and started loosening
Belinda's corset. By the time Clive got back Belinda was
coming round. She struggled into a sitting position.

'I'm sorry, Belinda,' Jake said. 'Didn't mean to give you a
turn.'

'I've got some Rescue Remedy in my bag,' Phyllida offered.
'You know, the Bach Flower Remedy. It's good when someone's
had a shock.'

'Might be better than brandy,' Stan agreed.

'Or a nice cup of tea,' Clive said.

'I don't want anything,' Belinda wailed. 'Please. I've got to
go. Kevin needs me.'

144

I saw Stan and Clive exchange glances as if this merely confirmed something that they had suspected.

'There's nothing you can do for him, lovey,' Stan said gently.

'Oh yes, there is. I know where Kevin was that night. I've got to tell the police.'

Stan and Belinda went off to the police station, leaving behind them a buzz of speculation. I needed to get away from that and be alone for a while. I slipped out of the stage door and for a few moments I was dazzled by the midday sun. It was disorientating, like coming out of the cinema when it's still light. The world outside seemed less real than the world of the theatre.

Without really thinking where I was going, I set off at a brisk walk down Maid's Causeway towards the centre of town. When I got to the roundabout, I hesitated. King Street or Jesus Lane? How could I put as much distance as possible between me and the theatre before I had to collect Grace from the nursery? I had an impulse to get on a bus and ride out to the edge of Cambridge and back. No sooner had the thought entered my head, than a bus appeared at the far end of King Street. I was only fifty yards from a bus stop. As I ran towards it and the bus slowed down, I saw that it was an open-topped tourist one, the kind that goes round and round Cambridge in a continuous loop. I'd never been on one before. Well, why would I? I'd never been a tourist here. The bus stopped, the doors opened with a pneumatic sigh and the driver looked questioningly at me.

'How long does it take?' I asked.

'About an hour or so.'

I got on board, paid the fare and climbed up the stairs. I've never quite got over that childhood excitement of finding the front seat free. I settled myself down on it with a sense of relief. I'd escaped. This was a little holiday from real life. I thought of Melissa. Was this how it had begun with her? Had she found out about Kevin and Belinda and felt a compelling need to step out of her life for a little while, to leave her unfaithful husband, and perhaps to punish him?

The bus hadn't moved off yet, and I was just wondering why, when I heard someone coming up the stairs.

A shadow fell over the seat. I looked up to see Geoff standing next to me. He gestured towards the space beside me and raised his eyebrows in enquiry. My heart sank, but what could I do? I shifted over to make room for him. When he folded himself down in the seat next to me, an aura of tobacco came with him. He was breathing hard.

'You were going a heck of a lick down that street. Didn't you hear me calling after you?'

I shook my head. With a jerk, the bus set off.

'Jake wasn't allowed to go to the police station,' Geoff continued. 'He asked me to run after you and see if you'd chat about what's happened. On camera, of course.'

'Oh, of course,' I said sardonically. 'Something along the lines of "friend of missing woman denounces cheating husband as love-rat"? Is that the kind of thing he has in mind?'

'That'll be a no, then?'

'I'd rather go over Niagara in a barrel. So I'm afraid you're wasting your time.'

'Oh, I wouldn't say that. A nice sit-down in the sun, a quiet cigarette, the company of an intelligent woman. What better way to pass the time?'

'Don't you have to get back to the theatre?'

'I'll tell Jake I had to track you half round Cambridge.'

'Will he believe you?'

'Nope. But he needs me too much to make a fuss. And anyway I've paid my fare. It would be a terrible waste of money to get off at the next stop, now wouldn't it? We Scots are notoriously stingy, as you well know.'

He seemed a different person away from Jake and I was charmed in spite of myself. I stole a sideways glance at him. He winked and settled back on the seat. He had an open face with a blunt nose, like an amiable dog, a retriever maybe. The lock of heavy tow-coloured hair that hung over a broad, bony forehead reinforced that impression. I've always liked that particular variety of West Coast Scots accent. I had a boyfriend, once . . . but that's another story.

Geoff shifted his hip and pulled a surprisingly smart silver cigarette-case out of his back pocket. He flipped it open and offered me a cigarette. I shook my head. He got out a cigarette, tapped it on the case and put it in his mouth. He produced a lighter that matched the case and glanced at me for permission. I nodded. He lit it and took a deep drag.

The bus turned down Jesus Lane and followed the route Joe and I had taken earlier in the week. The bus swayed as it turned into Bridge Street, throwing me and Geoff briefly together, but neither of us spoke. The bus toiled up the hill past Kettle's Yard Museum and then made a dog-leg back to the Madingley Road. This was the point at which it headed out of Cambridge, to do a loop around the American Military cemetery. We picked up speed and swept past my own college, St Etheldreda's, pristine in its Neo-Georgian red brick and white paint. We went on past the University of Cambridge Veterinary School and over the flyover that crosses the M11, and quite suddenly we were in rolling, green country.

A relaxed silence had established itself between us. It was as though we did this all the time; we were like two colleagues jolting along on the bus to work. It was curiously restful: virtually as good as being alone. I leaned back in my seat and yawned. The sun on my face, the warm little breeze ruffling my hair, and the rhythm of the bus had a soothing effect.

Geoff pulled *Thus Spake Zarathustra* out of his jacket pocket and began to flick over the pages.

'When you visit a woman, do not forget to take your whip,' I said.

Geoff raised his eyebrows.

'Wasn't that Nietzsche's advice?' I asked.

'If I had to choose a philosopher to take as a practical guide to life, I doubt it would be Nietzsche.' He gave a grim little smile. 'Mind you, I do sometimes wonder if he was so far off the mark. You see it again and again: the biggest bastards have the most women hanging around.'

'Kevin?'

'What do they see in him?'

I shrugged. 'Energy's always attractive.'

'That's what Nietzsche thought. Amongst other things.'

We were nearing the cemetery. The brilliance of the summer day gave an extra poignancy to the neat rows of white crosses that covered the sloping lawn. The bus slowed down. It stopped to let a group of American tourists off, and to take others on board. This was the limit of its journey.

Geoff sighed and took off his glasses. His eyes, a greenish hazel colour, looked small and defenceless without them, and they'd left a red mark on his nose. He massaged his temples, then replaced his glasses. He lit another cigarette, inhaled deeply and blew out a cloud of smoke.

'And do you know the cream of the jest?' he said. 'Kevin was jealous of *her*!'

'How do you know that?'

'Oh, Melissa and I know each other from way back. We're old friends. Even more than friends at one time.'

I looked at him in surprise.

He smiled. 'Oh, it was never very serious, but I met Véronique – that's my wife – through her. The three of us used to see a lot of each other.'

'Melissa never said.' I felt piqued that she hadn't confided in me.

'No, well, she was careful to keep it quiet. Kevin's the kind of guy who wants to believe his wife was a virgin when he met her. When I showed up here, Melissa took me aside, told me Kevin would give her a hard time if he realized that we were once an item. And all the while he was giving Belinda one. Christ.' He shook his head in disbelief.

148

The bus was moving off again now. As we headed back towards Cambridge, I thought over what Geoff had said.

'You know, I'm not as surprised as all that,' I said. 'If you're the kind of person who grabs a bit of easy sex whenever you get the opportunity, then you probably assume that everyone else is the same. Kevin was having it off on the sly, so he probably thought Melissa would do too, given half a chance.'

'To a man with a hammer, everything looks like a nail,' Geoff said.

'Nietzsche again?'

He nodded. 'What a bastard. Kevin, I mean. And another thing that makes me mad . . .' his voice trailed off. He took one last drag on his cigarette, dropped the stub on the floor of the bus, and ground it out with the heel of his shoe.

'What?'

'Oh, well, no harm in telling you, I suppose. Melissa wanted to think about Agnes, you know, who would look after her if anything happened to them? He just didn't want to think about it. Got offended and told her she was anticipating his death.'

This was another new light on Kevin, and by now I wasn't surprised to hear that underneath the *bonhomie* was a solid core of selfishness.

Geoff was still pursuing his own line of thought. 'When a man's got a kid, he's got responsibilities.'

'Stephen made a will after Grace was born. Actually we both did.'

'It was weighing on Melissa's mind. She asked if I'd consider being guardian to her wee girl. She knew she could trust me to make a good job of it. I brought up my son on my own after my first wife scarpered.'

I looked at him with respect. There was far more to Geoff than I'd originally thought. It occurred to me that Melissa could have done much worse than to stick with him. In fact, wasn't it now apparent that she *had* done much worse? I was so absorbed by these thoughts that I hadn't noticed that we were back in the centre of Cambridge, travelling down Queen's Road along the Backs.

As the bus slowed down for the next stop, Geoff got to his feet.

'This is me,' he said. 'I ought to get back to the theatre. Mustn't leave the boy wonder on his own for too long.'

'I'll come with you,' I said. 'We can cut across through King's College.'

We got off the bus and set off across the grass. In spite of what Geoff had said, he seemed to be in no hurry. The warmth of the day and the beauty of the view were conducive to dawdling. Before us lay a stretch of tree-fringed meadow, then the river and beyond that the gardens of the five colleges that back on to the Cam: St John's, Trinity, Clare, King's, and Queens'. The picturesque variety of architectural styles, the glimpses into secluded gardens and the vistas of lawn and open grass were enchanting. The magnificent Gothic tracery of King's Chapel was outlined against an intensely blue sky and below it the lawn dropped down to the river with an effect like a ha-ha. The punts and their passengers were hidden from view and the top half of a young man wielding a pole and wearing a beribboned boater appeared to glide through the long grass at the river's edge.

As we walked towards the bridge, the river gradually came into view, and we heard the cries and laughter of inexperienced punters trying to avoid collisions. We paused on the bridge to watched the punts floating underneath, and then we made our way up the side of the sloping lawn towards the Front Court of King's College. Geoff had lapsed into silence again. For both of us, I guessed, the shadow of Melissa's absence lay across the beauty of the day and the setting. I thought of her as I had last seen her, waving goodbye as I drove down the track from the cottage.

We emerged into the big open space of the courtyard, its central lawn a little faded now in late summer. This wasn't the oldest college, but it was perhaps the most imposing. The chapel on the north side was one of the finest medieval buildings in Britain, the spectacular tracery screen that separated the court from the street was a bravura display of Gothic revival, and the west side had the calm authority of the eighteenth century. Unusually we had arrived at a moment when there were no tourists. The quietness was broken only by the rhythm of our footsteps on the path that skirted the lawn. A new idea about what might have happened to Melissa was forming in my mind. I wondered if it had occurred to Geoff, too. I looked sideways at him. He was walking slowly along, deep in thought, his hands thrust deep into his trouser pockets. I was reluctant to break in on his reverie, but at last, as we stepped out of the court into the busyness and noise of King's Parade, I said what was on my mind.

'Do you think Melissa found out about Belinda?'

Geoff shot a glance at me. He pursed his lips and nodded.

'That would be my guess.'

'I can understand her leaving, but why didn't she take Agnes with her?'

He shook his head, 'I've been wondering about that, too.'

We threaded our way along groups of tourists and strolling shoppers. We turned right and cut across through the market place. Geoff didn't speak again until we were passing W.H. Smith's.

Then he said, 'Maybe she thought that leaving the baby with Kevin would cramp his style.'

'It's done that, all right. But I don't know . . . Would she have let it go on for so long? I mean, it's been two days now, more than two days. What if . . .' I hesitated.

'Yes?'

'It sounds stupid, I know, but what if she doesn't know that she's got a baby?' Geoff stopped and stared at me. 'I mean, what if she's suffering from amnesia brought on by the shock of finding out about Belinda. It does happen, doesn't it? I think it's called a fugue.'

'I suppose it's not impossible,' Geoff said slowly.

'It might explain why she abandoned the car near the flat in London. Maybe she drove there on automatic pilot, then didn't know why she was there. Maybe she's sitting in some hotel or boarding-house, wondering who she is.'

Geoff didn't seemed to be listening. He was looking past me now. A new expression had appeared on his face, as if he had suddenly spotted someone he recognized, but hadn't expected to see. I turned to look.

He was gazing at a newspaper-stand, heaped up with piles of the lunch-time edition of the *Cambridge Evening News*. I found myself looking into Melissa's eyes. A life-size photo of her covered almost the entire front page. From newspaper after newspaper her face stared out at me.

'You could be right,' Geoff said, 'but I don't think she'll stay incognito for long, do you?'

Chapter Twelve

THE fine weather broke that evening. The wind threw hand-fuls of rain at my bedroom window. Sitting up in bed against the pillows, I tried to read, but my thoughts wandered. Stephen hadn't rung me yet that day. He'd be at work now. I pictured him in the head office of some vast conglomerate, all glass atrium and huge indoor plants. I still didn't know the name of the company. I thought about the suddenness of Stephen's departure for LA. I thought about how disconcerted I'd been when I rang the hotel and they told me he'd cancelled his booking. For a day or two I'd had no idea where he was. Did I really know now? I had a phone number, it was true, but I'd never tried to ring Stephen there. He always rang me. He wouldn't be there during office hours. Or would he?

Another picture was forming in my mind: a swimming pool shimmering in the heat like the ones in the Hockney prints, palm trees, a bedroom with sun striking in through the slats of the blind. I got as far as rolling over in bed and putting my hand on the phone, before I changed my mind. Stephen lying to me? Being unfaithful? The thought was absurd. A little voice in my head said: that's probably what Melissa thought, too, and remember how your second marriage ended. You came home to find your husband in bed with one of his students. I told the little voice to shut up. Call it instinct, call it the triumph of hope over experience, but I did trust Stephen. Once I started checking up on him, I might as well throw in the towel.

I turned my attention back to my book. After a few minutes I was yawning. A few minutes after that, I was asleep.

It seemed that I was woken by an unexpected sound. At first I thought I'd been dreaming, but no, when I opened my eyes, I could still hear it, a faint sussuration, a kind of sucking and sighing. I got out of bed and went over to the window, and stood looking out towards Ely, the floorboards cool under my bare feet. Under the full moon the fields glimmered with a strange radiance. They absorbed the moonlight and reflected it back to a sky that was awash with pallid light. The strange sound was that of water lapping against the side of the house. I was gazing out at a flooded landscape. A great sheet of water stretched out as far as the eye could see. I could make out the dark irregular shape of Ely and its cathedral standing proud of the water.

The little city was again an island, just as it had been before the fens were drained. The scene was so silent, so beautiful, so mysterious that at first I felt only awe. I looked down into the garden and then came the first prickle of fear. Only the tops of the tallest shrubs were poking out of the water. The water had almost reached the first floor of the house and it was still rising. How had all this happened so suddenly?

All at once I realized that it hadn't happened at all. This was a dream. Yet curiously that knowledge didn't at all diminish my terror. I ran over to the other window, and looked out towards Journey's End. On that side too, there was no land to be seen. It was as though my house were a ship adrift in an ocean. I was stranded here alone with Grace.

I snatched up the binoculars and trained them on Journey's End. The house was dark, but as I lowered them I caught a glimpse of movement. I raised the binoculars again. There was a rowing boat, heading towards me. There was only one person in it, pulling the oars in long smooth strokes. I went on watching through the binoculars, but as I watched, relief gave way to a sense of unease. There was something I didn't like about that figure. The boat was making steady headway. The figure was growing more distinct now. I saw a black coat, dark hair. The figure stopped rowing and leaned on the oars to rest. I saw that the hair was really a hood. And now it was turning towards me. . . .

With a prodigious effort, I forced my eyelids open. The room was full of light. I was lying flat on my back in bed. The T-shirt I'd been wearing as a night-dress was drenched with sweat and sticking to my body. I got out of bed and went over to the window. The rain had stopped during the night. There was that intensely still, newly washed feeling of early morning.

I thought about the dream. Much of it could be explained by the book I'd fallen asleep reading. I opened it and read the end. 'The sun was rising now, and the wide area of watery desolation was spread out in dreadful clearness around them . . . The boat reappeared but brother and sister had gone down in an embrace never to be parted: living through in one supreme moment the days when they had clasped their little hands in love, and roamed the daisied fields together.' George Eliot's *The Mill on the Floss* was on one of the courses I was teaching in the autumn, but it was comfort reading, too. It was far from being her best novel, but the stupendous and pathetic ending in which Maggie Tulliver rows across the flooded fens to rescue her brother Tom had thrilled me as a girl and I still found it moving. But the hooded figure in my dream hadn't been Maggie Tulliver, I knew that. I wondered whose face I would have seen if I hadn't managed to wake myself up.

I went downstairs to check on Grace. She was yawning and making the preliminary little noises that meant she'd be crying in earnest soon. I badly needed to talk to Stephen. It was six o'clock in the morning here, but evening in LA. I rang the number he'd given me. The receiver was picked up straightaway at the other end.

'Cass!' He sounded delighted. 'I've just got in. I was going to ring you, when it got a bit later. Any news about Melissa?'

155

I told him that the car had been found and that Belinda had given Kevin an alibi.

'Can't say I'm very surprised to hear that Kevin was playing away,' Stephen said.

'Well, I was! I mean, they've got a baby!' I realized how naïve I sounded.

'Oh, Cass, it's a classic set-up. A man like Kevin, he's used to being the centre of attention – of his wife's attention especially. He probably felt neglected. Started to feel sorry for himself.'

'Did *you* feel that?'

'No! Grace is the apple of my eye, you know that – and I'm not exonerating Kevin in the slightest. It was a shitty thing to do. But sorry as I am about Melissa, you're the one I'm most concerned about. How are you bearing up?'

'OK. At least I thought I was.' I told him about the nightmare I had just had.

'I wish I was there. I don't like you being on your own. You know, if you really felt you needed me . . .'

'I feel better now that I've spoken to you. I'll be fine. What will you be doing this weekend?'

'I'm going with Bob and the family to Big Sur tomorrow. Won't be back until Monday.'

'What's Big Sur?'

'It's like a national park. Up the coast, north of LA. A big expanse of wilderness and forest. It's where they have the giant redwoods. They say it's huge. Two hundred and fifty square miles, would you believe? We'll he staying at the Big Sur Inn. Let me give you the number.' I heard him shuffling papers. 'Here it is.'

I wrote it down on the pad by the bed.

'How are you going to spend the weekend?' he asked.

'I said I'd look after Agnes today—'

'Oh, you didn't! Why can't Kevin take her to the nursery?'

'It's Saturday.'

'Oh, Lord, so it is. It's still Friday here. You know, you

156

shouldn't be running around after Kevin. He doesn't deserve it.'

'I'm not doing it for him, I'm doing it for Agnes.'

We'd hung up before I realized that I still hadn't told Stephen about meeting up with Joe. Recent events had pushed him to the back of my mind and anyway it somehow wasn't the kind of thing to mention over the phone. He'll only worry unnecessarily, I told myself. Not that there was anything to worry about, of course. At least that's what I told myself. . . .

After I had fed Grace, she fell asleep again. I took advantage of that to have a bath. The doorbell rang just as I was getting out. I pulled on my dressing-gown and looked out of the bedroom window. Kevin's red hire-car was parked below, even though he wasn't due to drop Agnes off for another half an hour. I went down and opened the door. He was standing there with Agnes in his arms, and the bag containing all her paraphernalia at his feet.

'Cass, I'm know I'm a bit early . . .'

'Well . . .' I couldn't pretend I was pleased to see him.

'Can we talk? Please? I just want to explain.'

'It's not me who's owed an explanation.'

'I know that! Don't you think I've wished a thousand times that I could talk to Melissa.'

Agnes's eyes were fixed on my face. She gave me a big smile and stretched out her arms towards me. I stretched out my arms and Kevin handed her over.

'Oh, all right, you'd better come in,' I said.

The truth was that, angry as I was with Kevin, I did want to hear what he had to say for himself. And on the level of simple, vulgar curiosity, I did want to know more about what had happened at the police station.

Kevin picked up the bag and followed me into the kitchen. 'I've brought all her stuff,' he said, 'and I've made up a couple of bottles. I'll put them in the fridge, shall I?'

I nodded. 'Want a coffee?'

'I don't want to put you to any trouble.'

'I was about to make some anyway.'

'Let me put the kettle on.'

When he'd done that he sat down opposite me at the kitchen table. The strain was really starting to show. There was a stain on his white T-shirt and his hair was greasy. I'd never seen him so dishevelled. His eyes met mine, then he looked down. There was silence for a few moments.

He said: 'When Melissa was ill, and the baby, too, of course, it was a terrible time and then afterwards when they came home from hospital. Things hadn't been the same between us. I don't know what it was. Not just sex, though it was that, too. Melissa was worried that she'd get pregnant again. I was worried about that too. I don't know. The whole thing just seemed so much more . . .' He hesitated. 'Oh, I don't know, more difficult, complicated than before. And Melissa just wasn't herself. She used to be so much fun. And then on Tuesday, Belinda more or less invited herself round to the flat. Said she wanted to talk about the play. Of course I knew what that meant . . .' He sighed and shook his head. 'I don't know how I could have been such an idiot.'

'Did Melissa find out?'

'Bloody Belinda. It was when I was talking to Melissa on the phone. Belinda didn't realize. She picked up the extension in the bedroom. Melissa heard the click. She said "You've got someone there, haven't you?" '

The kettle switched itself off, but neither of us moved.

There was something about this story that puzzled me. You'd have to be very jealous or very suspicious to decide that your husband was having an affair on evidence as slender as that. Unless . . .

'It wasn't the first time, was it,' I said.

'Once before, just once, years ago, I swear to you that's all it was!' He was blinking back tears.

'Oh, Kevin,' I said wearily. I got up with Agnes in my arms. As I passed her over to Kevin so that I could make the coffee, she reached out for a book that was lying on the table. I pulled her back but she had got a grip on it. It was my copy of *East Lynne*. It was too heavy for her. She let go and it toppled off the table. It landed with the pages open and the spine bent. A slew of paper markers spread themselves over the kitchen floor.

'Oh, Christ. Hang on to her. I'll sort this out,' Kevin said. He got down on his knees and began to gather up the pieces of paper.

Agnes was dismayed by his raised voice. She screwed up her face, ready to cry.

'All right, all right,' I said gently. 'Not your fault.'

I put her into Grace's highchair and gave her a plastic spoon to suck while I made the coffee. When I turned round to put the cafetière on the table, Kevin was still on the floor, sitting back on his heels. He looked up at me.

'I'm losing it, Cass,' he said. 'There are times I think I'm going out of my mind.'

He got heavily to his feet and put the book on the table. It still had a few old envelopes and bits of scrap paper sticking out of it. He put the pieces that had escaped in a pile beside it. He sat down.

'Perhaps I really am going crazy,' he said. 'Last night I thought Melissa had come back to the house. I woke up, thinking that I'd heard someone in the next room. I was certain, *certain*, that if I got up, I'd see her there leaning over Agnes in her cot.'

'Did you go and see?'

'I couldn't. It was as if I was paralysed. I was just completely unable to move. I think I must have fallen asleep again. I woke up a bit later and then I did get up. There was no one there, of course.'

'You were dreaming,' I said.

He shook his head, not so much in disagreement as in perplexity.

'It seemed so real.'

'Could anyone have got into the house? Could Melissa have got into the house?'

He was on the verge of tears. 'I don't see how. The house was all locked up. I'd even put the chain on the front door.'

I moved my chair round so that I could put my hand on his shoulder. There wasn't much I could say. In the end all I could manage was:

'Look, if she is staying away to punish you, then that's a good thing really, because it means she could come back any time.'

'Do you really think so? I know I've been an absolute bastard.' Tears were rolling down his face again. 'But if she knew how sorry I am, how much I regret it. I've told the police that I'll do a public appeal.' He pulled a handkerchief out of the pocket of his jeans and scrubbed his face.

I busied myself with the coffee. Kevin, sniffing now and then, gazed out of the window. The morning sun was streaming in through the long, floor-length window that looked out over the stream. Agnes had stopped banging her spoon and was sucking it again. When she saw I was looking at her, she waved the spoon and chuckled. The sunlight was falling across her head, illuminating hair as fine and blonde as thistledown. I yawned and my eyes filled with tears. I reached for my bag to get out a tissue. That was when I noticed the envelope that had been shaken half out of the book on the table. Part of a typed name and address were visible, but I couldn't quite see . . . I wasn't really thinking as I began to spell out the letters. ADOWS and on the next line S END. The next moment I knew what it was. I saw myself in Melissa's dressing-room, holding a letter in my hand, the door was opening, Kevin was appearing. I saw Melissa giving a tiny shake of the head. And that was it. That was what I'd done with the letter. I had slipped it between the pages of *East Lynne*.

I looked sideways at Kevin. His gaze had followed mine.

'That's addressed to Melissa,' he said. He looked at me as if to ask permission, but without waiting to receive it, he reached forward and plucked the envelope out of the book. He took out the letter and scanned it.

'This is Melissa's anonymous letter. But how did it get there?'

'I, um, I think I must have just slipped in there after she'd shown it to me. Without really thinking what I was doing. On automatic pilot, you know. I'm always doing that these days.' It was the truth, but how lame it sounded.

'Like with your car keys the other night.'

I nodded. 'That's right. Can I see the letter?'

He handed it over. It was just as I remembered it. When I looked up again, Kevin was examining the envelope.

'I still don't know what Melissa thought was odd, apart from the signature,' I said.

'Well, I do. How did the writer get hold of this address? I was in London at least once a week – or Melissa was – so we didn't bother to have mail forwarded. Hardly anyone had the Journey's End address.'

'Couldn't they have found out from the theatre?'

'Fred wouldn't have given out a home address. And anyway why couldn't they just have left the letter at the theatre?'

'We'd better let the police have this.'

Chapter Thirteen

'THE King of Cups?' Joe said thoughtfully. 'You know, that's kind of familiar.'

'Really? You think it means something specific?'

It was early on Sunday evening. Around six o'clock Joe had rung me from Ely, where he had been sightseeing, to suggest going for a walk. Kevin had taken Agnes to the theatre for Tilly to look after, so Grace and I had had a quiet day alone. I was ready for some fresh air and some adult company and more: I badly wanted to talk to someone outside the overheated world of the theatre, someone who had nothing at all to do with it. I'd been sucked so far into it that everything outside seemed colourless and unreal. I needed to get some distance on it. And of course I was still curious about Joe and his life in the years since our divorce.

I picked him up at Ely station. He got into the car and when he leaned over to give me a peck on the cheek, I remembered the kiss he had given me in my dream. I was amused to find myself feeling affectionate, even a little proprietorial, as if we really had embraced.

The day had been very hot but there was just enough of a breeze now to make it pleasant to be out walking. We drove over to Wicken Fen. It's a National Trust nature reserve, the last remnant of the watery wilderness that once covered East Anglia. The place was almost deserted. As we strolled along a boardwalk towards the old waterway that winds through it, the trees and shoulder-high reeds that pressed in on both sides blocked our view and created a sense of seclusion.

'The King of Cups,' Joe said again. He shook his head. 'I just can't quite put my finger on it. Maddening. It'll probably pop into my head when I'm thinking about something else.'

We walked on without speaking. The wind in the swaying, sighing reeds and in the fluttering aspens was like a continuous murmured conversation being carried on around us. Our feet echoed on the boards. Joe had his hands deep in pockets of his linen trousers. He was wearing a white cotton shirt with rolled-up sleeves that showed off his tan. He'd always gone brown very easily. For once I'd got out of my jeans into a summer dress, with a pattern of green and blue, like forget-me-nots on grass, and I had actually ironed it. Grace was wearing a T-shirt, little dungarees and a sunhat. Her push-chair rumbled over the boards. We turned a sharp bend which brought us out into the open near the junction of the two waterways, Wicken Lode and Monk's Lode. On the opposite bank was moored a red-and-green barge with the window boxes full of geraniums. A window was open and a man in a gingham apron was frying sausages.

We paused for a moment to enjoy the view. The water was tranquil in the evening light. There was an iridescent flash above the surface and a blur of wings.

'Wow, what was that?' Joe said.

'A dragonfly. It's the Emperor, I think. I sometimes get them over the stream in my garden.'

'This is a terrific place. And what an evening!'

'It's glorious,' I said sadly.

Joe glanced at me. 'But you could enjoy it a whole lot more if you weren't so worried about your friend? How long has she been gone? Five days?'

'About that.' I told him about Kevin's one-night stand with Belinda.

'There you are then. Dollars to donuts she'll turn up safe and sound, when she thinks her husband's had time to learn his lesson.'

'That's what everyone at the theatre thinks.'

'But you're not so sure?'

'Well, I can understand her letting Kevin dangle. But it seems odd that she hasn't been in touch with anyone. I mean, she must know how worried I am, for instance. Why hasn't she at least rung me? And the fact that she left Agnes behind in the first place . . .'

'That's easy. She wanted to cramp his style. And it has, hasn't it?'

'And then there's the play . . . Stan rang me – she's the stage manager – this morning. She said you could cut the atmosphere with a knife. Everyone thinks it's Kevin's fault that they're in this fix, Belinda's going around looking all pale and red-eyed. They're all exhausted, Phyllida – she's stepped in at the last minute to take Melissa's place – still doesn't know her lines. . . .'

'What can I do to make you feel better? A decent meal somewhere?'

I couldn't help laughing. 'You haven't changed much, Joe. Food is still the answer to everything.'

'Well, you know, it generally is.' He patted his belly. 'And I have to say that raising two boys hasn't done much to dispel that notion. So: dinner? How are you fixed?'

'Well, I do know a nice pub by the river, the unreconstructed sort that serves pub grub and good beer from the barrel.'

'Perfect. Now have we got time to see – what's it called?' He unfolded the map of Wicken Fen that he'd bought from the visitor's centre. 'Yeah, the tower hide. It says here that there are good views in all directions.'

'There's plenty of time.' We'd reached the end of the boardwalk by now. 'But what about the push-chair?'

Joe frowned.

'The ground does look a bit rough,' I said.

His face cleared. 'Oh, we can manage that. Sure we can.

That's not what's bothering me. It's the King of Cups. I thought I was about to remember, but it's slipped away again.'

He shrugged and took hold of the handles on the push-chair and bumped it off the boardwalk on to the earth path. I was about to take it back, but then I thought, What the hell? Joe was already manoeuvring the push-chair with practised ease along the river bank and Grace was wriggling and crowing, excited by the bumpy ride.

The hide is a three-storey weather-boarded building, shaped like a windmill with a thatched roof. The upper floors are reached by narrow wooden ladders. They had handrails, admittedly, but all the same . . .

'I'm not sure about this,' I murmured.

Joe was already bending down, unbuckling Grace. He lifted her up. She chortled and grabbed at his hair. He laughed.

'What a cutie! Brings back memories. I loved it when the kids were small.'

'You should feel flattered. She doesn't take to everyone.'

He handed her to me. 'You go first. I'll follow on behind. It'll be perfectly safe if we do it that way.'

Inside it was cool and dim. After a minute or so, I emerged into the light of the viewing-room, out of breath. There were high narrow windows looking out in all directions giving a wonderful view over the fens. Raised wooden seats – like pews and about as comfortable – ran round on all four sides. I sat down on one and looked out over the mere. Joe sat down next to me. He took out a handkerchief and wiped his forehead. The landscape was growing hazy in the evening light. Here and there long straight rows of trees, now in full bloom, had been planted as windbreaks. There seemed something strangely significant about their arrangement, as though the geometry of the huge plain had some meaning beyond itself, like a mathematical formula or the organization of an abstract painting.

'I think it was Lewis Carroll,' I said, 'who wanted to have a life-size map of England, so that he would always know where

165

he was. That's how I sometimes feel here in the fens: as though I'm moving around on a gigantic map. The landscape's so flat that it almost seems two-dimensional.'

'Yeah, it's kind of weird,' Joe said. 'You know, it's not really how I think of England at all.'

'Perhaps more like Holland,' I agreed. 'And those lines of poplars. They always make me think of France. Perhaps that's why I like it so much: it's almost like a foreign country.'

'I hired a car and drove up to Boston the first weekend I was here. Thought I ought to be acquainted with the namesake of my home town. We always meant to do that, remember? And you know what I found myself thinking as I drove north. This is just like the Midwest. Iowa, maybe. No, really,' he said, seeing my smile. 'The huge skies, the wide open spaces. The long straight roads. Those farmhouses set back from the road. And nothing else – absolutely nothing – as far as the eye can see.'

I thought of my dream of a flooded landscape.

'It was once all covered with water from here right up to the Wash. That must have been amazing and it wasn't so long ago, either. There's a bit in Tennyson's *In Memoriam*: that always makes me think of the fens:

> There rolls the deep where grew the tree.
> O earth, what changes hast thou seen!
> There where the long street roars, hath been
> The stillness of the central sea.

Although actually it's the other round: trees are growing where the sea used to roll. Ely was an island – the name comes from the eels that were the staple diet of the monks.'

'Hence all those watery names, I suppose,' Joe said. 'Waterbeach, Horningsea and the like. Cass . . .'

I waited, expecting him to go on. He didn't. I looked sideways at him. He was staring out into the distance.

'What?' I said.

'Have you ever wondered about how things might have worked out if you'd joined me in Denver?'

I had, of course, more often than I wanted to admit, especially when my second marriage broke up.

'I did sometimes wonder if we should have tried it for a year or two longer, given things more of a chance.'

Joe sighed. 'I knew you didn't want to go to the States. Or not to Denver anyway. You know how it was, I was too young and ambitious to compromise.'

'Me, too.'

'Guess you always wonder about the road not travelled. I'm kind of at another crossroads now.' He pulled his handkerchief through his fingers.

'Tell me.'

'It's Amy. She wants to make a clean break, get married again. You know, I took the job at Columbia because she complained that I wasn't spending enough time with her and the kids – and she was right. Then I found out that she'd been having an affair. It had been going on for a year or two.' He shook his head and bit his lip as if he still couldn't quite believe it. 'We split up and now we're at different sides of the continent. Hell, there's even a four-hour time difference.'

'God, that's difficult.'

'Difficult! Yeah! Imagine sharing child custody over two thousand miles. And that's the problem. It's giving her the perfect excuse not to share.' I glanced down at his hands. He was pulling the handkerchief taut between his fingers. 'She wants to marry this other guy and have the kids with her all the time. Visiting rights only for me. And I'm thinking, maybe I should let them go. Catch up with them later.'

'What do you mean, catch up with them later?'

'When they're older, old enough to decide if they want to live with me. You know what a lot of guys in my position would do? They'd find some cute postgrad, young enough to be their daughter. They'd start over; new wife, new family. People do it

167

all the time in the States.'

'They do it here, too,' I said.

He must have caught something in the tone of my voice, because his head shot up and he turned to look me in the face.

'But you don't think it's a good idea?'

'Getting married again? How could I possibly say? But with your boys: I'm sure, really sure, that you should do everything you can to be with them.'

'Amy doesn't come right out and say it, but she thinks this guy will be a better father than I am to my own boys. He's the outdoor type, takes them camping, plays baseball with them.'

'Good for him. No, really,' I said, as Joe grimaced. 'It's good that he does that and that they like him. But he's not their father, you are. And they need you.'

'I guess you're right. I hope you are.'

We sat gazing out over the water. A couple of geese rose slowly in the air and flew honking away. The sun went behind a cloud.

'Grace needs her cardigan,' I said. 'We'd better go back down.'

Joe speared a chip. 'You and I, we were just kids really, weren't we?' he said. We were sitting at a wooden table only feet away from the river. It was around eight o'clock, and though it wasn't dark, the air seemed to be getting stiller and heavier. And the sky was a deeper blue. Iron lampposts with fluted columns and peeling white paint marked the edge of the towpath. Strings of coloured light bulbs – green, amber, cream and red – were slung between them and shed a soft light over the lawn and the weeping willows around it. There was a festive feeling that came from the proximity of the pleasure boats and water and the coloured lights.

We had almost worked our way through enormous plates of scampi and chips. I had fed Grace while we were waiting for the food and she was asleep in her push-chair. Our conversation had been wide-ranging, sixties pop music, academic life, politics – I wasn't surprised to learn that Joe was a Democrat – but now we were back to the old days.

'That crummy apartment we had, that first winter. That wallpaper.' He laughed and shook his head. 'We'd been living there for – how long? – before we realized that it was upside down.'

'That was the least of it. I've never ever been so cold in my life.'

'We had to heap our coats on the bed at night.'

'That gas fire. My toes were burning while the back of my head froze.'

'And it was so damp.'

'Oh God, yes.'

'Those were the days,' I said, laughing.

'They really were,' Joe protested.

A boat came chugging up the river and moored beside us. Two swans with a couple of cygnets bobbed up and down in its wake.

'None of those things seem to matter when you're young,' Joe said.

I was off on my own line of reminiscence. 'Remember when I got that rash on my chest? You wouldn't believe it was chickenpox.'

'I didn't think grown-ups could get it! Do you remember that wedding – where was it now? Yes, Jersey . . . paddling in my tuxedo . . .'

'Yes . . .' I saw, not the event itself, but Melissa and myself poring over a photograph. I heard her saying, 'Aren't you dying to know what he's like now? You are going to meet him, aren't you?' I put down my beer and rested my hand on the table. I had managed briefly to forget about my worries. Now it all came flooding back and I felt guilty for enjoying myself.

'Hey, sweetheart . . . What's up? It isn't upsetting you, is it, this reminiscing?' Joe reached over and put his hand on mine.

'No . . . it's not that . . .'

Joe's fingers closed round mine. His hand was warm and

supple, a comfortable fit. I remembered that he'd always been good at holding hands. Some men grip your hand too slackly, others too tightly so you feel like a small child being towed along by daddy. With Joe I'd felt anchored and protected. I looked across the table at him. His face was growing indistinct in the gloom; the pinkish-orange glow from the lights smoothed out the lines on his face and made him look younger. I wondered if I looked younger too.

'It's Melissa,' I told him. 'Just a few days ago everything seemed to he going wonderfully well for her. Career going well, new baby, happy marriage – or so I thought – and now . . . well, who knows.'

Joe squeezed my hand.

I said, 'It just makes life seem so uncertain. It makes me think of that image in medieval literature: the Wheel of Fortune. One moment you're at the top, the next moment . . .'

'Can I clear those plates and get you some dessert?' said a woman's voice.

I gave a start. The waitress's footsteps had been muffled by the grass and we hadn't heard her coming up behind us. Joe released my hand and leaned back from the table.

'Er, no thanks, I think I've had enough . . .' I mumbled.

'Me, too.' Joe said. 'But I'd like a coffee. Can I get an espresso?'

The waitress nodded and went off to get it, leaving Joe and me in a silence that wasn't comfortable.

Don't they say that every cell in our body is replaced every seven years? It was twice as long since the last time Joe and I had made love. Psychologically, too, the years had changed us into different people. And yet how different were we really? Weren't those young selves still buried deep inside the middle-aged people we had become? Like layers of geological sediment the years had covered them up but hadn't obliterated them. I remembered the erotic charge of hearing 'My Funny Valentine' on the radio, the way it had propelled me into the past. I felt a

pang of desire like a gentle punch low in the belly. My face grew
warm. Stop it, I told myself, it's not as if the hand-holding *means*
anything, Joe's just a very tactile person.

I angled my watch to catch the light.

'Ought to be going soon, if I'm going to drop you off at Ely
station to get home in time to watch Kevin's appeal on TV.'

It was too dark for Joe to see me blushing, but in any case he
was gazing off over the water.

'Joe?'

He looked at me. 'Sorry,' he said, frowning. 'What did you
say just then?'

'That we'll have to go soon.'

'No, before that?'

'That I didn't want any dessert?'

He shook his head impatiently. 'Before the waitress came.'

'Oh, um, yes, something about medieval literature and the
Wheel of Fortune?'

'Yes, yes, yes!' Joe thumped the fist of one hand into the palm
of the other. 'That's it! Yes! It's the tarot.'

'What?'

'The King of Cups. It's the name of a tarot card. And so is the
Wheel of Fortune. *And* the Tower, now that I come to think of it.
That must be why I almost remembered earlier on.' He started to
laugh.

'The tarot? That's the last thing I'd have expected you to
know about.'

'Oh, I had this wacky older girlfriend at Berkeley. Before I
came over here. God, it must be well over twenty years ago. She
used to read the cards. There were different suits: Cups and
Coins and Swords and something else I can't recollect. They
stand for different types of people. I was the Knight of Swords,
I do remember that. Something to do with my colouring, I
think.'

'So what do they mean, these suits?'

'Sorry. Can't tell you. I was never all that interested, to tell

171

you the truth. I know how we can find out, though. It's bound to
be on the net.'

The phone rang as I was coming in through the door. I was still
lost in thought as I picked it up.

'Hello. Is this Dr James?' It was an unfamiliar male voice. I
could hear a subdued hubbub in the background as though the
speaker were in a pub.

'Yes.'

'I am calling on behalf of Safe Homes Security. You have
been selected for a free assessment—'

'How did you get my name? I'm ex-directory.'

'You are on our list of privileged clients. Now, I wonder if you
are aware that the crime rate is rising in your area—'

I suddenly felt absolutely furious.

'This is outrageous. You're trying to frighten me into buying
something.'

The voice continued smoothly, 'We are offering you an
inspection, completely free—'

'Look: I'm just not interested!' I slammed the phone down.

This kind of approach was unethical even by the standard of
cold calling. Was there a code of conduct? If not there ought to
be. I could at least complain to the company. I dialled 1471 only
to be told that the caller had withheld their number. I went
upstairs still seething. To ring on a Sunday evening, too. I looked
at my watch to see how late it was. Oh, Lord, I was going to miss
the news if I didn't hurry up.

I switched on the television. There was a platform with a long
table set with microphones and a row of chairs behind it. After a
moment or two Kevin came on to what I couldn't help thinking
of as the stage. He was accompanied by Detective Sergeant
Vickers and a female officer whom I didn't know. Someone
came forward and pulled out a seat at the centre of the table.
Kevin sat down and rested his clasped hands on the table. The
concerned faces of the police, flash-bulbs going off, rows of

journalists . . . it was so much like other occasions when I'd watched distraught relatives appeal for help that I almost felt that I had seen it before.

Detective Sergeant Vickers explained how long Melissa had been missing, described her car and gave the registration number.

Then it was Kevin's turn. He spoke in a low self-possessed tone that suggested reserves of emotion barely kept under control. He said how worried he was. How much he missed Melissa, and how much their baby daughter needed her. He spoke of the stress she had been under, rehearsing for the new production. He knew their life together hadn't been perfect, he could have been a better husband, but he did love her. If anyone had seen her, or if she herself was listening . . . He looked down at the table. He seemed too overcome to continue. The camera panned in close. There was a moment of suspense. He lifted his head and looked straight into the camera.

'Melissa, if you can hear me . . .' his voice faltered. The policewoman put a hand on his arm. He swallowed and went on:

'I don't want to believe – I can't believe – that any real harm has come to you. And I won't rest until you're home again with me and Agnes. I'll never stop looking for you.'

There was a moment or two of silence, then a barrage of questions. I heard fragments: 'Any idea at all where . . .' 'true that Belinda Roy. . . ?' Vickers held up his hand and shook his head. Then the policewoman was helping Kevin to his feet and they were turning to go.

A number to call if you had information came up on the screen. I switched the TV off. Kevin wasn't at home, I knew. This had been recorded earlier and he had intended to go back to the theatre for the final dress rehearsal. He might be there until the early hours.

I went over to my computer and switched it on. It made its usual plangent twang and the screen lit up. As I sat in front of it watching the various icons appearing one by one, a hollow feel-

173

ing developed in the pit of my stomach. Years and years ago, even before I'd met Joe, someone at university had told the tarot for me. I could remember virtually nothing about it except that she'd warned me about an unhappy love affair and a broken heart. That's probably pretty inevitable when you're eighteen, but it had left a shadow over me all the same. I'd steered well clear of any type of fortune-telling ever since. I felt sure there was going to be something sinister about this pseudonym.

I called up my favourite search engine, Google.com. I keyed in 'tarot' and sat drumming my fingers impatiently. A list of references scrolled down the screen. I was spoilt for choice. I called up the first one. The website offered a large range of options: history of the tarot, how to register for a course, where to buy books. I wandered around it for a while, but there was nothing about the meaning of individual cards. I returned to the search engine and typed in 'King of Cups'.

This took me straight to a page on a website. At the top was an image of a card similar to a court card in an ordinary pack of playing-cards. It was designed to look like a rather crude wood-cut filled in with bright primary colours: red, yellow and blue. It showed a man with a white beard, seated on a throne and holding what I assumed was a goblet though it looked more like a sceptre. I scanned the text below it. 'This card represents a mature, intelligent man, probably a business or a professional person. A calm and pleasant manner can conceal strong emotions. He can be a source of good advice for the querant.' That last wasn't a word I was familiar with, but I guessed that it meant the person whose cards were being read. There didn't seem to be anything sinster about this. I pushed back my chair with a sigh of relief. It was an odd pseudonym, but a benign one. I wondered why the police hadn't thought of checking up on it this way. Then it occurred to me that perhaps they had. No reason why they should have told me.

The phone rang. I picked it up with my eyes still on the screen.

'Joe?'

'Hi. You tracked it down OK?'

'Yep, I am reading about it right now on . . . let me see . . .' I read out the name of the website.

He laughed. 'That's exactly what I've got up on my own screen.'

'Then you'll know this card represents a 'mature man in authority who gives sound advice.'

'Yeah . . .' he said, drawing the word out doubtfully, 'but didn't you say it was typed upside down?'

'Does that make a difference?'

'All the difference. If the card's the right way up, it's referred to as "dignified", but if it's upside down, its "ill-dignified" and the meaning of the card is reversed. You need to scroll down. It's underneath the part that you've heen reading. Can you see?'

As I moved the mouse, an inverted image of the King of Cups appeared along with a whole block of new text. I read it with mounting unease.

'Deception and underhand behaviour are signified by this card reversed. Now this character combines intelligence and authority with dishonesty and unscrupulousness and represents someone who could be a major threat to the querant. This is someone who is not what they seem. They should be avoided at all costs.'

Chapter Fourteen

'A thought came over me today as to whether Lady Isabel really was dead,' said Barbara Hare.

In the silence that followed you could have heard a pin drop. The tableau on the stage seemed frozen. For an awful moment I thought Clive had dried.

Then he shook his head, passed a weary hand over his forehead, and said:

'It's all too true, alas.'

The curtain came down. As the house lights went up there was a murmuring sound like the rustling of the wind in the trees. It was as if the entire audience had been holding its breath. What was it that Stan had said? *Theatre folk are so superstitious.* Well, you didn't need to be very superstitious to feel a frisson at those words. Before the performance began I'd wondered it I'd be able to suspend my disbelief. After all I'd written the script. I'd heard the lines again and again. I knew the actors as real people. But I hadn't seen the whole thing come together and I hadn't seen the costumes. I was entranced. The colours of Lady Isabel's dresses were startlingly brilliant – magenta, lilac, emerald green. The corseted bust, the nipped-in waist, and the breadth of her hips in the crinoline created an exaggeratedly feminine silhouette. As she moved around the stage, the crinoline swayed to the rhythm of her walk and her skirts rippled and surged around her, now and then offering a glimpse of an elegantly laced boot.

Archibald Carlyle and Captain Levison wore close-fitting frock-coats and narrow tapering trousers which broadened the shoulders and narrowed the hips. And this was quite right, I thought, because the costumes reflected the contemporary polarization of male and female roles, and anyway *East Lynne* was in its way one of the sexiest novels of the nineteenth century.

Joe put his hand on my arm.

'Where was it that Belinda saw the figure in the cloak?' he asked.

I pointed out the place. From our box we could see virtually the whole auditorium. It was packed, every seat taken. There was the usual interval bustle, people standing up to let others pass, a buzz of conversation.

'Someone's down there looking at you.' Joe pointed to the stalls.

'Oh, that's Tim Fisher. The policeman.'

When he saw me looking back he half-raised his hand in a gesture of greeting. I'd spoken to him on the telephone that morning to tell him about the King of Cups and I had felt that he was holding something back. I had that impression even more strongly now. But I had to admit to myself that this might just be paranoia. The discovery of the meaning of the 'ill-dignified' tarot card had disturbed me. I hadn't slept well. Add to that getting up twice to feed Grace and it was no wonder I was looking at everyone with a suspicious eye. *This is someone who is not what they seem. They should be avoided at all costs.* But if they weren't what they seemed, how did you know whom to avoid? And anyway I was surrounded by people who weren't what they seemed: they were actors, for God's sake. . . .

'Sure you don't want a drink?' Joe said.

'Don't think I can face the crush, but if you want one . . .' I didn't admit that I didn't want to emerge until it was all safely over in case I overheard a derogatory comment about the play.

'No, I'm fine. But how about an ice-cream?'

'That would be nice.'

When he'd gone to get them, I rang home to check with Tilly that the babies were all right.

'They're both asleep,' she reported. 'They look so sweet . . . oh, hang on, one of them's crying. Honestly, they're fine. Oh, that's set the other one off. I'd better go. Please don't worry, Cassandra.'

Joe came back with two choc-ices and, as we were unwrapping them, the curtain rose again.

Lady Isabel in her disguise of Madame Vine was sitting by the bedside of her son. I knew perfectly well that the sick boy was in tact a boisterous twelve-year-old football fan from a stage school in London. I knew that Phyllida was as tough as old boots. Part of me was even aware that she wasn't word perfect. But, by God, she could act after all and I felt a catch in my throat.

'This cannot be death so soon,' she said, gathering the small body up into her arms.

Tears rolled down my cheeks. Joe fumbled for my hand and squeezed it.

As the play went on, I found myself ever more riveted by Phyllida. Her face had been made up to look hectic and flushed and she had a scar. I had never seen her in her full costume as Madame Vine. She was unrecognizable under the tinted spectacles, the grey wig and the all-enveloping black dress and bonnet. A bizarre thought darted into my head. This could just as easily be Melissa. What if it was? The idea was absurd, but once the idea had occurred to me, I couldn't shake it off. The figure on the stage flowed from one identity to another like a shape-shifter from Lady Isabel to Phyllida to Madame Vine to Melissa. I tried to get a grip. The truth was that my tired eyes and my tired brain were playing tricks on me and I was seeing Melissa everywhere. Only that afternoon, I'd seen her walking down the street. When I'd caught up with the woman, I realized that she didn't look remotely like Melissa. There had been something about her walk and her build that was just enough for my eye to fill in the rest and create what I wanted to see.

All the same it was a relief when Madame Vine was stripped of her disguise and revealed to be Lady Isabel – and Phyllida.

'You've been here all this time? As Madame Vine?' Archibald stammered.

'I could not live away from you and my children. But I've suffered the torments of the damned, living in this house with your new wife, watching you caress and kiss her. I've never loved you so passionately as I have since I lost you.'

She fell back on her pillows exhausted.

'Archibald, I am on the very threshold of the next world. Surely you will forget and forgive.'

'I cannot forget. I have already forgiven.'

'Will you not say a word of love to me before I die? Only a word of love! My heart is breaking for it.'

Even though I knew what Archibald was going to say I was sitting on the edge of my chair.

He leaned over her and brushed back the hair from her forehead.

'You nearly broke mine when you left me,' he whispered.

'But you will . . . you will keep a corner in your heart for me . . .'

'You're growing faint. Let me call for help.'

'No, it's too late. But it is hard to part! Farewell, farewell, my once dear husband. Just one last kiss. Surely that can't be a sin . . .'

Archibald hesitated. Then he bent down and put his lips to hers.

'Until eternity,' he whispered.

Her head lolled back on the pillow. It was all over.

There was a moment or two of silence followed by a tumultuous burst of applause.

'You were magnificent, Clive. I think I've fallen in love with you myself.'

179

'Bless you, my darling.' He hugged me. 'It all came together in the end, didn't it? Let me get you a glass of champagne. And, then, alas and alack, I must mingle.'

Joe and I had joined the cast in the circle bar with the cast for the first night bash being thrown for the patron and friends of the theatre. The room was packed. There had been some debate about the propriety of throwing a party in the circumstances. But Richard had pointed out that without the support of local business people, and above all the Friends of the Everyman Theatre, there wouldn't have been a production in the first place. It wasn't fair to deprive them of their treat – and it would be very bad for business. So that was that and here we all were, wolfing canapés and smoked-salmon sandwiches and swigging champagne.

And looking around it struck me that the performance hadn't ended yet. Phyllida was talking in an animated way to a large man with a paunch and a pin-striped suit. She caught my eye and gave me an ironic little smile. Clive had been seized – literally, she was hanging on to his arm – by the chair of the Friends. You wouldn't have guessed from the way he was smiling into her face that the one thing he longed to do was to get into his car and drive back to Hampshire to his wife and daughters. He would be commuting now that the play had opened. When I looked his way, he caught my eye and gave a scarcely perceptible wink. Kevin at the far end of the bar was surrounded by admiring middle-aged women. Jake was hovering beside him with Geoff and his camera in attendance.

I put my glass down on a bracket on the wall and stifled a yawn.

'Tired?' Joe asked.

'Fit to drop. And these shoes . . .' I slipped one of my shoes off and rubbed my foot on the back of my other leg. Whatever had I been thinking of, buying heels like these?

'Why don't you let me drive you home?' Joe had hired a car in preparation for a trip north to see his old supervisor.

I hesitated. Kevin had given me a lift in, but it looked as if he was going to be quite some time.

'It'd be no trouble, Cass,' Joe went on. 'I like driving at night. Less traffic. So I'll be heading north after I've dropped you off. I've booked a room at the George in Stamford. Nice old coaching inn, I believe. Just the kind of thing we Americans go for.'

I fumbled for my shoe and swayed as I tried to slip it back on. Joe put his hand above my elbow to brace me.

'Anyway,' he went on. 'I'd rather see you safely home. I'm sure that's what Stephen would want me to do.'

There was something disquieting about that thought.

'The new outfit looks terrific,' said a voice behind me.

I turned to see Stan smiling at me. Her hair was piled up in a complicated arrangement, and she was wearing what looked like a Lurex tent.

'I want you to meet someone,' she said.

My eyes slid past her to the woman standing behind her. My heart seemed to miss a beat. For a instant I thought it was Melissa. It wasn't, of course. This woman was older, by perhaps as much as five years, nearer to my age than Melissa's. Her face was fuller, fatter, and her body was heavier. And yet the resemblance was striking: the shape of the nose was the same and the line of the jaw. The effect was disconcerting: it was as if Melissa had become bigger and blurred and out of focus. I realized that I was staring at her and looked away in confusion.

She stepped forward and held out her hand. I took it.

'You must be Cassandra.' She smiled at me but I could see that it was an effort.

'That's right and you must be Maire. Can I introduce you to Joe?' I said. 'Joe, this is Melissa's sister, Maire.'

'Glad to meet you.' They shook hands.

Stan was looking Joe up and down with obvious interest. She leaned towards me and lowered her voice.

'Is this Buttons – or is it Prince Charming?' She gave me a sly smile and I realized that she was a little drunk. 'You are going to

181

introduce me, aren't you?' she said out loud.

'Of course, Stan, this is Joe. Joe, this is Stan, she's the stage manager, you remember. . . ?'

'Hi.' He stretched out a hand. I watched with amusement as he switched on the old Baldassarre charm. I knew Stan was wondering why I'd never mentioned him before. 'Cass has told me all about you. You've done a great job. What a fantastic production!'

I left them to it and turned to Maire.

'When did you get in?' I asked.

'Just a few hours ago. Couldn't stay away any longer. I managed to get a cancellation.' The way her voice went up at the end of every line made her statements seem uncertain and provisional, as though she was testing out my reaction. 'Came straight to the theatre. Stan's been great. Managed to find me a seat at the last minute.' She lowered her voice and put a hand on my arm to draw me closer. 'You know, I had a hunch that Melissa might show up for the first night? She's always been such a professional.'

'I somehow thought she might be here, too,' I admitted. I was fascinated by her. My eyes kept straying back to Maire's face. I found myself comparing her with Melissa, trying to work out where their features overlapped and where they didn't. And it wasn't just that: it was her mannerisms too, the way she had of glancing sideways at me as she spoke. There was something uncanny about it.

'I have a very bad feeling about all this, Cass, very bad. And I don't mind telling you, I think the police are dragging their feet. Something's happened to my sister and I'm determined to get to the bottom of it.' She scanned the room behind me as if she might spot a clue to Melissa's disappearance – or even Melissa herself. 'I've already rung that police sergeant and I'm going round to see him in the morning. I'm going to give him a hard time.'

'Have you spoken to Kevin?'

'Kevin! Huh!' She spat the words out. 'Briefly. He is not

pleased to see me, I can tell you that. I never did think he was good enough for Melissa and now I know I was right. Stan here has brought me up to date with what he's been up to.' A kind of spasm seemed to pass over her face and her grip tightened on my arm. She swayed a little.

'Are you all right?' I asked.

'Jet lag. I always suffer really badly. Just felt a little dizzy there for a moment. Guess I should be heading back to my hotel.'

'Would you like us to take you?'

'No, no,' her voice was firmer now. 'I've ordered a taxi.' She looked at her watch. 'In fact he'll be waiting right now.' She hesitated, then took one of my hands in both of hers and squeezed it. 'You know, I'm so grateful for what you've been doing for Agnes. I'll ring you tomorrow, OK?'

'You're sure you're all right?'

'I'll be fine.' She looked round. Stan and Joe had drifted a little way off and were deep in conversation. 'I'll just slip away. Say goodbye to Stan for me.'

I watched her make her way to the exit, attracting puzzled looks from several people, who obviously thought she looked familiar.

As I turned to Joe and Stan I heard Stan say:

'So how long have you and Cass known each other?'

'Oh, we're very old friends,' he replied, giving me a sideways smile.

'Really?' Stan gave an enormous yawn. 'Oh, do excuse me.'

'What time did you manage to get to bed last night?' I asked.

'The dress rehearsal didn't finish until one o'clock. And that wasn't the half of it. I had Belinda crying on my shoulder half the night. I was seriously worried about whether she'd be able to go on tonight.'

'She's as upset as all that?'

'Well, you knew it had been going on for about six months with her and Kevin?'

'No!'

'Apparently it started when she auditioned for her part in the play. The good old casting couch!'

'You mean. . . ?'

'Yes, that's right. When Melissa was in hospital with Agnes.' Her voice was grim. 'Aren't men bastards?'

'Kevin gave me the impression it was a one-night stand!'

'Oh, no, no, no. Belinda was in deep. She's not the sharpest knife in the box and she really thought he cared about her. All that languishing with unrequited love in the first act? Well, let's put it this way. Not much acting skill was required there. They never learn, do they? Kevin dropped her like a hot potato when Melissa disappeared.'

I thought about those anxious days in the premature baby unit, those vulnerable little bodies in incubators, Melissa and me in dressing-gowns. My heart ached just thinking about it. And all the time Kevin was . . .

'You know,' I said, 'this kind of thing really does make me think men must be a separate species – or even from a different planet.'

'A lower form of life, that's for sure,' Stan said, smiling sweetly at Joe.

'Hey, leave me out of this,' he protested. 'I'm as disgusted as you are.' He looked it too. I'd forgotten about that scowl of Joe's. 'Any decent guy would be. But there's something I don't understand. Kevin ended up spending hours at the police station. Is that right? Well, why didn't he tell the police straightaway that he had an alibi. Surely he wasn't trying to protect Belinda?'

'God, no.' Stan gave a snort. 'Don't you see? There he was, playing the pathos card, the devoted husband, clutching his motherless baby to his breast, hardly able to hold back the tears. He certainly wasn't going to admit – unless he absolutely had to – that when Melissa did a bunk, he was between the sheets with another woman. That wasn't going to play very well with *Hello* magazine, was it?'

'Would you believe it?' Joe shook his head.

'Oh, well, according to Richard, we must look on the bright side,' Stan said.

'There's a bright side?' I said.

'Oh, yes.' She gave a cynical laugh. 'The accountants are wetting themselves with excitement. We couldn't have got more press coverage if we'd paid for it. We're sold out for the entire run.'

'I thought people might ask for their money back now that Melissa's not in it.'

'Well, Phyllida's pretty well known, but really of course it's Kevin they're interested in. The drama offstage is even more fascinating than the one on it. They're hoping to get some of both. Oh, well, I'd better go. I only popped in for a glass of champagne. I'm going to check that everything's in order backstage. Then I'm going off home.'

'Shall we be going, too, Cass?' asked Joe.

I nodded. I looked around for Kevin. He was nowhere in sight, but I could leave a message at the stage door. The bar was packed now and loud with the buzz of conversation. Joe turned sideways and began to edge his way through the crowd. We were briefly separated when Phyllida's pin-striped friend ploughed in front of me on his way to the bar. I reached forward to grab Joe's hand. We threaded our way through to the double doors that led to the red-carpeted stairs down to the foyer. They'd been propped open. People had spilled out of the bar and were standing chatting in little groups on the landing. We were on the top step when I felt a hand on my shoulder. I looked round to see Kevin.

'You're not going yet, are you?' he said.

He came closer – close enough for me to smell a very expensive cologne – and put his hand on my waist.

'Cassandra's tired. I'm taking her home,' Joe said.

'And you are?' asked Kevin. His voice was cool. His eyes flicked down to where Joe was holding my hand and flicked back to Joe's face. The two men stared at each other as if I wasn't there. I made an effort to take control of the situation.

'Kevin, this is Joe Baldassarre. Joe, Kevin.'

Joe nodded curtly, his face impassive. His gaze dropped to where Kevin's hand was still on my waist.

'Take your hand off her,' Joe said. He spoke as if this was some unremarkable neutral request. He could have been asking Kevin to pass the salt.

'I thought I was giving you a lift home,' Kevin said to me, his eyes fixed on my face. It was as if we were alone together. His voice was low and intimate. The people nearest to us had stopped talking and were looking around as though they had sensed the tension. Behind Kevin I saw Jake and Geoff, Jake's eyes widening in avid interest.

'Did you hear me?' Joe asked pleasantly. Kevin looked at him. His hand stayed where it was. I was intensely conscious of the heat of it though the thin material of my blouse. I looked at Joe and saw what Kevin was seeing: a middle-aged man, over-weight, balding, about the same age as Kevin but much shorter and without the muscular definition that comes from working-out in a gym twice a week. Something about the way he was standing triggered a memory twenty years old: a party at which a drunken rugby player had tried to get too friendly with me. He'd laughed when Joe objected, not imagining that he had anything to fear from a little guy with a physique like Woody Allen. Kevin was about to make the same mistake. Another moment and he'd be sprawling down the stairs.

I shook myself free of both of them and stepped between them.

'I'm getting a lift home with Joe. I'll speak to you tomorrow, Kevin.' For a moment or two it was as if hadn't spoken. They went on staring at each other like two dogs facing each other in the street. Then Kevin turned and without a word began to shoulder his way through the crowd.

Chapter Fifteen

'THE son-of-a-bitch,' Joe said. 'Seems to thinks he owns you.'

It was only then that I realized I had been holding my breath. I let it out.

'Oh, and you don't?' I said. 'You're not married to me now, you know, and even if you were—'

'Oh, come on, Cass, he was completely out of order.'

'That's not the point. I'm a big girl now. I'm capable of fighting my own battles.'

'I hope you're right. Because to my mind what that guy needs is a smack in the face.'

'Joe!'

'Sorry, sorry. Look, I guess I'd better take you home.'

We didn't say much as we went out to Joe's hire-car and set off on the half-hour journey into the fens. The adrenaline rush that I'd felt when Kevin and Joe were confronting each other had subsided, leaving me deathly tired. I kicked my shoes off and slumped back in my seat. A wave of depression swept over me. I felt empty and depleted. It wasn't only Melissa being missing, and the episode between Joe and Kevin. It was that something was finished, something which had taken up everything that I had to spare from Grace over the last few months. The first night was over and with it my close connection with the theatre and the group of people I'd seen virtually every day for weeks. I felt a pang at that thought. Soon I'd be back in college and the world of the play and the company would be distant and unreal.

And Melissa, how long could I go on worrying about her at this level of intensity? If she didn't show up soon, would I start to forget her, too? No, not while there was Agnes. Surely, surely there'd be a phone call soon, a message from Melissa . . . The lights of the car on the road, the rhythm created by the broken white line: the effect was hypnotic and I felt my eyelids sinking. The next thing I knew Joe was shaking my shoulder. We were at the Old Granary. I stretched and yawned.

Joe reached over and put a hand on my arm.

'Cass . . .'

'Mmm . . . what is it?' I was still half-asleep. When he didn't reply, I turned towards him. It was so dark that I could see only his profile.

His voice was serious. 'What you said earlier. I know I'm not still married to you, but sometimes I wish . . .'

It was like a warning bell going off. I was suddenly wide awake.

'Don't.' I put my hand on his mouth.

He put his hand on mine, pressed my fingers to his lips. We sat there like that in the dimness of the car. Then the security light outside my front door came on, flooding the car with light. Tilly had opened the door and was standing on the doorstep, shielding her eyes against the glare with her hand.

'I must go,' I said.

Joe nodded and released me.

'Look,' he said, 'I'll be back in a few days. Don't know exactly when yet, but if you want to talk, ring me on my mobile, OK?'

I nodded. 'Thanks for coming to the opening with me.'

'My pleasure.'

I got out of the car.

He called after me. 'Hey, no chance that Kevin will be hanging around here, is there?'

I shook my head. 'His car isn't here. And anyway I'm sure he won't want to see me after what's happened. He'll have already collected Agnes.'

I watched him reverse and drive off. It was only as his lights disappeared and I turned to go into the house that I realized that I hadn't got his mobile number.

I tiptoed into my study where Grace was asleep in her cot. Tilly had changed her and fed her shortly before I'd got back, so with any luck she'd sleep for a few hours. Kevin had been and gone as I'd guessed. He'd arrived a full quarter of an hour before me: he must have driven like the clappers. I bent over Grace in the semi-darkness and breathed in the warmth of her sleeping body. When I kissed her she gave a little whimper. Then with a sigh she lapsed back into sleep.

I climbed up the narrow stairs to my bedroom leaning heavily on the handrail. I left my new clothes on the floor where they fell and got into bed without taking my make-up off. Sleep came instantly but it was far from restful. Scenes from *East Lynne* played themselves over and over in my head. It was like the sensation you have of the road coming up to meet you when you try to sleep after a long drive. I was stuck in a loop, going through the play over and over again. The thing was that the performance had to be perfect. If there was even the tiniest mistake we had to go back to the beginning. I was playing Lady Isabel. Again and again we got nearly to the end but then I would forget a line and realize with a sinking heart that we had to do it all over again. At one point I woke up and knew that I had been dreaming. But immediately it seemed, I was back on stage, again as Lady Isabel. And this time Melissa was there in costume as Madame Vine. I was puzzled: Lady Isabel and Madame Vine couldn't be on stage together, could they? Then I forgot about that, because Melissa was telling me something very important. She was explaining that acting was terribly dangerous, because it involved the transfer of souls. The risk was that you would

189

change into the character you were playing and not be able to get back into your own body. And even as she spoke her own features were dissolving and reforming. . . .

I came out of the dream with a jerk. The clock said ten past seven. Downstairs I could hear Grace making conversational little noises. She was talking to herself. She would soon get tired of that and demand to be fed, but I had a few minutes respite. I settled back on the pillows and thought about the dream. What could it mean? Why was I playing Lady Isabel, the jealous wife who had abandoned her children? That was Melissa's role – in *East Lynne* and in real life. But then a startling thought occurred to me. It wasn't Melissa, was it, who was living with a nice reliable lawyer like Archibald? That was me. And was I also being tempted into adultery by an old love? That idea gave me a jolt. A moment or two's reflection and the analogy with *East Lynne* broke down. I couldn't see Joe as a murderer and the villainous seducer of young women. And how old was Lady Isabel? Twenty-five, tops, when she runs off, whereas I was nearly forty and had been married twice. And why was I entertaining these ridiculous thoughts anyway? I wasn't Lady Isabel and neither was Melissa, because Lady Isabel didn't exist. She was a character in a work of fiction. It was time I returned to the real world and got up and fed my baby.

But for all my rationalization, one question still remained. What was I going to do about Joe? If I wasn't going to let things go any further, there was something I had to do, and the sooner the better. After breakfast my chance came. The phone rang. At first there was just a crackling sound.

Then: 'Cass? It's me. How did it go last night?' It was Stephen.

'Fine! It went fine. Well, up to a point. I mean there's still no word of Melissa. But Phyllida came up with the goods in the end.'

'Oh, I'm glad.' His voice faded away and I caught only snatches of what he was saying. '. . . fantastic here . . . the silence . . . bigger than the Statue of Liberty.'

'The silence is bigger than the Statue of Liberty?'

'Don't be silly. The redwoods. Some of them grow taller than the Statue of Liberty.' His voice came back so loudly that I had to hold the phone away from my ear. '– left the Big Sur Inn this morning. We're spending a night in a cabin in the forest. Going back to LA tomorrow. I'm on Bob's mobile.'

I took a deep breath. 'I've got something to tell you.'

'I can hardly hear you. The signal's not very good.' His voice seemed to be flickering on and off. It was like listening to a badly tuned radio.

'I said, I've got something to tell you!'

'Speak up then!'

'I took my ex-husband to the opening last night!' I shouted.

'You exhumed what?'

'No, no! my ex-husband, my first husband. You remember! Joe! He's in Cambridge on sabbatical and he came to the opening with me.'

There was no response, but I couldn't tell whether it was because the signal had faded or because Stephen hadn't spoken.

'Hello! Hello!' I bellowed. 'Are you there?'

Stephen's voice came back weakly . . . 'a turn-up for the book . . . nice that you weren't on your own . . .'

'Also: he lost his rag with Kevin and nearly punched him!'

There was a brief buzzing sound, then quite suddenly his voice was as strong and clear as if he had been standing next to me.

'Tell him not to hold back next time. He can land one on Kevin for me. Oh, God, the signal's going again. I'll speak to you again very soon. When I get back to LA. Miss you. Love you. Love Grace.'

'Love you, too. Take care.'

'You, too. 'Bye then.'

' 'Bye.' And he was gone.

As I hung up, I didn't know whether to feel relieved or

affronted. Didn't he realize that I had been on the point of falling in love with another man? Or perhaps he didn't care? But I knew I'd be kidding myself if I pretended I thought that. I knew what he'd say if I pressed him. If I don't trust you, then that's the whole foundation of our relationship gone. Sure, you might let me down – my ex-wife did after all – but a life lived in fear of that happening again is no life at all. Wasn't that more or less what I'd decided myself a few days ago?

I went down to the kitchen to put the kettle on. While I waited for it to boil, I wondered if it's better to have a man who's too interested in you – or not interested enough? When I was twenty the question would have seemed absurd. I'd taken possessiveness and jealousy as signs of love. It's flattering to have all someone's attention. But would I really like Stephen to be the kind of man who wanted to know where I was and what I was doing all the time? It would be intolerable. And how close really was I to falling for the Joe of today? It was the Joe of twenty years ago that I was longing for – and the Cass of twenty years ago: the young woman who had been ardent and carefree, who could spend hours reading *War and Peace* in the bath, topping up the water again and again until her fingers were as wrinkled as prunes; the Cass who had been able to survive for days on bacon sandwiches and apples and black coffee; above all the Cass who had everything before her. I was mourning my lost youth, it was as corny and as clichéd as that. I was grieving because I'd lost my flat belly, my chin was getting blurry, and I'd never again go to a party and end the evening slow-dancing with a stranger. I felt an aching nostalgia for those days. But would I go back even if I could? What was that saying? that if everyone's life was put on the table, most people would pick up their own? A life without Grace was unthinkable. Stephen too was part of that life and he'd soon be home.

I grinned to myself. I liked black coffee now. In the old days I'd only drunk it because I thought it was more chic than white.

I decided to go out into the garden for a while and sit in the sun. When I went to get Grace out of her cot she was fast asleep and I decided not to risk waking her by shifting her to the garden. Instead I opened the study window, so that I'd hear her if she cried. I'd only be a few feet away. I locked the front door and took a rug and my coffee and *The Mill on the Floss* into the garden. I stretched out under the shade of a big elder-tree. I closed my eyes. The stream was making a gentle sound just on the edge of hearing. Minutes later, the coffee undrunk, I was asleep.

I woke up feeling that something had disturbed me. The sun was hot on my face and glowed red-orange on the inside of my eyelids. I yawned and opened my eyes. The sun had moved round while I'd been asleep. I looked at my watch. My God! Half past twelve. I sat up abruptly. I'd been asleep for three hours – no, nearly four. And Grace hadn't woken up. Or had she? Was it her crying that had woken me up? I listened intently. The house and garden lay silent under the midday sun. All the fears I'd had when Grace was a premature baby came rushing back. She never slept this long during the day. What if she wasn't asleep – what if— Oh God, how could I have let myself sleep so long? I ran into the house. It was cool indoors. I rushed down the stairs to my study, my heart beating fast. The cot was over by the window. I could see that Grace was hugging Woolly Bear to her chest with one hand. With the other she was pulling her foot up to her face. She was cooing to herself. I felt a flood of relief. I bent down into the cot to pick her up. She looked up and smiled at me. I froze in mid movement. For a few moments I didn't believe what I was seeing. I thought I might be hallucinating. I blinked and looked again. Nothing had changed.

It still wasn't Grace in the cot. It was Agnes.

My own baby had gone.

Chapter Sixteen

'OH. Oh. Oh.' It seemed to be someone else who was gasping in shock. I looked round inside the cot as though I could have somehow overlooked Grace. I felt giddy. I groped for the swivel chair by my desk and collapsed on to it. I was trembling and my mouth was dry. How could this have happened? Might it be – was it possible – was she somewhere else in the house? Had I put her somewhere and forgotten about it? Had Kevin left Agnes here earlier?

My heart in my throat, I ran up to my bedroom, knocking over a pile of books on the study floor and nearly taking a tumble down the stairs. The duvet lay on the bed in a series of hummocks. I hadn't straightened it that morning. I searched the bed pulling the duvet this way and that. She wasn't there. For a crazy moment I wondered if I'd left her in the car. Could I really have left her shut in there on a warm day like this? I looked out of the window. The car lay inertly in the sun outside the front-garden gate. It was empty. No baby strapped in the car seat.

I couldn't delay the full realization any longer. Someone had taken her.

I wanted to run round the house screaming. But I walked back down to the study, forcing myself to slow down and think. Agnes was mumbling to herself in the cot. I looked down on her scarcely seeing her. I shouted, 'Grace! Grace!' as if she might be somewhere nearby and could hear me and reply. Agnes was startled. She began whimpering. She tried to pull herself up into a sitting position. I couldn't bring myself to touch her. What was she doing here in the place of my own baby? Someone had come into the house while I was asleep in the garden and had taken Grace, substituting Agnes for her. But if Agnes was here, then. . . ?

I went to the phone and stabbed in Kevin's number with a quivering finger. Almost immediately the phone was picked up at the other end. A familiar voice said hello. It was Melissa. My hand flew to my throat. The voice continued: 'We can't come to the phone at the moment.' It was a recording. Kevin had left the answering-machine on and he hadn't changed the message. Perhaps he was there, all the same. I waited in an ecstasy of impatience for him to pick up the phone, but the message played itself out.

I slammed the receiver down and ran upstairs to the study. Agnes was crying, but it was a far-off sound that didn't have much to do with me. I scrambled up to my bedroom. I seized the binoculars and directed them towards Journey's End. I saw the boot of Kevin's red hire-car sticking out round the side of the house. He was at home. I grabbed my car-keys from the bedside table and ran to the study. The moment Agnes saw me, she whimpered. She lifted her arms imploringly. I paused. Could I leave her here? No, she'd have to come with me. When I lifted Agnes up, she sensed my anxiety and impatience and began to howl. I felt a flash of anger, of hatred, even.

'Stop it, stop it,' I muttered through clenched teeth.

I just wanted to get rid of her and get my own baby back. Everything seemed to take an age. I fumbled with the clasp on the baby-seat. I stalled the car. And all the time Agnes was screaming with hunger and fear. Then I was off down the rutted track, driving as fast as I dared. The light was red at the level-crossing. Unable to sit still, I got out of the car, and stood by the gate to the track biting the skin around my fingernails. The train was coming from Ely. It advanced across the flat plain with infuriating slowness. After it had passed there was a delay before the light went green, then I was pumping the barriers up, running back to the car, driving through. I didn't wait to pump the barrier back down.

At Journey's End I pulled up sharply in a spray of gravel and leaped out to lean on the doorbell. Nothing happened. No one came. I put my ear to the door. Silence. I rang again and I rattled the doorhandle. The door was open. I ran through the dim sitting-room and up the stairs. I pushed open the door to Agnes's room. The curtains had been pulled back. Sunlight was flooding in the room. There in the cot was Grace. She was awake and sitting up. She had Agnes's felt snake in her hands and was sucking one of the baubles attached to it. When she saw me, her eyes opened wide and she chortled. I snatched her up. Standing there with my arms wrapped round her I felt that I would never let her out of my sight again for a single moment. But was she really all right? I held her out from my body to examine her. She grinned and wriggled, urging me to joggle her up and down. She was fine, absolutely fine, as perfect and lovely as ever.

As I stood there drinking her in, I heard the door behind me click shut. I turned round. Kevin was leaning against it.

He was wearing his usual uniform of jeans and a white T-shirt. His feet were bare. As I stared at him he drew one foot up and rested the sole of it against the door. His arms were folded across his chest in a way that made the muscles bulge. His lower face was dark with stubble.

'What are you doing, Cassandra?' His voice was cool.

I pulled Grace back to my chest. She protested and struggled, but I held her close. 'How did my baby get here?' I said, trying to keep the tremor out of my voice.

'I'm sorry?'

'How did Grace get here?'

'Grace? But that's Agnes you've got there.'

I stared at him, unable to speak. He smiled.

196

Grace put her hand up to my face. Without taking my eyes off
Kevin, I pressed her fingers to my face and kissed them.

'They do look very similar, don't they?' Kevin said gently.
'And you've been under a lot of pressure, haven't you?'

He continued: 'Come on now, who'd do something like that?
You really think someone came to your house while you were
asleep? That someone took your baby away and left another one
in her place? Who would that have been? The fairies, perhaps?
Bit of a mad idea, isn't it?' He unfolded his arms and let his
hands drop by his sides. 'Who's going to believe you, do you
think? Post-natal psychosis, that's what they call it, isn't it, when
a woman with a baby goes off her head?'

The ground seemed to fall away beneath my feet. Was it
possible, could he be right? Was this really Agnes? Was I going
mad?

Grace made a little noise of complaint and gripped my T-shirt.
I was back on solid ground. Of course this was my own child. It
wasn't something there could be any doubt about. She was part
of me. The connection between us was like a gravitational pull.

'I don't know why you're doing this,' I said. 'But I'm taking
Grace home now.'

He went on as if I hadn't spoken. 'You're overtired, getting a
bit muddled up. Giving birth can do funny things to a woman. I
mean, look at Melissa.' He shook his head. 'I mean, who would
have thought it? Running away from a perfectly good home and
husband. That is: if she did run away? What do you think,
Cassandra?' He was still smiling but he was clenching and
unclenching his right hand, stretching the fingers out in a rhythmic flicking movement then squeezing them into the palm of his
hand. The knuckles were white.

'I don't know what's happened to her! I wish I did.'

'No idea?' he asked. 'None at all?'

I shook my head.

'Mmm. Do I believe you? I'm not sure. You know, Cassandra,
until last night I thought you were a decent woman. I should

have known better: there aren't any decent women, are there? It's a contradiction in terms. No sooner is Stephen out of the way than another man is sniffing around. You're like a bitch on heat.'

He was looking into my face, but he didn't really seem to be seeing me. He was still clenching and unclenching his hand.

'Does anyone know you're here, Cassandra?' he asked.

For half a beat there was silence.

'I rang Stephen before I came out,' I said.

'Oh, no, I don't think you did. I think you came hot-footing it straight over here. Just as I intended. I want you to tell me what you think has happened to Melissa. Is she alive?' He paused for effect. 'Or is she dead?'

I shook my head, too frightened to speak.

'Perhaps this will concentrate your mind.'

He stepped forward and grabbed Grace under her arms. I hung on to her, but he pulled her towards him. Grace let out a protesting bleat. Kevin tried to wrench her away from me. I hung on to her. We were pulling her in different directions and she started to scream. I had to let go.

Kevin stood back and held her away from him. She looked at me, uncertain whether or not this was a game. I reached out for her. Kevin hefted her above his head.

'Is Melissa alive, do you think?' Grace giggled. He lowered her. 'Or is she dead?' He lifted her again, this time making a whooshing noise. 'Alive?' She giggled even more. He brought her back down. 'Or dead?'

I put my hand on his arm. 'Kevin, please.'

'Not until you tell me about Melissa. You do know, don't you?'

'No, no, I don't! I swear I don't. Please, my baby.'

I heard the pleading in my voice and I hated him. If I'd had a gun to put to his temples or a knife to slip between his ribs, he would have been a dead man. I'd even have twisted the knife as it went in.

'Can't you at least hazard a guess?' He lifted Grace up again.

This time he let go of her for a split second. He caught her as she came down but she was jolted. She wasn't used to being treated so roughly. She hiccuped and screwed her face up. She began to cry. Kevin smiled and lifted her on to his shoulder, patting her back. His eyes were on my face.

'There, there, Daddy's got you now.' Her eyes goggled, she leaned forward, there was a gurgling noise, and she vomited down his back.

'Oh, Christ, you foul little brat.' He thrust her away, his face contorted with disgust. I snatched her from him. He pulled his T-shirt up over his head. In the second that his eyes were covered I saw my chance. I stuck my leg between both of his and brought my knee up as hard as I could. He gave a high-pitched scream and collapsed on to his side on the floor. He brought his knees up and his hands went down to his balls. The T-shirt was still attached to his head like a burnous. I ran down the stairs. Out of the corner of my eye, I saw something gleaming on the chest by the door: Kevin's car-keys. I grabbed them and ran outside. I wrenched open the back seat of my car and flung Kevin's keys in. I was astonished to see Agnes was still in the car seat. I'd completely forgotten about her. What the hell was I going to do? I fought down an urge to unbuckle Agnes and fling her on the grass verge. There wasn't time and anyway I couldn't leave her with this madman. I clambered into the front seat with Grace and pressed down the button for the central locking. I pulled the seat belt over both of us, and started the car. I crunched the gears into reverse and swung the car back into the turning-space.

Kevin appeared at the door of the house. I caught a glimpse of his bare chest, densely covered in dark hair. One hand was nursing his crotch and in the other he was holding a shoe. Adrenaline surged through my body. I swung the wheel back round. The wheels skidded in the gravel, throwing up stones that pinged on the side of the car. Kevin was coming towards me. But the gravel was slowing him down. He was staggering, hopping, trying to put on the shoe. Then he was alongside me, grabbing at the door.

I put my foot down. The car shot forward, pressing me to the back of my seat. I veered out of the gateway, clipping my front right bumper. The car swerved and bumped down the track. I put an arm round Grace and steered with one hand. Grace was trying to pull herself up my chest. Her hands were over my mouth and I had to lift my chin to see over her head.

The light at the level-crossing was green and the gates were still open. The car clicked over the rails. As I cleared the other side, I glanced in the mirror. The track was visible right back to the gate of the house, but Kevin was nowhere to be seen. All the same I didn't risk stopping until I was back on the metalled road. By then I was shaking so much that I had to pull over to the kerb. I looked into the back seat. Agnes was waving her hands about and smiling. She'd been enjoying the ride. I leaned my head back against the head-rest and sat there stroking Grace's head and trying to take deep breaths. She whimpered and snuggled into me.

There was a flicker of movement in my wing mirror. A figure was advancing towards me. I sat up with a jerk, my heart beating fast. But I saw it wasn't Kevin. This was a middle-aged woman walking a small dog. As she passed, she glanced at me. I followed her train of thought, as she went on for a yard or two and paused. She turned on her heel, came back and looked at me. I lowered the car window.

'Are you all right?' she said. She was older than me, about fifty, with a weather-beaten look and an upper-middle-class accent. A horsy woman, I guessed.

'Yes, yes, I'm OK,' I told her.'

I saw her looking at the baby fastened to my chest. She took in my dishevelled appearance and the smell of vomit.

'I know I shouldn't be carrying her like this,' I said. 'I'm afraid it's an emergency.' I groped about for a plausible explanation. 'My friend's been taken ill and I have to look after her baby. That's her in the back. I only live a mile or two down the road.'

'You don't look very well yourself, if you don't mind me

saying so.'

'I'm fine. Really.'

She looked doubtful. 'Well, if you're sure.'

'Yes. Yes, I am.' I smiled at her and started the engine.

As I drove off, I saw her in my mirror, standing on the pavement staring after us, while her Yorkshire terrier strained at its leash.

I drove the rest of the way to the Old Granary very slowly and very carefully. I got out of the car on legs that wobbled and took Grace into the house. I put her in her cot and went back for Agnes. I fished Kevin's car keys out from where they'd slid under the passenger seat and put them in the pocket of my jeans. It was only as I unbuckled Agnes from her car seat, that I asked myself what on earth I was going to do with her? Her enjoyment of the car ride was over and she was beginning to grizzle. I took her inside and locked the door behind me. I put her in the cot with Grace. They were both cross and hungry. Any moment now they'd be screaming their heads off.

I climbed the stairs to the top of the house and picked up the binoculars. I looked out first along the track in the direction of Ely. I almost expected to see Kevin advancing towards me on foot, but there was no one there. I crossed to the other window and looked over to Journey's End. The hire-car was still there. I patted the pocket of my jeans and felt the reassuring outline of Kevin's car-keys. He wouldn't have more than one set and to walk round by road would take him an hour or so. It was much shorter across the fields, but I couldn't see him wading through the drainage ditch up to his thighs in stagnant water. I opened the window. A waft of air carried in the scent of hay and a brief snatch of birdsong. The Cambridge to Ely train was trundling across the landscape. Ordinary people were on board, tourists perhaps, going to Ely to walk round the marina and the antique shops, to stroll through the narrow streets, maybe even go to evensong. I told myself I could relax now. There was plenty of time to ring the police. The important thing was that the children were safe. And so was I.

And with that knowledge came the reaction.

I began to shake again. A wave of nausea swept over me. I staggered into the bathroom and lowered myself on to the floor by the toilet bowl. I retched but nothing came up. I managed to lie down on the bathroom floor before I passed out completely and lay there gazing at the ceiling. Little lights exploded in front of my eyes. In the room below, first one baby then the other began to scream. Gradually the nausea ebbed away. After a few minutes I sat up slowly I got hold of the side of the bath and pulled myself clumsily to my feet.

I heard the sound of a car approaching. I looked out of the window towards Ely. My heart lurched. A car was coming down the track. The next moment I recognized the car. It drew up outside the garden gate and Joe got out.

Chapter Seventeen

THE doorbell rang as I was making my shaky way down the stairs from the study to the ground floor.

I opened the door. Joe had prepared what he was going to say and he launched straight into it.

'I woke up this morning feeling a total jerk – that business with Kevin, and what I said later on. I just had to come back to apologize. I mean, we're not kids any more, are we? We can't turn back the clock. But, gee, I hope we can be friends – I'll hate myself if I've spoiled that . . .'

His voice trailed off as he took in my dishevelled appearance.

'Jesus, Cass, what's happened? You look as if you've been in an accident.'

I looked down at myself. My shirt was filthy and there was a large rip in it.

'Oh God . . .' I suddenly wanted to cry.

'Cass? What's the matter? It's not Grace, is it?'

'No, she's here, she's all right.' I was blinking back tears.

'Stephen?'

'No, nothing to do with him. Come in. Please.'

He stepped inside and I closed the door quickly behind him. I turned the key in the lock and pushed home the bolt with fingers that still trembled a little.

'Wait a minute.' I tested the door to make sure it really was locked. I turned to see Joe watching me with an expression of concern and curiosity.

'What in God's name. . . ?' he said.

'He stole her. Kevin stole my baby! He was going to hurt her.' Tears were welling up and spilling over now.

'Jesus! Have you rung the police?'

'Not yet . . . I was – just – about to.' The words were jerked out between sobs.

'Hey, come on, now.' He took hold of my hands. 'You're so cold. I think you're in shock.' He steered me into the kitchen and sat me down at the table. He looked around, located the kettle, filled it at the sink and plugged it in. Overhead the wailing continued.

'What a racket,' he said. 'I can't hear myself think.'

'They're hungry.'

'They?'

'Agnes is here, too. Melissa's baby.' I started to get to my feet.

'I'll get them. You stay here.'

He brought Grace down. 'This *is* Grace, isn't it?' he said.

I nodded and he put her in my arms. I opened my shirt and she latched on to my breast.

Joe reappeared with Agnes.

'Have you got any baby food?'

'Baby food?'

'You know, gunk in jars.' He was fitting Agnes into the high chair.

'That cupboard there.' I pointed. 'I usually purée our own food for her, but I do keep a few . . .'

'Hey, no need to apologize. This stuff's just fine,' he said, holding up a little glass jar containing a red paste. 'Penne with roast tomato and courgette. Or what have we here? Porridge oats! Yum-yum.' Agnes had stopped crying and was listening wide-eyed to his running commentary. 'So what's it to be?' he asked her. 'Porridge oats? Good choice, Agnes!' She gazed at him in wonder. 'And tea for you, Cass, right? No, don't you move, I can find everything.'

He made the tea and put a mug in front of me.

As I drank it I began to feel more like myself.

Joe sat down next to Agnes. He opened the jar and began to spoon puréed porridge oats into her mouth.

'You know,' he said. 'I've often wondered over the years what it would be like if we ever met up – you know how you do?'

I nodded.

'I could never have imagined it would be like this,' he said, gesturing to both babies with the spoon. 'If the bottom falls out of the academic market, we can always open a kindergarten.'

I gave a weak smile.

'Feeling better now?' he asked me. He wiped Agnes's mouth with a piece of kitchen roll. 'Want to tell me more about what happened?'

I told him how I had woken up and found that Grace had gone and Agnes had been left in her place.

'How did Kevin get in?' Joe asked. 'Did you leave the door open?'

'No, it was locked.'

'Does he have a key?'

'A key? No.'

'And it's a deadlock, isn't it? He'd need to have a key. Are you really sure you locked it?'

'Yes, I remember unlocking it when I went in from the garden.'

'So how did he get in, Cassandra? I presume there's no sign of a break-in?'

'No, there isn't.' I hadn't had a chance to think about this. I thought about it now. Grace had stopped feeding. I fastened my bra and buttoned up my shirt. When I looked back at Joe he was looking pensive. And quite suddenly I knew exactly what he was thinking. How reliable was I? Sure, he'd once been married to me, but for how long, two years? Three years? And that had been a long time ago. How well did he really know me now? And back in the old days hadn't I always been dreamy and impractical, a bit off the wall, as Joe used to put it? I was forever losing things, locking myself out of our flat. And that 'Cassandra': he'd only ever called me that when he was pulling seniority on me. I'd rather liked that in the past, had felt protected and reassured. Well, I didn't like it now.

'What are you saying? That I left the door open? Or that he didn't swap Agnes for Grace? That I don't know my child?'

'Hey, now.' He spread out his hands in a placatory gesture.

'Or that I made it all up? That Kevin isn't a psychopath who might even have murdered his own wife and—'

'What?' Joe stared at me. He was on the point of saying something else, but I didn't find out what it was, because just then the phone rang.

For the first couple of rings neither of us spoke. Then Joe said, 'Shall I?'

'I'd better . . .' I got up and handed Grace to Joe.

'Dr James?' It was a masculine voice, cultured, pleasant, light in timbre.

'Yes?'

'We're doing a survey on behalf of the Law Society. Have you got time to answer a few questions?'

'Sorry, no—'

'Just one question then. It's this: have you made a will?'

'What?' I thought I must have misheard.

'Have you made a will?'

I gasped and hung up.

'What the hell was that about?' Joe was standing beside me with Grace in his arms. She was trying to grab his hair.

'I think it was a threat. Someone asking me if I'd made a will.'

'Kevin?'

'It didn't sound like him, but . . .' I was remembering the other phone calls: the man selling security, the double-glazing saleswoman with the husky voice, the man from the holiday company. They hadn't sounded like Kevin either, but perhaps

. . . I didn't know which were real and which weren't.

'I think perhaps this isn't the first time he's rung up pretending to be someone else. Look, I've got to ring the police. I should have done it before.'

'You're going to have to explain how he got into the house. Think, Cass. He *must* have got his hands on a key somehow. Are you sure that you haven't ever done any of that good neighbour stuff, watering each other's house plants or whatever.'

Something stirred in my memory.

'Wait a minute. There was a time a couple of months ago. Stephen and I went to visit his sister down in Devon for a weekend. Melissa fed Bill Bailey for me. But she gave the key back. And anyway, it's the kind that key-cutting places aren't supposed to reproduce.'

'Hell, there are ways of getting round that. And don't forget. He's the one with the missing wife. The police will still be looking at him very carefully. Do you think he did kill her? Did he say that he had?'

Grace was stretching out her arms to me. Joe handed her to me. It was hard to remember what Kevin had said exactly. I had been so afraid for Grace. It was only much later that I reconstructed that conversation in detail.

'I don't know. But I think he's capable of it. But it doesn't matter. I still have to ring the police.'

I found the card Tim Fisher had given me. Joe punched in the number, but when he handed the phone to me there was nothing. I joggled the receiver.

'There's no dialling tone,' I said.

Joe took the phone from me and listened.

'You know what? That sick bastard hasn't hung up. You won't be able to ring out until he does.'

'I'll have to use my mobile.' My handbag was hanging on a chair. I fished about in it. 'It's not there. I had it last night. What can have happened to it? Realization dawned. 'Oh, no . . .' I looked at Joe.

He read my face. 'Oh shit. Kevin's taken it, hasn't he?'

'It doesn't matter, does it? You've got one?'

There was a strange expression on Joe's face.

'What?' I said.

'Yep, the battery's dead. I wanted to ring you earlier on. Wasn't able to.' He shook his head. 'I don't believe this. Here we are in one of the most technologically advanced nations in the world and we can't make a goddamned phone call.'

'One of us will have to drive over to the farm next door.'

'You'd better go. I'll baby-sit. They know you – and anyway I wouldn't want to leave you on your own here with that madman on the loose. Just let me try the phone again.' He lifted it up and listened. He shook his head.

An unpleasant feeling was stealing over me. 'Perhaps he is on his way over here right now? I mean he doesn't know that I'm not alone. I'm going to look out of the bedroom window to see if his car's still there.'

'Good idea. And Cass – take a look in the mirror while you're up there.'

I went up to my bedroom, taking Grace with me. I propped her up on the pillows and gave her Woolly Bear to suck. I picked up the binoculars and focused them on to Journey's End. The car was still there, thank God. I went into the bathroom and looked in the mirror. There were smudges of mascara around my eyes and I was very pale. I looked like Dusty Springfield. My hair was sticking out in all directions. No wonder Joe had been so taken aback by my appearance earlier on. I washed my face and put on a clean shirt.

Joe shouted up the stairs.

'Cass, there's some weird shit going on. Is there an extension up there? Pick up the phone.'

I did, but I couldn't make sense of what I was hearing: a clattering, a banging, shouting. And then someone picked up the receiver and a hoarse voice said:

'Cass, Cass. Please? Cass?' I dropped the receiver as if I'd been stung.

I yelled down the stairs for Joe and ran back to the window. I heard him thumping up the stairs as I raised the glasses back to my eyes and trained them on the windows of the cottage. The ivy around them sprang into Pre-Raphaelite detail. As I watched the back door opened. I gave a start that almost sent the binoculars flying. A figure came stumbling out of the back door, a figure that was wearing Kevin's jeans, but the face . . . it was just a red blob. I thought there was something wrong with the focus of the glasses. By the time I realized that there wasn't, he'd disappeared round the corner of the house.

Joe was standing beside me now.

'What is it? What's happening?'

I gave him the binoculars. He lifted them and fiddled with the focus.

'I can't see anything!'

'Give them to me!' I snatched them back. I looked through them just in time to see the figure emerge from the other side of the house where the car was parked. He was staggering now. It was like watching a film without a soundtrack. I could see exactly what was happening but I couldn't hear a thing. Kevin was heading down the drive. He had a hand up to his throat and he was weaving erratically from side to side. I followed his progress as he reeled along the path. What was going on? He tripped and fell. He struggled to his feet and stretched out groping hands like someone playing blindman's buff. He disappeared behind a hedge and I could see just his head bobbing along.

'What's going on?' Joe said. 'Tell me!'

While the scene was unfolding before me I was mesmerized by it. When Joe spoke, suddenly I understood what was happening.

'His allergy! He's gone into anaphylactic shock, but why hasn't he taken his adrenaline?' And then I knew why not. I clapped my hand to my thigh and felt the outline of the keys through the denim of my jeans. 'Oh God! Oh God!'

I pulled the keys out of my pocket and held them up. 'It must be in the car! And I've got his keys.'

Joe stared at the keys, then at me.

'You want me to. . . ? Is this for real? How do we know it's not another trick?'

How could we be sure? Somehow I was sure, but I didn't really know, did I? I looked into Joe's face. He held my gaze. I'd like to say I didn't hesitate at all, but that wouldn't be true. It was no more than a second, but it was still time to think what a contemptible shit Kevin was and that the world would be a better place without him. I looked at the keys. I registered the number of serrations, the texture of the leather fob, the name of the car-hire firm stamped in gold.

'Your call,' Joe said.

'Go!' I dropped the keys into his hand.

Joe thudded down the stairs behind me. I turned back to the window. As I raised the binoculars again, I heard the front door slam below me and then an engine revving. At first I couldn't work out where Kevin was. Then I spotted him. He was moving more slowly now and his head was only occasionally visible above the hedge. The blood was thudding in my ears, a rhythmic pounding. A moment later I realized that the sound wasn't in my head. I lowered the binoculars and looked in the direction of Ely. Far off down the line I could see the Ely to Cambridge train advancing. The gates! I hadn't closed them. I lifted the binoculars. Kevin had emerged from the cover of the hedgerow. He was tottering this way and that as if he were drunk, his hands now covering his face. Surely he could hear the train? But he was moving towards the railway line. I leaned out of the window and yelled a warning at the top of my voice. It was hopeless at that distance, but to do nothing was impossible. The train was thundering up the track. Kevin was swaying now. He fell down and began to crawl on his hands and knees up the slight rise that led to the gates.

'No, no, no,' I screamed.

Kevin got to his feet again. He staggered and the momentum

210

spun him round. He moved his head around uncertainly. The train was fifty yards down the track. I gripped the windowsill. He seemed suddenly to be conscious of danger; his head was moving from side to side, but he must have been dizzy and disorientated. He turned and stepped straight on to the line.

I heard the screech as the driver tried to brake in time.

At the very last moment I closed my eyes.

Chapter Eighteen

'I'VE made you some tea,' Stan said.

I pulled myself up on the pillows. I was still groggy, but the long drugged sleep made me feel as if my brain had been washed clean.

'That's sweet of you,' I said.

It was the following morning and I was in bed at home. The police had questioned me briefly after Kevin's death, then a doctor had arrived and given me a sedative. Joe had arrived on the scene of the accident shortly after it had happened, and he was in an even greater state of shock. He'd actually been kept overnight in hospital. So had the driver of the train. Stan had arrived soon after the police and had stayed to look after the children.

'Stephen rang a couple of hours ago,' Stan said. 'He wouldn't let me wake you. He was at the airport in LA, hoping to get a seat on standby. He'll ring again when he's managed to get a flight.'

'That's great.' Hearing his name made me long to see him.

'Could you eat something?' Stan asked.

'Perhaps in a while, but first, I'd better feed Grace.' I was leaking milk and Grace in her carry cot beside the bed was making little mewling noises.

'She won't be awfully hungry. I gave her some of those porridge oats a bit ago.' Stan lifted Grace up and handed her to me. She settled down at my breast and began to suckle. For me too, there was comfort in the familiar contact.

Stan sat on the edge of the bed. Neither of us spoke.

My brain was still working sluggishly, but after a bit it threw up a question.

'Is Agnes OK?'

'Oh, Cass – I was waiting to tell you. After you fell asleep last night, someone came from Social Services. They've taken her into care.'

'Into care?' I was horrified. 'But what about Melissa's sister? Couldn't she take her?'

'She wants to. I rang up and told her about it. She was hopping mad. Talking about employing a lawyer.'

'And there's still nothing from Melissa?' It wasn't really a question. I knew that Stan would have told me if there had been.

She shook her head.

'I did hope that when she heard about Kevin . . .' I said.

'Yes, so did I. But it's not too late. It only hit the late news last night. She might not see it until this morning.'

If she was still alive. That thought hung unspoken between us.

'Cass?'

'Mm?'

'There's something else I've got to tell you. After you'd gone to bed last night, the police came back and they searched the house. One of them, a woman, even had a quick look round in here.'

'Whatever for!'

'I don't know. I didn't want to let them do it, but they had a warrant and everything. And, well, they took your computer away. I'm sorry.' Her face was creased with concern.

'Don't look so worried. You couldn't help that. I just can't think why they want it.' I said. I stretched out my hand towards her. She put her hand in mine and I squeezed it. 'I just so much appreciate you coming over like this. What's happening at the theatre?'

'Don't you worry about that now. I'll have to go and see Richard in a bit and find out what's happening. But let me get you some breakfast first.'

She got up from the bed and went downstairs.

Stan was right. Grace wasn't very hungry. It was the contact she'd wanted as much as anything. When she stopped feeding, I got out of bed and went over to the window. The sight of the binoculars gave me a queasy feeling. I left them where they were. I didn't need them to see that Journey's End was still a focus of activity. There were several police cars and a white van parked around it. The previous day, before I'd been sedated, I hadn't been able to stop myself running obsessively through the events that had led to Kevin's death. That was beginning again: the horror of finding my baby gone, Kevin taunting me, the feel of the car keys as I snatched them up, the screeching of tyres, my arrival back at the Old Granary, Joe spooning food into Agnes's mouth, Kevin reeling out of the door of the Old Granary. I shook my head as if I could shake the memories loose.

I got back into bed with Grace and pulled the covers up. Stephen would be home soon. Things wouldn't seem so bad then. And yet he was still so far away. Perhaps it was best to think of the distance in time, not miles. Every minute that passed brought him closer. I tried to count the hours before he would be here, but I found it hard to calculate. The dregs of the sedative were still clogging my thoughts. Time and space, were they really the same thing? I couldn't quite think. If only I could go back to sleep until Stephen got here, just to escape back into oblivion once more. I thought perhaps I could. . . .

The doorbell rang. The bedroom door was ajar and I could hear the front door being opened. There was a murmur of voices, then the clattering of several pairs of feet coming up the wooden stairs to the study on the floor below. Then a single pair of feet came up the stairs to my bedroom and Stan appeared in the doorway.

'Detective Sergeant Vickers and Detective Constable

Pritchard want to talk to you,' she said.

'I'll come down.'

I heaved myself out of bed and put on my dressing-gown. I went into the bathroom and splashed cold water over my face. When I felt more awake, I went down.

The study was full of people. Detective Sergeant Vickers was sitting on the swivel chair by my desk. Detective Constable Pritchard was sitting on the little two-seater sofa next to the desk. Stan was standing by the window. There was a tension in the air that I didn't fully understand. No one spoke.

Then Stan said, 'I'll go up and keep an eye on Grace.' She disappeared up the stairs.

Detective Sergeant Vickers said, 'You're well enough to speak to us, now, Dr James?'

'Yes,' I crossed the room and sat on the window seat. 'I suppose you haven't heard anything – about Melissa. I mean?'

'Miss Meadow?' He shook his head. 'I'm afraid not.'

'Is Agnes all right?'

He nodded. There was another little pause.

He said, 'There's no point in beating about the bush, Dr James. Yesterday afternoon one of our officers, Tim Fisher, received a phone call from Mr Kingleigh. It's logged at about forty minutes before he died. He appeared to be in a state of considerable distress. He claimed that you had taken his baby and were refusing to return her. That you had in effect abducted her.'

'What!' It came out as a shriek. 'But that's exactly the opposite of what happened!'

'Agnes *was* here with you yesterday, wasn't she?'

I felt a chill. There's was no getting round the fact that the police had turned up to find Agnes sitting in the highchair in my kitchen.

'Well, yes,' I said, 'but . . .'

Vickers went on. 'He also claimed that you assaulted him and stole his car keys. He said he was stranded at his cottage.'

'Yes – but – you don't understand! He threatened Grace!'

'You don't deny assaulting him and taking his car keys?'

'I had to stop him following me!'

'Can you tell us where you were on the afternoon of Tuesday the tenth of August?'

'What?' I was bewildered by this change of direction. 'Last Tuesday? The afternoon before Melissa went missing? Well, let me think. I picked Grace up from the nursery at two o'clock. And then I was at home. That's right, I stayed at home until I went over to Melissa's.'

'Any witnesses to that?'

'Well, no, but . . .'

Vickers turned his head very slightly and nodded to Pritchard. Detective Constable Pritchard was getting to her feet and stepping forward. She pursed her lips and looked me full in the face.

'Cassandra James, I am arresting you on suspicion of the murder of Melissa Meadow and Kevin Kingleigh.'

'Tell me again about the last time you say you saw Melissa,' Detective Sergeant Vickers said. 'What time did you arrive at the house?'

'Quarter past nine? Half past?'

'And you left at. . . ?'

'About half past ten, twenty to eleven, something like that.'

'And you don't remember passing anyone on the road either coming or going?'

'Really – I just can't remember now.' I rubbed my forehead. The heaviness of earlier in the day was changing into a headache. It was stuffy in here. I'd seen interview rooms like this on TV a hundred times. I couldn't believe I was actually sitting in one.

'Do you really think Melissa's dead?' I asked.

Vickers said, 'We found bloodstains in the bathroom at the cottage. They'd been scrubbed with bleach but there was still enough to get some DNA. We're testing it right now.'

He sat back and tapped his ballpoint pen on the table, but his eyes never left my face. Probably he was hoping that when I heard that, I'd break down and confess.

There were four of us in the interview room. Vickers, Pritchard, me and Rod Loomis, Stephen's partner in the firm. He was the only solicitor I knew except for the woman who'd done the conveyancing for the Old Granary. He was a short, balding man, rather dapper. Today he was dressed in a linen suit and a bow tie. He didn't look at home here.

Vickers went on: 'Our problem is this, Dr James. We haven't been able to discover any independent corroboration that you did actually see Miss Meadow that evening. In fact we can't find anyone who saw her or spoke to her after she collected her daughter from the nursery at two o'clock that day. Several people did ring the house but they only got the answering-machine.'

'I can explain that. She was asleep. She told me earlier that she was going to put the answering-machine on.'

'Strange that she didn't return any of the calls.'

'But anyway, Kevin said that he spoke to her. The phone company must have a record of that.'

'A call was made from the cottage to the flat in London at ten forty-five. Belinda Roy confirms that Mr Kingleigh answered the phone call at that time. She overheard part of the conversation.'

'Well, then.'

'But we don't know that it really was Miss Meadow on the other end of the line, do we?'

I was having trouble focusing on what he was saying. I kept worrying about Grace. I'd been allowed to leave her with Stan, but she'd need feeding again soon.

'Who else could it have been?' I asked.

'It could have been you, Dr James.'

There was a silence.

'But it wasn't.' I was glad that my voice at least was under

217

control. Under the table my knees had started to tremble.

Vickers sighed. Then he leaned forward and put his clasped hands on the table.

'We have another problem,' he said. 'There's no real evidence, is there, that you yourself were at home that afternoon?' His voice was affable but firm. 'I want to suggest to you, Dr James, that on the day of Melissa Meadow's disappearance you went over to Journey's End much earlier than you've led us to believe.'

'You can't really think that I murdered Melissa!'

'Cassandra,' Rod said. He laid a hand on my arm. 'Wait. This is a preposterous allegation, Sergeant. My client is happy to help in any way she can, but she cannot submit to this line of questioning.'

'No, no, Rod, it's OK,' I said, putting my hand on his. 'I've got nothing to hide and anyway I want to know how Detective Sergeant Vickers thinks I disposed of her body with a six-month-old baby in tow.' I corrected myself. 'Two six-month-old babies actually, because I would have had to deal with Agnes as well.'

'Oh, I'm not suggesting that you did it on your own,' Vickers said. 'If we don't take it for granted that Miss Meadow disappeared after eleven o'clock that evening, then we have a gaping great hole in Mr Kingleigh's alibi. No one appears to have seen him between the time he left his agent in central London at four o'clock and nine o'clock when Miss Roy arrived at the flat in Camberwell. In fact, it's my suggestion that Kingleigh was the instigator and probably the perpetrator of this crime. I see Dr James playing a supporting role, assisting him particularly in the establishment of an alibi.'

'But why? Why would I do that?'

'Perhaps you regarded Miss Meadow as a rival for Mr Kingleigh's affections.'

I couldn't take this in at first. When I did, I actually laughed.

'That is a deeply offensive suggestion,' Rod burst out.

Vickers said, 'I don't think Dr James can deny that she spent the night with Mr Kingleigh at Journey's End only a few days ago. I myself saw her there.'

The breath was jolted out of me. I looked at Rod. He was staring at Vickers with his mouth open. He was after all a good friend of Stephen's as well as his partner. Then he got a grip.

'I would like to speak to my client alone, Sergeant.'

Vickers looked at me. I nodded. Vickers recorded the break in the interview and switched off the tape recorder. He and Detective Constable Pritchard left the room.

'Cassandra, just what is going on here? You didn't, did you?'

'What, murder Melissa? Or sleep with Kevin? What do you think!'

'Oh, Christ, I'm sorry, of course I know you haven't murdered anyone, but did you really spend the night there?'

'It's not what he's suggesting. Kevin rang me up. He said he thought Agnes was ill. She was screaming the place down. I went over there with Grace. When I'd got Agnes settled, I was just so exhausted that I fell asleep. Kevin slept downstairs on the sofa.'

Rod let out his breath in a noisy exhalation.

'Look, Cassandra, I'm not sure that I'm the best person to be dealing with this. I've never done any criminal stuff. But I do know enough to advise you that you shouldn't answer any more questions.'

'Look, Rod, you wouldn't be human if you weren't wondering, but I haven't done anything criminal. Nothing at all. I swear. I've got nothing to hide.'

'Nothing? Really nothing?'

'Unless you count stealing his car keys as a crime. And that was self-defence. The bastard had my baby.'

Rod groaned. 'I don't like the way this is shaping up. It's not just how things *are*, but how they can be made to *look*. You know that as well as I do.'

'If I don't say anything, they'll keep me here, won't they?'

'They can hold you for twenty-four hours without charging

219

you. With a serious crime like this they can extend it for another twelve.'

Thirty-six hours. A day and a half. Grace had never been away from me for more than a few hours. My breasts began to ache at the very thought of it.

'If I do answer their questions, could they still hold me?'

'I'm afraid so.'

'They can really do that? They can separate me from my baby even though I've done nothing wrong?'

'You know they can.' He paused and then said unwillingly, 'They know that it won't look good if you turn out to be innocent and anyway they're not monsters . . .'

'So they might let me go if I answer their questions?'

'I'm still advising you not to.'

'Tell them to come back in.'

Detective Sergeant Vickers and Detective Constable Prichard came back into the room and I explained how it was that I had come to spend the night at Journey's End.

'So you felt sorry for Mr Kingleigh, left alone with his baby?'

'I felt even sorrier for Agnes.' It dawned on me now how easy it had been for Kevin to get a hold over me through her.

'But you stopped feeling sorry for Mr Kingleigh, didn't you?'

I nodded.

'After you found out about his affair with Miss Roy?'

'No! Or at least, yes, but it wasn't what you're implying. I felt angry on Melissa's behalf. I thought that might be why she'd left.'

'I understand you had an altercation with Mr Kingleigh that almost ended in a brawl in the bar at the theatre? What was that about?'

'Kevin was supposed to be driving me home. But then I decided to get a lift from my ex-husband, and Kevin was annoyed.'

He nodded. 'Did he have cause to be jealous?'

Rod opened his mouth to object. I said, 'No, it's OK, I want to answer. The answer is no on both counts, Sergeant. Kevin would not have been justified, because I was not having a sexual relationship with either him or my ex-husband.'

'So why was he upset?'

'He liked to manipulate people and he thought he was manipulating me. It wasn't working any more and he was angry.'

Vickers flicked over the pages of his notebook. He said, 'And according to what you told me earlier, Mr Kingleigh came over and swapped your baby for his. When you drove over to remonstrate with him, he threatened you and your baby. You managed to escape and took his car keys with you.'

'That's right.'

'Did you know that Mr Kingleigh was allergic to nuts?'

I bit my lip and nodded.

'Let me tell you what we found at his cottage. The sitting-room was in chaos. The telephone had been knocked on to the floor. A briefcase had been tipped up and papers were scattered around. Books had been pulled off shelves. The kitchen was the same. Worse, even. Stuff all over the floor. Broken crockery, milk, flour. Things had just been swept out of cupboards. Evidence of a desperate search for the adrenaline that could have saved his life. We don't know yet what he ate – cereal, a biscuit? – that contained nut, but given the strength of his reaction, it's amazing that he stayed on his feet as long as he did. He was a dead man – maybe even literally – before the train hit him.'

'A biscuit?' I was seeing myself in the kitchen on the night Kevin had called me over to care for Agnes. My hand was on a tin in the cupboard.

'It must have been an accident,' I said. 'Perhaps he got hold of something belonging to the landlord and ate it by mistake.'

I tried to remember. Had I actually taken that tin out? I didn't remember doing that, but I'd been so tired ... on auto-pilot really ...

'There should have been a rescue kit in the kitchen,' Detective Sergeant Vickers was saying. 'His GP says that Mr Kingleigh

221

was punctilious about keeping the antidote on hand. When he couldn't find it anywhere in the house, there was one last chance. There actually was another rescue kit in the glove compartment of the car. We found it there. But he didn't have the car keys, did he? Because you'd taken them. And by then he didn't have the strength to smash the window.' Vickers held my gaze. 'Can you imagine what that could have been like?' he asked.

'Oh, Christ.' I was seeing a blind staggering figure, a swollen face.

'The keys weren't all you took, were they?' he said quietly. 'You took the adrenaline from the kitchen, didn't you? You found out he'd been carrying on with Miss Roy behind your back. You were beside yourself with anger. You'd helped Mr Kingleigh to dispose of his wife because you thought he loved you . . .'

Rod raised a hand. 'Stop there! This is outrageous. Dr James categorically denies that she had any kind of sexual relationship with Kevin Kingleigh or that she was involved in his death.'

Vickers seemed unperturbed. He nodded.

'Let's go back, shall we, to the disappearance of Miss Meadow and some of the events surrounding it? This business of the cloaked figure in the dress-circle. I'm not sure what lies behind that, but perhaps you can enlighten me. You and Mr Kingleigh were acting in concert there, weren't you?'

'Oh, please! I was the one who found the cloak in the costume store. If I was involved, why would I have brought that to Stan's attention?'

'Did you find it? Or were you discovered putting it back?'

I stared at him. I seemed to have stepped into a looking-glass world, where everything was reversed. It was all an absurd mistake, of course it was, but the picture he was building up was curiously compelling . . . I missed what Vickers was saying next and had to ask him to repeat it.

He did so with no sign of impatience.

'I said, how do you account for the fact that Miss Meadow didn't tell anyone except you about the anonymous letter?'

'I can't account for it. But the letter does exist. You know that. Kevin handed it over to you.'

He leaned back in his chair.

'Ah, yes, the letter.'

There was a pregnant pause. The silence lengthened. Then Vickers leaned forward and leafed through the folder on the table between them.

'*This* letter,' he said, holding up a piece of paper in a plastic wallet.

'That's right.'

There was a theatrical pause. Vickers put the wallet on the table and slipped it across to me. All of a sudden I knew what he had been going to say, incredible though it was. Just in time I stopped myself from saying it for him.

'Perhaps you'd like to explain how this came to be written on your computer,' he said.

Chapter Nineteen

SOMEONE must have been telling lies about Joseph K., for with-out having done anything wrong he was arrested one fine morning. The opening lines of Kakfa's *The Trial*, so chilling in their matter-of-factness, kept running through my mind as I sat on the thin police-cell mattress. Joseph K. never did find out who had set in motion the train of events that led inexorably to his execution, but I knew who had been lying about me. I'd been maligned by a dead man.

The cell was the shape of a shoe box and it didn't feel much bigger. At least I was alone and I had a lavatory all to myself, even if it was the sort you wouldn't fancy using without putting toilet paper round the seat. And I did have a book. I'd found it in my bag and had been allowed to keep it with me. I always carry a World's Classic around with me. They're so small and light and you never know when you're going to need something to read. I did wish though that the current handbag book wasn't Gogol's *Dead Souls*. Not that it really mattered: there was no natural light and the central light bulb didn't give off enough light for me to read. The book's importance was more as a talis-man, a reminder of the outside world and of my real self.

When Detective Sergeant Vickers told me about the letter, something monstrous had loomed up before me. It had been deleted, of course, but computer experts can retrieve documents that have been thrown way. There's no doubt about it. It had been written on my computer. I had even found myself wondering whether I really could have written that letter and forgotten about it. That was the first moment that I fully understood I might be charged with murder. One by one, it seemed, the routes of escape had been blocked. The evidence was only circumstantial – *could* only be circumstantial, for God's sake – but it was compelling. Even the fact that I was a lecturer in nineteenth-century literature – could there be a more blameless occupation? – was suspect now. Who better to know where to put their hands on a poem by Byron? *We'll go no more a-roving* . . . The irony of it wasn't lost on me.

I found myself doing a mental review of prison literature. Someone would surely have written a book on it. Oscar Wilde's *The Ballad of Reading Gaol*, Arthur Koestler's *Darkness at Noon*, *The Jail Diary of Albie Sachs* . . . There was a sudden burst of drunken singing and the clanging of a door down the corridor, and I came back to the present. I recognized these thoughts for what they were, a way of distracting myself from the seriousness of my situation, of avoiding the thing I was most afraid of: being separated from Grace. I wasn't living in a totalitarian state and I hadn't done anything wrong. So there must be a way out. *Stone Walls doe not a Prison make, Nor Iron bars a Cage; Mindes innocent and quiet take That for an Hermitage.* I must stop this: literature couldn't help me now. And yet I couldn't help trying to bring to mind the rest of the poem.

> When Love with unconfinèd wings
> Hovers within my Gates
> And my divine Althea brings
> To whisper at the Grates:
> When I lye tangled in her hair
> And fetter'd to her eye,
> The Gods that wanton in the Aire,
> Know no such liberty.

Stone Walls do not a prison make,
Nor Iron bars a Cage;
Minds innocent and quiet take
That for an hermitage,
If I have freedome in my love
And in my soule am free;
Angels alone that soar above
Injoy such liberty.

Sir Richard Lovelace, the Cavalier poet, was a more sanguine prisoner than Oscar Wilde or Arthur Koestler. Well, I didn't think Stephen would be whispering at the grates: getting on the phone to the best criminal lawyer in London would be more his style. But there must be something I could do for myself. Just one loose thread in the tissue of circumstantial evidence and the whole thing would unravel. It struck me then that maybe Lovelace was right in a way. I didn't have to be in prison. If only I could relax, empty my mind of all this anxious clutter and let it become 'innocent and quiet'. I lay back on the bed and closed my eyes.

I saw a hot August day, clouds of wheat dust far out in the fields. I was driving home on the day that Stephen left for the States. It was so vivid that when the dog sprang out in front of me I pressed my head back against the pillow. I went on as slowly as I could, trying not to miss a single impression, trying to see everything as it had happened. Again Melissa smiled at me in her dressing-room, again she handed me the letter, again we leaned over a cot to watch our sleeping babies.

Tears pricked my eyes. She must be dead. What else could keep her from Agnes? There were bits of our conversation that I couldn't remember. I hadn't known I would need to remember them. I pressed on. I saw Joe sitting across the lunch table, felt the coldness on my fingertips as I drew a line in the condensation on my wineglass . . . .

The effort of concentration had an unexpected effect.

I fell asleep.

I dreamed that I'd lost Grace. I could hear her crying somewhere, but I couldn't find her. I ran around the Old Granary, bumping into things and looking for her in the most unlikely places, in cupboards, even inside the washing-machine. It was not until I had run back upstairs to my bedroom that I realized. Yes! There was a room I hadn't searched. The secret room. I must have put her there to keep her safe. Relief surged up in me. But the next moment I realized that my problems weren't over. Because the secret room wasn't always in the same place. Where was it today? I examined my bedroom walls carefully, running my hand along them to find the hinge of the door. A phone began to ring and I hesitated, not sure whether to answer it or not. Grace was still crying. I had to find her. But the phone was so insistent and I knew that Grace was safe. And anyway this was a dream. Grace wasn't really there. And I had to answer that phone before I woke up. I would learn something terribly important if I did. I willed myself to stay in the dream. I went over to the bedside table. The dream was slipping away, growing fuzzy round the edges. I lifted the receiver. It was Joe. His voice was very serious:

'Didn't you realize, Cassandra, that they are all nothing but a pack of cards?'

And with that the world of the dream vanished. I was lying on my bed in the cell breathing hard. A phone was still ringing somewhere close by. And it was all all right now. I'd found the loose thread. You could say that it was Grace who got me out of the prison cell. I was rescued by a crying baby. Of course, they would have been bound to release me sooner or later. Wouldn't they? That's what I tell myself now, but it wasn't how I felt at the time.

'I can prove that Melissa was still alive at around half past ten that evening,' I told Detective Sergeant Vickers back in the interview room. 'My ex-husband rang my mobile phone. I was

227

upstairs changing Grace's nappy. So Melissa answered it for me! He actually spoke to her. They had a conversation.'

He considered this. 'You could have faked that,' he said at last, but I could tell that his heart wasn't really in it.

'Oh, come on, Sergeant, I'm one of the few people involved who isn't an actor. And don't you think Joe would have realized? I mean, the man used to be married to me.'

Vickers opened his mouth to speak.

'And no,' I added hastily, 'we weren't in collusion. I hadn't seen or spoken to him for at least fourteen years before we met up last week.'

Vickers heaved a sigh. He looked exhausted. I looked past him to Detective Constable Pritchard. She gave a sympathetic little smile.

'So can I go?' I asked. 'Or do you have to speak to Joe first?'

'That's not going to be a problem,' Detective Sergeant Vickers gestured wearily towards the front of the police station. 'The professor's out there along with a posse of others eager to proclaim your innocence. Though eager doesn't really describe one of them, hangdog is more like it. I suppose it would be stretching a point to charge him with wasting police time by not coming forward earlier, though there's nothing I'd like better.'

I had no idea what he was talking about. I looked from him to Detective Constable Pritchard. She got to her feet.

'I'll go and speak to Professor Baldassarre, shall I, Sarge?'

Vickers nodded. When she'd left the room, he switched off the recorder and leaned back in his seat. We sat in silence for a bit and then he said:

'Might as well tell you that one or two other things have come to light. Mr Kingleigh's alibi for that night has collapsed. That young actress – Belinda Roy – has now admitted that she went home around midnight. We found a copy of your house key in a drawer at Mr Kingleigh's cottage, so he had access to your word processor. He could have typed that letter. And then there's Mr Harcourt-Greaves . . .'

For a moment I couldn't think who that was.

'The documentary man,' Vickers explained.

'Jake?'

'That's right.'

Behind Vickers, the door opened. Detective Constable Pritchard put her head round the door. 'It checks out,' she said.

I was on my feet before she'd had stopped speaking.

'Yes, yes, you can go,' Vickers said. 'I'll need another statement at some point . . .'

I didn't hear what else he was going to say, because I was out of the door.

In the waiting-room there was a crowd of people. There was Stephen with Grace in his arms. Joe was talking to him in a confidential manner, Stephen was nodding. They looked like old friends. Amongst all the emotions jostling for dominance, I found room for a twinge of irritated surprise. Stan was standing off to one side looking uncharacteristically grim and Jake was beside her. I easily recognized the description of hangdog in his drooping shoulders and glum expression.

The next instant Stephen saw me.

'What an earth have you been up to?' he enquired. 'I can't turn my back for a moment, can I?' And then I was hugging him and Grace both at once. I felt I could never get enough of them, but I did at last pull free. Grace clung to me and I held her close.

Through the window I could see the wide green expanse of Parker's Piece. There was a cricket-game in progress. People were sitting on the grass in little groups. A toddler was lurching uncertainly along chased by his mother. A summer's day in Cambridge. Had it had ever looked more beautiful?

'Cass,' Stan said, 'Jake has something to tell you.' She pushed him forward.

'I'm sorry, Cassandra,' he muttered. 'I really am.'

'What? What's the matter?' I asked.

He bit his lip and looked at Stan.

229

'Let me give you a clue,' she said. 'Who was that masked man?'

'You mean – it was Jake who was dressed up in that cloak!'

'Oh, God, oh, God,' he moaned.

'I can't believe it! Why did you do it?'

'It was a joke more than anything.'

'Oh, no, it wasn't,' Stan said. 'You did it to stir up excitement for that bloody documentary.'

'How could you sink that low?' I said.

'I didn't really do any harm.'

'No harm! The police thought I was involved!'

Stan said, 'And he wouldn't have owned up even now, if I hadn't finally realized what the cloak smelled of: that poncy aftershave he uses.'

'If it gets out, it'll ruin me professionally,' he whined, 'and anyway Geoff—'

'You little shit,' Joe spoke quietly, but the hairs went up on the back of my neck. I knew what was going to happen next and this time I wasn't going to try to stop him. But as it happened it wouldn't have done any good if I had.

Because it was Stephen who stepped forward and sent Jake sprawling.

Chapter Twenty

THE blood in the bathroom turned out to be Melissa's. After a tussle between Maire and the social services, Agnes was released into the care of Maire and Geoff, who had been named as joint guardians in Melissa's will. Kevin had died intestate.

'Kevin killed Melissa. I'm sure of that,' Maire told me. 'And that's what the police think, too. They're not looking for anyone else. Of course that's not enough for the bloody social services. I want to take Agnes home and raise her with my own kids. But they won't let me take her out of the county until Melissa's been declared legally dead. Geoff and his wife'll take care of her until then.'

We were sitting in my kitchen on an autumnal day in late September. A blustery wind was lashing the trees and now and again a handful of raindrops splattered on the window. Maire's hair was untidy and she had lost weight. In that respect she looked more like Melissa, and yet now that I'd got to know her better, the resemblance didn't seem so strong. She was a coarser, but stronger character. Where Melissa had been vague, even a little fey, Maire was blunt and decisive.

'The lying, manipulating bastard,' she said. 'They'd have got to him sooner if it hadn't been for bloody Belinda. What was it with Kevin? He could make even the smartest of women think that the sun shone out of his arse. Not that Belinda is the smartest of women, mind you. You know what, I'm glad he's dead – prison would have been too good for him. Except now they'll probably never find Melissa's body.' Her eyes filled with tears.

'It's awful . . .' I reached over and rested my hand on Maire's arm. There was nothing more I could say. Melissa had to be dead. She couldn't have missed all the media coverage of Kevin's death in the papers and on the TV; if she was alive, why hadn't she returned to claim her child? And she hadn't drawn any money out of her account or used her credit cards.

'He buried her somewhere and she'll probably never be found,' Maire said. 'I won't be able to lay her to rest, to say goodbye properly. That's hard.'

It *was* hard. How long did I go on hoping even against my rational judgement for news of Melissa – or even that it might *be* Melissa – every time the phone rang? It's difficult to say now. In spite of everything life went on in the way that it does. My maternity leave ended and I began teaching again at the beginning of October. *East Lynne* finished its run with another actor taking the part of Captain Levison. Jake's black eye recovered, but his reputation didn't. His documentary was never broadcast and the plug was pulled on the rest of the series. Stan moved on to other productions and other theatres. She sent me a postcard from a theatre in the Midlands, where she was stage-managing *The Wizard of Oz*. All it said was: *This isn't Kansas, Dorothy.* Some days do stand out: Grace's first Christmas, of course, and my fortieth birthday in December, which was also the day Stephen and I got married at the register office in Cambridge. There can't be many people who have their first husband as a witness at their third wedding. As Joe remarked, perhaps I should have called on my second husband, too, and made it a hat-trick.

It was about six months after my conversation with Maire that

I drove up the track to Geoff's smallholding in North Wales. It was a cold March day and I was on my way home after giving a lecture at Bangor University. It was spring now in Cambridge, but here there was snow on the tops of the mountains and little drifts clung to the tussocky grass lower down. The farm was in a sheltered spot in a fertile little valley. I stopped by the side of the track and got out of the car. I took some deep breaths. The air was intoxicatingly fresh and cold. A stream swollen with melt-water ran down the valley, providing a constant background murmur.

I shivered. It was time to get back in the car and drive on to the farm.

At first sight the place seemed deserted and I wondered if I were going to be unlucky. As I walked across the yard, I glimpsed a car through the open door of one of the stables. Geoff's Jeep was nowhere to be seen. But that was all right. It wasn't Geoff I'd come to see.

The house was small, built of grey stone with a slate roof, a sturdy four-square building. I rang the doorbell. No one came. I wandered over to the wall by the side of the slope into the valley. A woman was emerging from a sheep-pen with a bucket in her hand. She saw me and stood still for a moment or two. I waved. She waved back and set off up the hill. When she got close enough for me to make out her expression, I saw the polite wariness that one adopts when a stranger arrives at one's door.

She unlatched the gate into the yard. 'Véronique?' I asked.

'Yes?' Her eyes flicked over to my car, as if to check whether I was alone.

'I'm Cassandra.'

'But yes! How delightful.' She was close to me now. She put down her bucket, wiped her hand on her overall and shook my hand.

'I've been milking the ewes. It's very good with coffee, ewe's milk. You'll have some, yes?' The French accent wasn't strong, but I was very conscious of the caressing cadence. 'You've come to see Agnes, of course.'

I felt a sudden qualm. 'She *is* here?'

'Yes, yes, she is here. She's asleep. She sleeps always after lunch. I take the chance to do some little jobs. Come, you can see her now.'

We went up the narrow stairs through the centre of the house and turned left into a bedroom. Like all the rooms in the house it was small and the windows didn't let in much light. But someone had worked hard to make it bright and welcoming. There was a sheepskin rug on the floor and yellow plastic crates of toys. The walls were white with a frieze of characters from *The Wind in the Willows*. I went over to the white-painted wooden cot. The child asleep inside looked less like Grace than she used to do. Her hair was still fair, while Grace's had darkened. The shape of her face was different. She wasn't a baby any more.

Véronique stood next to me looking down into the cot. She leaned in and brushed back the hair from the forehead of the sleeping child.

'And your own little girl?' she asked. 'You didn't bring her with you?'

'No, she's at home with my husband.'

'Ah, yes, your husband; Geoff told me. I have to congratulate you.' Her tone was warm. Her formality was only that of someone for whom English is not the first language.

We went down to the kitchen. There was an Aga, a dresser with willow-pattern plates and a big scrubbed kitchen table. The room was deliciously warm.

Véronique made coffee with deft and economical movements.

'I'm sorry you've missed Geoff,' she said. 'This is the first time he's been away on a job for more than a couple of days.'

'Yes . . .'

She turned from the Aga. 'You know – I think you are not sorry at all. I think you came on purpose. You wanted to check up on me, no?' She was smiling.

234

I found myself blushing. She was right. I'd chosen a time when Geoff wouldn't be there.

'No, no,' she said. 'I understand.' She put the coffee-pot on the table and sat down opposite me. 'It's good that you are looking out for her. And of course you don't know me. In your position I would feel the same. But, you know, I love her, *la pauvre petite*. How could one not?'

I felt almost drowsy in the warmth from the Aga. Véronique pushed her sleeves up her arms.

I roused myself.

'How long will Agnes go on living here with you?' I asked.

'For a while longer. It takes time, you know, for someone to be declared dead. But it will happen, I think. Melissa will not return.'

'No, I don't think she will.'

'You think it was Kevin who murdered her?'

'I suppose I could play with words and say that in a sense I think it was. But in the generally accepted meaning of the word, I have to say, no, he didn't kill her.'

'She killed herself?' Véronique's eyes were wide.

'Melissa is dead. The Melissa I knew, that is. But there was another Melissa, one I knew nothing about. Oh, don't worry,' I said, responding to the alarm in her face, 'That Melissa won't come back either.'

'She won't? But why not?'

'I think you know why.'

The air was electric. For a moment I wondered if I'd made a mistake coming here alone. Then Melissa sighed. She took off her glasses and rubbed her eyes. When she looked at me again, her whole face seemed different.

'I thought if anyone managed to work it out, it would be you,' she said. 'How did you do it?'

'I asked myself what I might have done in your position and who in the end was left holding the baby. I did wonder about Maire. Whether she was really you, if you see what I mean. But funnily enough, she was actually too similar to you in some ways. The mannerisms, that way she had of glancing sideways. No, you would have tried to bury that resemblance, if you were acting the role of your own sister. And then there was Geoff. He had to have known about Jake dressing up and scaring Belinda. Jake said as much, even implied that Geoff had put the idea into his head. That seemed so unlike him. Once I'd taken on board the idea that Geoff might not be quite what he seemed, everything started to unravel. There was nothing really that couldn't have been set up by you and Geoff, from the anonymous letter to the bloodstains in the bath.'

'But you weren't sure at first, were you? When you got here, I mean?'

'You're right. I did have a moment or two of wondering if I was about to make an almighty fool of myself. You're good, Melissa. Bloody good. The hair, the glasses – contact lenses too, to change the colour?' She nodded. 'But it was the acting, really. You didn't let up for a moment. And that accent . . .' I shook my head. 'Just brilliant.'

She shrugged. 'Not difficult when you've got a French mother. And it's the best possible way to disguise a voice.'

'That's why the photos disappeared from your dressing-room. That one of your parents . . .'

'Yes, standing outside the pâtisserie they used to run in Carcassonne.'

'I was virtually sure, and when you pushed up your sleeve, that clinched it . . .'

'The burn on my arm.' She looked at it and grimaced. 'Ah, yes, one of the mementoes of my past life. Kevin did that, of course. Among other things.'

'You know, Geoff was good, too. Of course, I was blind with lack of sleep and mother-love, but all the same I have to hand it to you. The pair of you played me like a fish. And of course, Maire was in on it, too, wasn't she?'

'I'm sorry.'

'Are you? Are you really?'

She thought for a moment.

'No,' she admitted. 'I'd do it all again. You found out what Kevin was like, didn't you? When we first met he was so charming, so clever, so sexy – I'd never known anything like it. He was a bit possessive even then, but I was flattered. He swept me off my feet. After we got married, it grew worse. He was suspicious of my male friends. Wanted me to account for every moment I wasn't with him. There were rows, he started to hit me. Oh, you can write the script yourself. Things improved a bit after Agnes was born. And then the worst thing of all happened. He tried to control me through her.'

'Couldn't you have left him?' As soon as the words were out of my mouth, I felt how inadequate they were.

'He said he would hunt me down and kill me. I believed him. I knew I'd never really be safe. Not unless he thought I was already dead.'

I thought of something I'd heard on the news a few months ago. A woman and her children had fled from a violent husband and gone into hiding. Her address was kept secret but the name of her social worker was given in court. That clue was enough. He'd tracked his wife down and murdered her.

'When did you actually leave the house?' I asked. 'I've often wondered about that.'

'I left it as long as I dared. Geoff cycled over and he arrived about an hour after you'd left. He helped me set the scene, then he took the car and dumped it in London. I waited until I knew people would miss me. I was actually still in the cottage when the phone started ringing. That was my cue. I cycled over to Ely station. I was wearing a wig, padding, the works, my own mother wouldn't have recognized me. I went straight to Wales and took up my new identity.'

'But weren't you afraid for Agnes? How could you leave her behind, knowing what he was like?'

'That was the worst part, but it was the only thing I could

think of that would convince him. I knew he wouldn't dare to hurt her with the police and social workers swarming around. And you'd be there, too. And he wasn't interested in her except as a counter in the game with me. I thought he'd soon get sick of looking after her and surrender her to Maire.'

'It didn't work though, did it? He didn't believe that you were dead. That TV broadcast did for him, didn't it? So then it was plan B. Was it you or Geoff who went round to Journey's End, planted the biscuits, removed the adrenaline . . . ?'

'Geoff didn't know until afterwards.'

'That's what I guessed.'

'And I didn't really think Kevin would die. It was more of a warning than anything else. I wanted to give him a scare. I mean, I thought there'd be another kit in the car.'

'And there was. If Kevin hadn't taken Grace, and I hadn't taken his car keys . . . I suppose you could argue that Kevin was hoist by his own petard.'

We sat in silence for a bit.

'Would you have let me go on thinking that you were dead?' I asked.

'I'm not sure. Maybe one day, when I felt it was safe . . .'

'An enigmatic postcard from some big anonymous city? Or perhaps a phone call that couldn't be traced?'

She nodded. 'Something like that.'

'But wouldn't even that have been a risk? How could you be sure I wouldn't give the game away? That I won't give it away even now.'

'I can't be sure, but—'

She didn't have to finish her sentence. I did it for her.

'But I'm a mother, too.'

'Kevin was a monster, you know.'

'What are you trying to say? The end justifies the means?'

'Sometimes it does. What it comes down to here is something very simple in the end. Agnes. You would have done the same for Grace.'

238

Was this true? I thought of the satisfaction with which I'd kneed Kevin in the balls. What if I'd had a knife in my hand? That was different from actually planning to kill him, but even so ... What was it Nietzsche had written? *He who fights with monsters might take care lest he thereby become a monster. And if you gaze for long into an abyss, the abyss gazes also into you.*

'I'm very fond of you, Cass,' Melissa was saying. 'I don't suppose we'll meet again, though, will we?'

'Better not.' I didn't say it unkindly.

'I'm not going unpunished, you know. I'll never act again. At least—'

'Not on the stage.'

'Exactly.'

I pushed my coffee away undrunk and got up.

'Better go, I've got a long drive home.'

Melissa got to her feet, too. She walked me to the door. We stood on the threshold and looked at each other.

'What about Stephen?' Melissa asked.

'He doesn't know. Or at least he can't admit that he knows. He's a lawyer after all. He'd feel he had to do something about it. I'll find a way of sharing it with him without actually telling him.'

She nodded.

'The police,' I said. 'They might still tumble to it ...'

'I know ... that's part of it.' Part of her punishment, I guessed that she meant. 'But every day it goes on is one more day I've had with Agnes.'

We walked out to my car. I got in and started the engine. Now at the last moment I somehow felt reluctant to say goodbye. I wound the window down. Melissa bent down.

'What are you going to tell Agnes when she grows up?' I asked.

A shadow fell across her face. 'Am I going to go on pretending not to be her mother? I don't know. Mother, but not mother. It's a bit like *East Lynne*, isn't it?'

I nodded and wound up the window.

As the car jolted down the track, I kept glancing into the rear-view mirror. Melissa was standing alone in the middle of the farmyard. She raised her arm in a gesture of farewell. I raised my own arm, though I wasn't sure if she could see it.

Then the track turned and she disappeared from view.

AUG   2005

DEMCO